59372083177967     MOSQ

D0382873

# kiss
## OF DEATH

## ALSO BY LAUREN HENDERSON

# kiss OF DEATH

LAUREN HENDERSON

DELACORTE PRESS

Text copyright © 2011 by Lauren Henderson
Jacket photograph copyright © 2011 by Jitka Saniova/Trevillion Images

All rights reserved. Published in the United States by Delacorte Press, an imprint of Random House Children's Books, a division of Random House, Inc., New York.

Delacorte Press is a registered trademark and the colophon is a trademark of Random House, Inc.

Visit us on the Web! www.randomhouse.com/teens

Educators and librarians, for a variety of teaching tools, visit us at www.randomhouse.com/teachers

Library of Congress Cataloging-in-Publication Data is available upon request.
ISBN 978-0-385-73779-1 (hc) — ISBN 978-0-385-90691-3 (lib. bdg.) —
ISBN 978-0-375-89948-5 (ebook)

The text of this book is set in 12-point Goudy.

Book design by Kenneth Holcomb

Printed in the United States of America

10 9 8 7 6 5 4 3 2 1

First Edition

Random House Children's Books supports the First Amendment
and celebrates the right to read.

TO MY DARLING GREG—
SCARLETT'S FOUND HER TRUE LOVE,
AND SO HAVE I.

LUCKY US.

# Acknowledgments

Sad as it was to write the last Scarlett Wakefield book, it was also hugely satisfying to weave all the threads together, and to bring all the characters together for the final showdown—especially as it meant that I got to spend some time with my sister and her family in Edinburgh researching locations! Holyroodhouse, the Scottish Parliament, Arthur's Seat, and the cemetery are all as described, as are Leith and the Shore bar and restaurant. My nephew Ewan Macintyre very kindly drove me to the quarry party location and gave his name to the Ewan of the book; like that Ewan, he's a very talented musician, singer, and puppet maker. You can find him at ewan-macintyre.co.uk. Thanks to Kim and Symon for putting us up—if you like puppetry, you should visit their site, puppetlab.com. And, not wanting to leave out anyone in their very artistic family, I should mention my niece Rachael's online magazine, Brikolage (brikolage.co .uk). If you're an aspiring artist or writer, it's a great place to submit your work. Nuala Kennedy is a real person, and her music is just as beautiful as I describe it in the book; you can find her at nualakennedy.com. The main license I've taken is to move the time and location of the Celtic Connections festival, which actually happens in Glasgow around January and is superb—I really strongly recommend it.

Right, that's all the Edinburgh info done! I need to thank Stephanie Lane Elliott, Krista Vitola, and Beverly Horowitz at Delacorte Press for being such strong supporters of Scarlett Wakefield's adventures. Delacorte are a real powerhouse, and I'm very lucky to be with them now and for the future. My American agent, Deborah Schneider, and her right-hand woman, Cathy Gleason, always have my back, and I love them both to pieces. Chanchal, Gabrielle, Bonnie, Lauren, Cecilia, Damaris, Heather, Brooke, Amanda, Paula, Maggie, Dyanhea, Rebecca, Erin, Carlie, Dyana, Kelly, Cynthia, Nikki, Lucia, CNH, Zoe, Gabriella, Magda, Starr, Chelsie, Stephanie, Laura, Lisa Marie, Tia, Carolina, your lovely messages on MySpace were a real source of encouragement to me as I wrote this series—thanks so much! Randon Burns, thanks so much for your unflagging, puckish support and enthusiasm for my YA books. And Claudia Gabel, without you Scarlett would never have existed. Thank you so much for your help, encouragement, and tough love!

Now that I've come to the end of Scarlett's adventures, I'm really excited to be starting a new series—set in Italy, featuring four English and American girls, mystery, adventure, sun-kissed days and sultry nights, dark family secrets, and, of course, quite a few hot Italian boys! Look for the first book in the series this time next year. . . .

# *one*

## BLAST FROM THE PAST

This is absolutely the worst thing that's ever happened to me.

In the dark, I look sideways at Taylor, who's staring straight ahead, her body stiff with horror. I can tell that she feels the same as I do. She and I have been through so much together; you'd think we'd be immune to anything life can throw at us. We were warned, I suppose. But nothing could have prepared us for this level of atrocity.

I pull out my silenced phone and glance down at it. Oh God. I turn the face to Taylor, nudging her, so that she can see it too. In the glow from the phone, her lips are stretched back over her teeth in a grimace, her eyes narrowed in almost physical pain. She looks like a gargoyle. The bluish light makes her seem even more eerie.

"I can't *bear* it!" she whispers.

"We have to," I say grimly, looking from side to side just to confirm what I already know: there's no escape.

The clock on my phone is telling me there are fifteen more minutes of this. Fifteen more minutes of sheer hell.

I close my eyes to block out the sight. But then I have

to listen to the sounds, and they're even worse without the visuals. Hell, I imagine, is probably something along these lines. Trapped forever, forced to endure this torture, without ever being able to put an end to your misery.

And—an extra twist of the knife—having to watch your best friend go through it too.

A particularly excruciating screech snaps my eyes open in reflex. Nails scraping down a blackboard are soothing compared to this. And yet, if I had to describe the single worst part of the scene in front of me, I actually don't think it would be the noise they're making, atrocious and ear-splitting though that is.

It would be the clothes.

I really don't know much about Norway. It has fjords, apparently, and lots of snow, and the people are tall and blond and very, very white: that was pretty much the limit of my Norway Fun Facts up till this moment. But now, looking at the four members of the Norwegian folk group Hürti Slärtbärten (or something like that—I may have got some of those umlauts wrong) sawing grimly away at their violins onstage, I can add that apparently, Norwegians have no access to anything resembling modern fashion. They look as if some major blockade isolated them in the late 1980s. The two girls are wearing deeply unflattering red taffeta dresses with square-cut bodices, drop waists, and flouncy skirts, the kind of frocks a vengeful bride would choose for the brides-maids she's being forced to include in her wedding. And the two boys, in shiny red shirts tucked into black pleated trousers, could be the waiters at the same event.

They *are* all tall and blond; I got that part right. And

2

they're smiling and nodding at each other as they stand in line, dragging their bows over the strings, deliberately saw-ing out the kind of noises that would make any normal per-son stop in horror, stare at their violin, and apologize to the audience for having completely forgotten to tune it before going out on stage.

Taylor and I are right in the middle of the row of seats, thoroughly wedged in by other Wakefield Hall girls. And Miss Carter has strategically placed herself on one end of the row, with Aunt Gwen on the other. To get out, we'd have to clamber over everyone, plus face the wrath of the scariest teachers in the school. I actually duck down and look under my seat, wondering if it might be possible to crawl underneath it—there aren't that many rows behind us, maybe I could sneak out that way. . . .

But then, as I'm curled over, head between my knees, I realize something's happened onstage. There's rustling all around me; people are sitting up straighter. The screeching of the violins is even shriller and less tuneful, if that's possi-ble. Narrowly avoiding cracking my head on the seat in front as I straighten up again, I catch sight of the stage just in time to join, gobsmacked, in the collective gasp as the girls fall back to one side, the boys to the other, and a fifth member of Hürti Slärtbärten appears from the wings.

He's wearing the same silky red shirt as the other two boys, but its sleeves are belled out, then gathered back in at the wrists, making it, technically, more of a blouse. And if that weren't bad enough, it's accessorized with a black bow tie at the neck. His hair is gelled up and spiked out as if a pine-apple had exploded on top of his head. And though he's tall

3

and blond like the other group members, I can't honestly say that he's as white as they are, because his face is a mass of acne breakouts that match the flaming red of his shirt.

He struts out to the middle of the stage, wiggling his hips and waggling his violin, like he's some sort of pop star. He ducks and grins and winks at both of the girls, flirting with them; then he dances over to stand with the boys and leads them in a trio, chasing the girls around the stage, following them like he's enacting some bizarre courtship ritual, all of them still sawing away at their instruments. Every so often, he turns to wink at the audience, as if he's convinced we're all hypnotized by his sexiness and charm.

I'm paralyzed. My jaw's still dropped. I think every single member of the audience is in exactly the same situation: unable to believe that this boy with a faceful of spots, dressed like a really camp ice dancer, is acting like he's so gorgeous we're going to start screaming and rushing the stage any second now.

And then, farther down the row, I hear something. The unmistakable, high-pitched sound of mocking laughter.

There's a first for everything, I suppose. I'd never have thought that I'd be grateful to hear Plum laughing sarcastically. But right now, the sound is manna from heaven, because it releases the pressure on my rib cage, which has been almost suffocating me. Like a line of dominoes toppling, every single Wakefield Hall girl starts laughing, giggling at first, and then increasingly loudly till we're howling with laughter. It's a wave, rippling through us, then spreading; I can see the shoulders of the people sitting in front of me rocking as they start laughing too.

4

"Sssh!" hiss Miss Carter and Aunt Gwen furiously. "Sssh! It's not *funny!*"

But that just makes us even more hysterical. The lead violinist is prancing now, up on his toes, making charges at the two girls as if he were a bull; they're turning away, looking back at him over their shoulders, and shaking their skirts in would-be seductive motions that cause Plum to reach a pitch almost as high as the wail of their so-called music. The violins squeak up the scale, and so does Plum; by the grand finale, as the spotty boy stands triumphantly between the two girls, both of them playing their violins frantically in his direction, tears are streaming from my eyes, I'm laughing so hard.

They end on a last, screeching, out-of-tune note so painful that I wince and choke momentarily on my own snot. The whole audience has the same reaction, I think; there's a split second of silence as we all wrestle with the impulse to clap our hands over our ears.

"Bravo! Bravo!" Plum is clapping wildly and making whooping noises.

She's a twisted genius. We all join in, of course. I drum my feet on the floor. Taylor contributes a cheerleader's "Yay!" that only Americans are unself-conscious enough to yell in public. The entire row of Wakefield Hall girls screams for Hürti Slärtbärten as if we're hard-core fans with posters of them on our bedroom walls covered in lipsticked kisses.

And Spotty Boy totally believes it. He flourishes a long bow, he winks at us again, he waggles his hips; and then, unbelievably, he takes his violin, puts it between his legs, and plays a few chords on it, thrusting it out toward us sexily.

We all collapse. The lights come up and Hürti Slärtbärten leave the stage, but we're past it now. We're lying limp in our chairs, our faces red and wet with tears, trying desperately to catch our breath.

"That was *shocking* behavior," Aunt Gwen says angrily.

"*Really*, girls," Miss Carter chimes in.

"To be fair," Miss Carter's girlfriend, Jane, says from her seat next to Miss Carter, "they weren't actually terribly good, Clemency. I mean, they weren't in *tune*."

"It's the Scandinavian folk-music style," Miss Carter says, sounding a little embarrassed. "The dissonance is deliberate, I believe."

"Well, if you're not used to it," Jane persists, "it does rather sound like them being out of tune. And when he put his fiddle between his legs, I couldn't blame the girls for getting a little carried away. . . ."

Plum shrieks with laughter, remembering this. And Plum's laughter, as I've said, is very distinctive.

"*Plum?*" exclaims a voice from the other side of the auditorium.

Taylor and I jump. Wiping our eyes, we look over to the other side of the aisle, where a girl is standing up, staring in our direction. And we recognize her immediately. It's Nadia Farouk. I'd know that stunning fall of shiny blue-black hair, that exquisite makeup, that gold jewelry and chic black-clad body anywhere.

I should. I went to school with her for seven years.

"Oh my *God*," Nadia breathes, her eyes narrowing.

Plum sits up as straight as if someone just rammed an iron rod down her spine, tossing back her hair as she always does before she declares war. The two girls are deadly enemies; last year, Plum had some dirt on Nadia, which Nadia convinced me and Taylor to steal and destroy for her. What we didn't know is that Nadia also had dirt on Plum, which she promptly deployed, causing Plum to be kicked out of her and my previous school, St. Tabby's, and end up at Wakefield Hall Collegiate with me and Taylor.

Basically, we shot ourselves spectacularly in the foot. Or feet.

As Plum and Nadia size each other up, my gaze slides beyond Nadia to the girls sitting next to her. I recognize several faces from my year at St. Tabby's. But I don't expect to see the two that make my heart stop for a moment, then speed up, pounding as if it's trying to escape from my chest.

Alison and Luce. My two best friends from St. Tabby's. I spent almost every waking moment with them: in class, gymnastics practice every day after school, then going back to one or other of their houses to do our homework and have dinner, staying out as long as I could because all I had to go back to was the converted attic of a friend of my grandmother's in Holland Park.

Alison and Luce took me in, befriended me, gave me something that resembled the family life I lost when I was four years old and my parents died. We were three leotard-wearing, totally uncool, hardworking best friends; going back on the bus after gymnastics training, sweaty and giggling. We always had each other's backs through multiple competitions; we watched each other flip and somersault on the terrifying balance beam, fall on our bums over and over again, and get shouted at by Ricky, our coach. We knew all each other's weaknesses, and we *definitely* knew each other's strengths.

And I rewarded them by dumping them cold the moment a more glamorous option presented itself. Nadia, prompted by Plum, asked me to a party she was throwing, making it clear that Alison and Luce weren't included in the invitation, and I went. Pathetic, but I got my comeuppance. I kissed a boy at that party—gorgeous, sexy Dan McAndrew, the boy I'd had a crush on for years—and he promptly dropped dead at my feet. *Huge* uproar. I got kicked out of St. Tabby's, packed off to Wakefield Hall—the boarding school my grandmother runs. And to Alison and Luce, I was as dead as Dan.

I was alone and friendless, thinking I'd killed someone, until I met Taylor and—after some head-butting—gradually bonded with her. Eventually, the two of us found out the secret behind Dan's death. But I don't blame Alison and Luce for my loneliness. Not at all. I let them down. We might have been three musketeers, but I definitely didn't come through with the crucial all-for-one-and-one-for-all part of musketeering.

Instead, I showed them that hanging out with the smart set meant more to me than my best friends.

I deserved to have them drop me like a stone.

And now I can't take my eyes off them.

Luce still hasn't got boobs. But then, she never thought she would; her mum's flat as a board. She looks so much more grown-up, though; she's a tiny little thing, with brown hair that she always used to wear in bunches that made her look years younger. Now her hair's been cut close to her head in a pixie crop like Audrey Hepburn's, and she's actually wearing makeup. She looks . . . *sophisticated.*

Amazed, I glance next to her, at Alison, who's undergone some sort of before-and-after, *Britain's Next Top Model* transformation. Her curly red hair has been straightened into a smooth curtain held back with a wide black velvet band, and not only is she wearing mascara, it looks as if she's darkened her eyebrows, too. The change is extraordinary; her pale ginger lashes and brows tended to wash out her face, making it hard to see her features. Now she's really striking, in a sixties sort of way.

They haven't seen me yet; everyone from St. Tabby's is focused on Plum, who, as usual, is relishing the drama of the confrontation.

"Hey, Nadia," she calls in an icy voice, raising one hand and fluttering her fingers dismissively in Nadia's direction.

I'm still staring at Alison and Luce, amazed by how different they look. And the intensity of my stare attracts their attention, because their heads turn a little more, beyond Plum, and their eyes meet mine.

I see their shock. And then, as the shock fades, I see their anger.

They're still furious with me.

I want to look away, but that would be cowardly. But I don't want them to think that I'm being confrontational either. So I'm incredibly grateful when the lights dim once more, Nadia sits down, and we settle back into our seats.

"Och, you've been a great audience!" coos the woman behind the mixing desk in the kind of lovely Scottish brogue that immediately makes you feel relaxed and happy.

"Thanks for coming to Celtic Connections. This is always a very special evening for us here at the music festival, because tonight's the showcase for upcoming young artists. It's a treat to see the folk stars of tomorrow, isn't it? And here come our last group, who already took first prize in the Stornoway Folk Festival's Young Talent category, five bonny laddies with a real future ahead of them. Put your hands together for Mac Attack!"

There's a snigger from Plum after "bonny laddies," and I can't say I blame her. Lizzie and Susan, of course, laugh along; Plum could be giggling and pointing to a mutilated corpse and they'd titter dutifully. But as the stage slowly, dramatically, becomes bathed in blue-green light, its edges touched with violet, and Mac Attack start to play, the laughter dies on their lips.

Sometimes you can tell straightaway that people are really good at what they do. An actor nails her first line, or a dancer lands onstage with a stunning leap. And from the first chord, we all know that Mac Attack are as good as Hürti Slärtbärten sucked lemons. The song is in a minor key, haunting and powerful, immediately capturing my imagination. And it hasn't escaped our attention that the keyboard player, the flautist, the guitarist, and the double-bass player are all boys, with really good legs. Which we can tell, because they're wearing kilts.

Boys in kilts, playing soulfully. The audience settles back, entranced already.

And then comes the sound of a violin, sweet and melancholy, like a voice singing sadly in the distance.

> If with me you'd fondly stray
> Over the hills and far away . . .

It's an old folk song I recognize. But I've never heard it sound like this before. The violin makes it seem like an enchantment, as if the melody is casting a spell to throw a net over your heart and drag you away, as if the fiddler were the Pied Piper of Hamelin. And as he walks slowly onstage, playing the song, a hushed ripple of excitement runs through the entire row of girls. We all lean forward as if pulled by invisible strings.

Because he's gorgeous. He's got that classic hot-boy body: wide shoulders, narrow hips, strong muscly legs (which, of course, we can check out easily because of his kilt). His calves, in woolly socks pulled up just below the knee, have Taylor raising her eyebrows in approval. I know she hates guys with skinny calves. He's wearing a T-shirt, and his arms, flexing as he plays the violin, are just as strongly defined with muscle as his legs. The idiot lead violinist of Hürti Slärtbärten was waving his fiddle around as if it were a toy in a vain effort to impress the audience, but this boy is playing it as sweetly as if it were a part of his body, his concentration entirely on the music he's making.

Wow. He's a total heartthrob.

And then, as he steps into the spotlight in the center of the stage, I get the shock of my life.

*Oh my God.*

Because now that he's fully in the light, I can see his face. His hair is cut very short to his nicely shaped skull, nothing to distract from his features, which are instantly familiar to me: the gray-green eyes, the straight nose, the high cheekbones. The full, pink lips. Which—*God help me*—I should certainly be able to recognize.

Since I've kissed them.

It's Callum McAndrew. Dan McAndrew's twin brother.

Of course, I'm not the only girl here who knows Callum. Taylor, beside me, stiffens in recognition: she came to Scotland too on our quest to find out who killed Dan. She met Callum in circumstances none of us ever wants to think about again.

And farther down the row, I hear an urgent whisper as Plum informs Lizzie and Susan of the identity of the lead fiddler in Mac Attack. Plum knew Dan really well—*really* well. He was a core member of Plum's It girls and boys-about-town, partying hard with them. Callum is Dan's opposite, not a party boy at all. But he certainly knows Plum; his ex-girlfriend, Lucy Raleigh, was one of Plum's whole superrich, supertrendy clique of entitled, glossy hair flickers.

I slump in my chair, unable to take my eyes off Callum as he coaxes sweet, hypnotic music from the violin tucked under his chin. You'd never know it was the same instrument that produced such awful screeches for Hürti Slärtbärten. And yet the sound inside my head is much closer to horrible screeching than to Callum's exquisite playing.

*How can this be happening?* I think hopelessly. *St. Tabby's girls and Callum McAndrew in the same auditorium?* I feel like my past is not only rearing up to haunt me, but slapping me in the face over and over again. I can sense Alison and Luce's anger as strongly as if it were a red mist hovering around me. And as if that weren't enough for me to deal with, up onstage is Callum McAndrew, looking like a god and playing like an angel, which means that no girl present is going to be doing anything but gushing on about him, Googling incessantly to find pictures of him, and giggling madly whenever his name is mentioned for weeks to come.

Talk about blasts from the past. Every time I think I'm free of Dan's murder, that I can make a fresh start, it pulls me back, and now it's as if I'm drowning in it.

The irony is, of course, that I brought this whole disaster on myself. I was the first person to sign up for the school half-term trip to Edinburgh. I was desperate for a distraction: my boyfriend, Jase, has been AWOL for almost two months now. He's texted me, we've Skyped every now and then, but those brief flashes of contact have almost made everything worse, like throwing crumbs to a starving person.

I miss him horribly. I miss holding him, kissing him, wrapping my arms around him, diving my nose into the smooth hollow of his neck to smell his body. I thought it would be easier the longer he was away, but it's only got worse; missing him is like a hole in my stomach, fist-sized, fist-shaped, as if someone put their hand inside me and pulled out an essential organ.

So I was hoping Edinburgh would give me a little relief from the pain. New sights, new scenery, and, most importantly, somewhere with no memories of Jase. Every time I turned a corner at Wakefield Hall, every walk I took in the grounds, I half thought I'd see him, sweeping leaves, pruning trees, or just striding toward me, his face lighting up at the sight of me.

Some distraction. Instead, I've dropped myself into a pit of snakes.

# Two

# "THEY'RE VERY FAMOUS IN NORWAY"

"They practically need bodyguards," Taylor says, looking over at Mac Attack, who, postgig, are sitting in the foyer of the arts center behind a table piled with copies of their CD. Girls are swarming them as excitedly as if they were the stars of the latest teen vampire movie. The organizers of Celtic Connections are trying to coax the mob into an orderly queue, without much success.

"They look pretty freaked," I say, nodding at the organizers; one of them just dared to get between a band of fourteen-year-olds and Callum, and nearly got trampled for his trouble.

"Yeah, they do," Taylor says. "But, y'know, they're asking for it. Wearing kilts in front of a bunch of girls."

I giggle, realizing she means Mac Attack.

"They probably didn't know that every single school in Edinburgh was going to bus in a load of kids," I offer, looking around the foyer; clearly, the idea of young people playing in up-and-coming folk bands has been marketed to as many schools as possible.

"Not just Edinburgh," Taylor says. "Us, and them, too." She nods over at Nadia, who's surrounded by a small coterie of equally well-groomed St. Tabby's girls, sipping drinks they've got from the foyer bar. I'd bet money Nadia's plastic glass doesn't just contain diet Coke. "Which ones are Alison and Luce?"

I point them out to her, and her eyes widen.

"I thought you said they were kind of sporty and scruffy," she says, staring at Alison and Luce. "Wow. If that's what the sporty girls look like at St. Tabby's . . ."

I shake my head.

"No, they've got really smart since I left," I assure her.

"I hate to say it," Taylor mutters, "but all together in a group, they're pretty scary. It's like Plum just kept replicating."

I nod, knowing what she means; it looks as if every single St. Tabby's girl not only traveled up to Edinburgh with hair straighteners, a bulging makeup bag, and a pair of killer heels, but took plenty of time before the concert to make herself perfect. The Wakefield Hall contingent, by contrast, came up from London on a train that was delayed a good hour and a half by some "youths larking about on the line" at Doncaster, to quote the train conductor.

"Keep going and run them over!" Plum had drawled. "Only language they'll understand!"

And after hearing various announcements ("The youths are still on the line. The police have been called," "The police are attempting to remove the youths," and, finally,

"I'm happy to report that most of the youths are now under arrest, but one is still proving obstreperous"), you couldn't help having some sympathy with Plum's position. Because those larking youths meant that we'd limped into Edinburgh after over six hours on the train, too late to go and drop our bags at the boarding school where we were staying for the half-term week; we'd had to come straight to the arts center where Celtic Connections was taking place. We felt dirty and travel-stained, and the contrast provided by the shiny, pretty St. Tabby's girls wasn't doing us any favors.

"Are you going over to talk to them?" Taylor asks.

I shake my head.

"Not like this," I say frankly, looking down at the jeans and hoodie I'd worn for traveling. "I feel all scummy."

One of the great things about Taylor is that she tells things as they are. Lizzie Livermore, fluffy, giggly Lizzie, would immediately have burst into streams of assurances that I looked absolutely fabulous and just needed a touch of lip gloss. Taylor, however, glances at me and nods.

"Yeah. I'm a bit stinky, and you probably are too," she says frankly. "I'd kill for a shower."

Even Plum, Susan, and Lizzie, who usually look as if they've stepped out of the pages of *Teen Vogue*, are a distinct step down compared with the miniskirt-wearing, high-heeled St. Tabby's girls. Plum and the Plum-bots' latest daily uniform is leggings, a long sweater, and slouchy boots, and that's what they all wore to travel in, but I'm sure that they all had much tighter and sexier outfits lined up for this evening's outing. There's a department store called John

Lewis that advertises that it's never knowingly undersold: well, Plum is never knowingly underdressed.

Till now.

"Girls!" Miss Carter says, waving us over to a small table beside the bar where her girlfriend and Aunt Gwen are standing. "I've got us in a scratch dinner, since our timetable's been messed up by the train delay. Tuck in!"

"Oh *God!*" Plum exclaims in horror, looking at the admittedly unappetizing wraps laid out on the table, lettuce as limp as a used tissue protruding from each one, grated cheese the color of a tangerine dribbling out onto the plates. "Is that *cheese?* I'm lactose intolerant."

"I'm lactose intolerant too," Lizzie chimes in. "*And* I don't digest wheat well at *all.*"

"Today is just one *gigantic* source of *misery* after the other," Plum says with a sigh. "I was hoping at *least* for a salad bar."

"What's this?" Taylor asks, picking up a bottle of something bright orange.

"It's called Irn-Bru," Jane, Miss Carter's girlfriend, informs her cheerfully. "It's like the Scottish version of Tango. Only a bit different."

"Looks like Sunkist," Taylor says. She twists off the top and tilts the bottle to her mouth. "Yum," she says enthusiastically, after sipping. "It's kind of weird, but yum."

"What's it taste like?" I ask, taking a bottle myself.

"Orange and coffee," Taylor says thoughtfully. "And water. Like I said, weird. But in a good way."

"Cool." I take a pull at the bottle. It's got a slightly Red Bull feel to it, like a mild energy drink. "Mmm! I like this!"

I look around as I swig from the Irn-Bru. The arts-center

foyer is really overdue for a makeover; it looks like it was built in the 1970s and hasn't been touched since. From a design module we did last term, I recognize the yellows, browns, and oranges of the swirly carpet, the low ceilings, and the Formica-covered tables and matching, equally chipped chairs as classic seventies. The lighting is fluorescent and about as flattering as a size-S tube dress on a size-L girl. The only positive thing to be said about the decor is that you could tip bucketfuls of lurid orange Irn-Bru onto the carpet and no one would ever notice.

"They could sell those CDs three times over," Taylor says, indicating Mac Attack, who are still signing away; even though quite a few girls are clutching their CDs, now adorned with the signatures of all five boys in the band, the table is still surrounded, because the fans are hanging around, staring adoringly at their new idols.

I can't completely blame them. Callum is by no means the only handsome one in the group. The flautist is a square-jawed, stockily built guy with impressive shoulders and a sprinkling of brown freckles over his wide nose; the guitarist is tall and lanky, with a tangle of dark red curls, and as he looks down at the fourteen-year-old girls eagerly holding out CDs to him, he has a twinkle in his hazel eyes that makes me warm to him. He looks like an older brother being nice to his younger sister's friends.

And then, of course, there's Callum, sitting in the middle, looking bashful at the attention.

"He doesn't look that happy," Taylor comments.

"He never looks that happy," I say. "Or at least, he didn't when I knew him."

"Yeah," Taylor says. "I only met him once, and it wasn't exactly . . ."

She trails off, but I know precisely what she means. Remembering the circumstances under which Taylor, Callum, and I all found ourselves in a ruined tower on his family's Scottish estate wouldn't bring a smile to anyone's face.

I feel sad all over again, thinking about what happened. And just at that moment, Callum happens to look my way. Our eyes meet, and I see the shock of recognition in his, followed, almost instantly, by a welter of confused emotions. Surprise, naturally; sadness, just like mine; and something else, too, something that echoes what I'm feeling now as I look into his gray-green eyes. Another memory.

Because the last time I saw Callum, we kissed.

But I knew, after Dan's death and what happened in that tower, that Callum and I could never be a couple. Too much baggage, too much bad, sad history. I thought it was best to close the door and move on quickly, never looking back.

And there it would have stayed. If it weren't for this accident of fate that's brought us together, staring at each other across the foyer of the Edinburgh Arts Center as a pack of fourteen-year-olds bay for his attention like yappy Chihuahuas.

"*Huh,*" Taylor says, reaching for a wrap, handing me one. "Here. Eat that. And when you've finished, you can fill me in on exactly what happened between you and Callum. I mean, I know you kissed, but from the way you're looking, it was more like what you'd call"—she pauses, concentrates, and attempts her best British accent—"*a full-on snogfest,*" she concludes triumphantly, sounding so funny that I crack up laughing. Which, mercifully, makes her cross enough to distract her from further speculation about Callum and me . . .

•  •  •

"Are you Scarlett?" says a male voice, just as I'm chugging the last drops of my Irn-Bru. I cough, wipe my mouth inelegantly with the back of my hand, and nod in the direction of the guitarist from Mac Attack, the redheaded one with the nice eyes. The teachers supervising the younger teens are rounding them up now, though it's like herding cats, and the Mac Attack boys have sold every one of their CDs and T-shirts; the table they were sitting at is completely bare.

The guitarist leans over, partly because he's a lot taller than me, partly because, from the way he looks quickly from side to side, he has something to say he doesn't want anyone else to hear.

"Callum's in the greenroom," he says. "He asked me to pop over and see if you'll come back for a word with him. It's a madhouse out here."

"Um, okay—"

"Ewan! Will you sign my T-shirt?" a girl asks, tugging at his arm, staring up at him adoringly. "You're my favorite out of all of them!"

"Wait here a wee minute," he says to her, rolling his eyes at me as he turns to shepherd me off. I dart a look back at Taylor as I go: her eyebrows are raised in two straight black lines, and she lifts one hand to her mouth, kissing her palm sexily in a reference to what she knows about me and Callum.

*Thanks*, I think sourly. *That really helps, Taylor.*

Ewan whips me in double-quick time through the auditorium doors, down the central aisle, and up onto the stage. I'm so busy skipping along to keep up with him, jumping over the wires and white tape on the stage floor and dodging the amps, that I have no time to anticipate what it will be like seeing Callum again; so when we nip down some stairs in the wings and push through a door at the bottom, I'm catching my breath, still unready.

Like Ewan, Callum is still in the black Mac Attack T-shirt and kilt—I assume his is the McAndrew tartan—which he wore for the gig. His wool socks are pulled up to the top of his calves, which means I can see his knees and part of his muscular thighs as he moves.

This doesn't help.

He's laying his violin in its case, wrapping it in a white cloth as carefully as if he were swaddling a baby.

"Package delivered," Ewan says breezily. "Um, I'd better get back, eh? There's kids out there still want their T-shirts signed. We're on fire, man!"

He nods at me and dashes back out again. Callum closes the violin case and snaps the clasps shut, making more of a production of it than he needs to.

I understand why. If I had anything to do with my hands, I'd be concentrating on it just as hard.

"Hey, Scarlett," he says eventually, finally meeting my gaze.

"Hey," I say back, shifting from one foot to the other, wishing in vain that I were wearing something a little smarter than jeans and a hoodie. "You were really good. All of you."

"Yeah?" He reaches up and rubs one hand over his short hair, looking sheepish. "It went okay, I thought."

"You should sing more," I offer. "We were all saying it."

"Oh, man." Callum looks really embarrassed. "I feel such an eejit when I sing. But it seemed to go over okay."

Callum doesn't have the ideal personality for the front man of a band: he's not someone who loves to be in the spotlight. His twin brother, Dan, was the one with all the charming, attention-seeking genes. Dan would have done a much better job than Callum of talking to the audience between songs, all that banter and joking that a good front man can do. Callum just mumbled the names of the songs before each one, and then raised his violin bow gratefully, like someone who would much rather be playing than talking.

So it had been quite unexpected when, called back for an encore, Callum had bashfully announced that they would be doing a traditional song called "The Blooming Bright Star of Belle Isle," cleared his throat, and started to sing, in a light, melodic tenor: ·

> "One evening for pleasure I rambled
> To view the fair fields all alone
> Down by the banks of Loch Erin,
> Where beauty and pleasure were known."

23

It was a sweet, romantic song; Callum did a surprisingly good job of it, with Ewan harmonizing very well. And naturally, it drove the girls in the audience wild.

"I had to psych myself up to do it," Callum admits now. "Ewan said he'd start singing and if I didn't join in, he'd look like an even bigger eejit, because he doesn't sing the tune. So I had to. *Man.*" He grins. "I'm really glad it's over."

"It won't be so hard the second time," I say.

"That's what Ewan said! He was slapping me on the back afterwards and saying I'd popped my cherry." Callum blushes. "Sorry," he mutters.

I wave my hand in what's supposed to be a sophisticated, knowing gesture, but I'm nervous that it comes out more like I'm a loony trying to flap away nonexistent flies.

"Did you want to—"

"I thought I'd just—"

We both start to speak at the same time, break off, and manage to laugh about it, which dissolves the tension a little.

"I thought I'd just see if we could say hi quietly," Callum starts again. "Because it's, you know, a bit crazy out there. We didn't really expect this. And I saw some of the girls Dan used to hang out with. Plum. And Nadia." He grimaces. "I know what they're like."

*Actually, you don't, I think. Boys never know how girls like that can behave. Because they keep the really bad stuff for when the boys aren't around.*

"Yeah," I agree. "They're nightmares."

"Like Lucy," Callum says, naming his ex-girlfriend. "I didn't realize what she was all about 'till later. *You* know."

I nod grimly. I do know, all too well.

"It's nice to see you, Scarlett," he goes on. "I— When you visited Castle Airlie, things were so messed up, you know? It's nice to see you somewhere that isn't, um, there."

He grins again, and it's like a shaft of sunlight hitting a stained-glass window; it lights up the room. I forgot how handsome Callum is when he smiles. Probably because I've barely seen him do it.

"That was really clumsy," he says. "But you know what I mean."

"It's nice to see you too," I say, truly meaning it.

And we stand there for a moment, just smiling at each other. It's the first time Callum McAndrew and I have ever been comfortable in each other's presence, I realize. Even when we kissed, it was painful, poignant, because we knew very well it was the first and last kiss there would ever be: a kiss goodbye.

But now there's an ease between us. We don't even need to say anything; it's as if the past is fading and we can start again.

I wasn't expecting this. And I like it a lot.

"Callum, *darling*! Why are you hiding back here? You should be out in the bar with your fans!"

Plum comes tripping into the greenroom, arms out-stretched. She's trailing a cloud of perfume, Valentino Rock 'n Rose: she must have just sprayed more on. It's her favorite at the moment and I don't think it suits her at all—Plum is neither sweet nor rosy.

She's also trailing her sidekicks, Susan and Lizzie. Until Plum came to Wakefield Hall, Susan was a diamond in the rough, a tall, slender blonde with beautiful features who looked washed out by her pale eyelashes and eyebrows, and slobby in oversized sweaters and loose jeans; now that Plum has made her over, Susan looks like an off-duty supermodel. Legs up to her armpits, hair down to her tiny waist, mascara and eyebrow pencil giving her stunning features definition—you'd hate her if she weren't so sweet.

While Lizzie, bless her heart, is a fluffy golden retriever of a girl desperately trying to prove she has a place in the smart set by flaunting the latest designer bag. Taylor and I are quite fond of Lizzie, all things considered, but she's so keen to please that she'll do whatever the last strong-minded person she bumps into tells her to do. Basically, she's a pinball that anyone can flip.

Susan and Lizzie stand back, knowing their places, as Plum sashays forward, purring:

"You were *fabulous!*" She kisses Callum theatrically on both cheeks. "*Especially* when you sang! We all got goose bumps!" She pulls back slightly, indicating Susan and Lizzie. "Didn't we?" she prompts, and they bob their heads in response like nodding dog mobiles hung from a rearview mirror.

"Yeah, um, thanks," Callum says, looking hunted. "I should really be getting out there. Like you said."

"Of course! Let's go back!" Plum takes his arm and swings round to face the door.

Which means that she sees me for the first time.

"*Scarlett?*" she exclaims, looking quickly from me to Callum. "What are *you* doing here?"

"We're just catching up," Callum says quickly.

"I didn't even know you two *knew* each other!" Plum says, dragging Callum out of the greenroom. "You're *such* a dark horse with the boys, Scarlett!"

I don't know how she manages it, without a word being said, but by the time she's escorted Callum back over the stage and through the auditorium, she's silently ordered Lizzie to nip ahead of her and push open the doors, holding one ajar so that Plum and Callum can make an entrance into the foyer. Heads duly turn; eyes light up on spotting Callum. Plum's gripping his arm for dear life, as if he's a human trophy she's just won. Taylor comes over, grimacing at me.

"I saw her heading back there," she says. "But I'd've needed a stun gun to stop her."

"We should probably get one," I say. "In case of emergency."

"Callum! Hi!" Nadia calls loudly, to summon as much attention as possible her way. Then she steps over to him like a runway model, narrow hips swinging, legs stepping high, hair tumbling around her shoulders. "You were *fabulous!*"

"Yes, thanks, I've done that bit already, Nadia," Plum snaps.

"Hey, Plum," Sophia von und zu Something says blithely, following Nadia over. Sophia, bless her, is an Austrian countess. Very titled, very rich, and very thick. I honestly don't think she would have been accepted at St. Tabby's if it hadn't been for the first two factors; St. Tabby's is a *much* snobbier school than Wakefield Hall. My grandmother, who's the headmistress of Wakefield, would never have dreamed of taking Sophia, who has the mental capacity of a newt that just got hit by a car.

While Plum's distracted by Nadia, Callum manages to slip his arm free and swivel toward me.

"Callum, you remember Taylor," I say, and he nods.

"Hey," he says. "Nice to see you."

"You too," she says, smiling at him, and I realize instantly that she means it; she's not just being polite.

*Phew*, I think, *Taylor likes Callum*. For some reason, that seems to be important to me.

"Goodness, Scarlett, was one McAndrew brother not enough for you?" Plum says nastily, swinging round on us. "What are you trying to do—collect the set?"

My mouth drops open at the sheer unpleasantness of this, and Callum must be similarly stunned, because he doesn't say anything either. It's Taylor who snaps at her:

"Hey! You're out of line!"

"Oh, Callum, have you met Scarlett's bodyguard yet?" Plum asks, narrowing her eyes at Taylor. "Careful—you don't want to get on her wrong side! She's *very* butch."

I'm not putting up with this kind of thing from Plum.

"Oh, you're just jealous because Taylor's so photogenic," I retort. "You wish you looked as good in photos as Taylor does."

This hits squarely home; I actually see Plum swallow. She's got very used to taunting Taylor, secure in the confidence that she knows a juicy secret of Taylor's that means her victim won't answer back. But Plum's forgotten that I now have something as equally juicy on *her* as she does on my best friend.

"*Right,*" she manages feebly, tossing her hair in front of her eyes so that she doesn't have to look at me. "As *if.*"

And Nadia's glossy blue-black head turns from me to Plum, her dark eyes alert. Nadia's shown herself to be a smart operator; she's managed to use me and Taylor in the past to get something she wanted, playing us as smoothly as Callum played his violin. Now she's picked up on an odd vibe between me and Plum, and, knowing Nadia, she won't rest till she finds out what's at the bottom of it.

Which is by no means what I want to happen.

*Maybe I shouldn't have taken Plum on in front of Nadia,* I reflect. The trouble is, I'm not brilliant at these girl-on-girl politics, the guerrilla warfare games, that Plum, Nadia, and their set are so expert at playing. I made a basic mistake: I didn't think before I opened my mouth.

And then I relax. After all, meeting here is just a freaky coincidence. It's not like our path and that of the St. Tabby's girls are going to cross at all in the future. God knows what they're doing here, anyway; Scottish folk music is much too earnest for St. Tabby's supersmart image.

"Well, hello!" says a voice with an odd accent, and when we swing round to see who it is, I find myself staring right at the skinny chest of the lead violinist from Hürti Slärtbärten. He's changed—mercifully—out of his bright red silk blouse, but the faded grayish-white T-shirt with the Rolling Stones logo that he's wearing instead isn't much of an improvement. Especially as I think we can all tell, by his cloud of body odor, that he got pretty sweaty during his gig.

Thank God, he's not talking to me; he's looking straight at Nadia.

"You are a very pretty girl!" he says.

As if this is going to be news to Nadia.

"I would like to ask you to come for a drink with me," he continues as all of us stare at him in absolute incredulity.

"Jeez, he has balls of *steel*," Taylor whispers to me.

It's true. This geeky boy with gelled-up hair and a flaming acne breakout, smelling strongly of sweat, is hitting on one of the reigning princesses of London society. Not only that, but he's acting as if her answer is a foregone conclusion.

"You perhaps saw me onstage," he continues, nodding in a patronizing way to the rest of us. "I am *very* famous in Norway. So!" He smiles at Nadia. "We go for a drink?"

Nadia is looking from side to side, her eyes flickering nervously, and I know exactly why: I know how these girls' minds work by now, even if I'm not an expert at their games. She thinks some frenemy of hers is setting her up—maybe getting ready to take a photo of Nadia and Mr. Hürti Slärtbärten that they can then post on Facebook, captioned *Nadia and her new sick crush!*

"Don't worry!" he says jovially to the rest of us. "I bring her back safe and whole!"

Lizzie, unfortunately, loses it at this point and starts to giggle, tossing her carefully straightened and highlighted hair from side to side. It *would* be Lizzie, of course.

"Right!" Ms. Burton-Race, St. Tabby's history teacher, bustles up to us. "St. Tabby's girls, with me! Time to go home! We have a busy day tomorrow!"

I don't think Nadia's ever been that grateful to see a teacher in her life.

30

# Three

## "GOOD FRIENDS TELL YOU THE TRUTH"

"*That* was worth the price of admission," Taylor comments as we curl up at the back of the coach.

"I've never seen Nadia lost for words before," I agree appreciatively.

"The thing is, in the normal world, a boy who looks like that would never dare to come near her," Taylor says thoughtfully. "I mean, she must be used to princes and kids with million-pound trust funds hitting on her."

"Sophia von und zu Whatsit's older brother's a Graf," I offer. "That's a count or an earl or something in Austria. And apparently he's always after Nadia."

"There you go. So when old Stinkyspots came up to her, she literally couldn't believe it," Taylor says happily.

"No one could. It'd be like Aunt Gwen thinking she had a chance with Johnny Depp," I say, much to Taylor's amusement.

Then I dart a glance up the aisle. Aunt Gwen's sitting right at the front of the coach: there's no chance she could have heard me. Still, better to be safe than sorry where Aunt Gwen's concerned.

"Scarlett?" Taylor says more seriously.

"Yeah?" I put my feet up, wedging them on the seat back in front, getting comfortable.

"That photo of Plum you have," Taylor continues, lowering her voice now. Most of the girls, still excited from the concert, are chattering away, and the coach is a thirty-seater, much bigger than we need, so we're all spread out; still, she's talking about something so potentially explosive that I totally get why she's taking extra precautions not to be overheard. "It's somewhere really safe, right?"

I nod. Last year, in the course of trying to find out how Dan McAndrew had died, I came across a hidden stack of Polaroid photos of girls in—um, well, sexy poses. Not (blush) really horrible, hard-core stuff, but certainly not the kind of thing that anyone would want shown round. Or scanned and uploaded to Facebook.

Nadia was in there. Lucy, Callum's ex-girlfriend. Sophia von und zu Whatsit.

And so was Plum.

I burned almost all the photos. But something told me to keep one of Plum. Just in case. Plum had been awful to me after Dan's death, had practically driven me out of St. Tabby's. I felt bad about it, because I knew that none of those girls would want anyone to see those photos but the person who'd taken them, but having some Plum insurance had seemed like a sensible precaution.

And I'd been right. To be honest, in all the mayhem that directly followed my finding that photo, I'd forgotten for a while that I had it. I'd shoved it in my back pocket, only coming across it again when I was stuffing my dirty clothes in the washing machine at Aunt Gwen's; it was sheer chance that the Polaroid didn't go through a spin cycle and get washed out to nothing. I put it in my desk drawer, burying it under a pile of boring old exercise books so that Aunt Gwen wouldn't come across it.

Only a few weeks ago, I showed it to Taylor. And that was because Plum has found out something about Taylor's brother that she's been using to torment Taylor. Taylor's family, it turns out, work for a secret U.S. agency. I'd say they were spies, but Taylor would whack me round the back of the head for using that word, so I won't. Taylor's brother, Seth, was on some kind of mission in Venice over New Year's, pretending to be a superrich trust-fund boy with more money than sense, when Plum met him and unfortunately—because apparently he looks really like Taylor—knew immediately that he wasn't who he said he was.

Plum has been using that knowledge to get at Taylor ever since. And it wasn't till I flashed the photo in front of Plum and told her that if she didn't play nicely with the other girls, it would find its way to all sorts of online sites, that she backed off.

(I may also have added that her tummy looked fat in the photo. And that there was some cellulite on her thighs. Neither of which is true, but there's nothing more likely to make a girl take your threat seriously than if you say you have a photo of her looking like she has cottage-cheese legs. I may not have a lot of experience at girl-on-girl politics, but I'm learning.)

33

"It's in the jewelry safe," I say smugly. "Inside the box with my necklace."

I inherited—sort of—a very valuable necklace from my mother. And once I found out how very valuable it is, I decided to keep it in the Wakefield jewelry safe, watched over by my grandmother's secretary, Penny.

"That's *very* smart," Taylor says approvingly. "Even if Plum knew where it was, there's no way she could *ever* get to that safe."

"I know," I say even more smugly as Taylor high-fives me.

"Girls!" Miss Carter says over the mike at the front of the coach, making us all jump. "We're driving along Princes Street! On your right, you'll see Edinburgh Castle, which we'll visit in a couple of days, and the National Museum of Scotland. . . ."

The castle's high on a hill, above a deep gorge, dark and looming, lit up from below with orange lights that make it look imposing and eerie in equal measure. It's hard not to be impressed.

"Ooh!" Lizzie squeals, looking to the left instead, which seems to be Edinburgh's main shopping street. "Topshop! And H&M! And Accessorize! They have them all here, too!"

"Of course they have the same shops here, Lizzie," I say, rolling my eyes. "We're still in the UK."

"Glad to hear you have your priorities right, Lizzie," Miss Carter says rather sarcastically. "Forget the centuries of history at Edinburgh Castle! Robert the Bruce; Mary, Queen of Scots, giving birth to James the First; Oliver Cromwell

34

invading Scotland and capturing the castle . . . But no, just focus on Edinburgh's shopping opportunities, why don't you?"

The coach turns to the left, dipping down an incline. Edinburgh is really striking; all the buildings are high and made of gray stone, and uplit against the black night sky. It isn't cozy or welcoming; it's too stark for that. But it's definitely stunning: wide streets, dark churches, imposing gray buildings.

And apart from Edinburgh's beauty, I feel a huge sense of relief at simply being somewhere new. Wakefield Hall has so many confused memories for me now; every place that Jase and I kissed, everywhere that was special to me, is overlaid now with fear and sadness.

Because I'm scared that Jase and I will never be together like that again.

Taylor and I stare out the window as the coach takes a turn at a large, impressive roundabout, and lumbers down a hill. Shuttered shops loom close to us, tall apartment windows rising high above them, golden light filtering from behind closed curtains relieving the starkness of the city's architecture.

"I had no idea Edinburgh was so steep," Taylor says as we grab the seat backs in front of us, bracing against the incline. "It's like San Francisco."

Eventually the hill levels off and we're driving along a road with stone walls on either side, turning into a short stretch of grassy parkland. Another coach passes us, coming in the other direction, flashing its lights briefly in acknowledgment as we veer slightly onto the grass verge to make room for it. And then we're pulling up outside yet another imposing gray stone building.

"This is Fetters School," Miss Carter announces as the doors open. "We'll be staying here for the half-term week. It's a boys' school," she adds, "so you may not find all the creature comforts you're used to."

There's a palpable stir of excitement at this news—boys!—which Aunt Gwen promptly crushes. Her favorite hobby is killing people's dreams.

"Of course, as it is half-term, the boys are off on holiday," she informs us with a note of triumph in her voice. "Fetters is empty apart from us and a skeleton staff."

"I think she *likes* giving us bad news," Lizzie says sadly to Susan as we clamber down from the coach and drag out our cases. I feel a sudden wash of exhaustion flooding over me; it's been a long day. We were up before seven this morning to give us time to get into central London and catch the train from King's Cross. I can't wait to pull my clothes off and fall into bed.

But the last surprise of today is still to come. As we bump our cases up the entrance stairs and through the main doors of the school building, the girls in front of us stop dead, causing a ripple effect; I bump into Lizzie, in front of me, who in turn bumps into Susan.

"What's going on?" Taylor says from behind me as her suitcase knocks painfully into my legs.

"I dunno," I say, wincing. "But *ow.*"

"Girls! Please!" Aunt Gwen calls impatiently, and we all tumble forward into the hall, stumbling on each other's suitcases.

You can tell Fetters was built as a school, not the stately home that Wakefield Hall was before my grandmother bowed to financial reality and turned it into an upmarket girls' penitentiary. Fetters's entrance hall is institutional-looking, painted pale blue, with noticeboards hung between each set of paneling, and lit with violently bright fluorescent strip bulbs that illuminate the hall so brightly there's no place to hide. Immediately, I spot the cluster of girls standing at the back, gathered around a reception desk.

That's what caused the Wakefield Hall girls to stop in their tracks. Plum, who's leading the way, is staring over her Vuitton suitcases at them, her body tense. Because it's the St. Tabby's contingent—Nadia, Sophia, Alison, Luce, and the rest of the smart set. They're staring at us with the same dismayed and appalled expression that I imagine our own faces are wearing.

"You're staying here *too*?" Plum blurts out angrily.

"Jane! Clemency!" Ms. Burton-Race calls from the desk, where she's flipping through pages on a clipboard. "Fast work, eh? We're on Corridor E, and you and your girls are on Corridor B. Just below us. Nice and cozy."

She beams at Miss Carter and Jane.

"I'm *so* glad we decided to join forces!" she says cheerfully. "It's going to be lots of fun all going round Edinburgh together! And *so* much better for the environment—we can share one coach, instead of using two!"

Plum's glaring at Nadia. Alison and Luce are staring scornfully at me. I try to give them an apologetic look in return, but they peg their chins high in disdain and turn away as soon as my eyes meet theirs.

"Oh *boy*," Taylor mutters behind me.

I couldn't have said it better myself. "Lots of fun" is *not* exactly how I would have summed up the coming half-term week.

· · ·

"Uh, Scarlett?" Taylor says, and if it were anyone but her asking, I'd call her tone distinctly nervous. Taylor doesn't do nervous. But still . . .

I turn my head, which feels as heavy as a ten-pound weight (actually, on reflection, it *is* a ten-pound weight, I suppose) and stare at her, my eyes glazed with exhaustion. She's sitting on the edge of her bed, dressed in the red pajamas with white Scottie dogs on them that she bought from Victoria's Secret in America. Taylor has lots of pajamas from Victoria's Secret, and I crave them all.

"Scarlett?" she says again, bending over to get a good look at my face, because it's tilted to one side on the pillow.

I'm completely drained. Turning my head used up the last surge of energy I had.

"I can't believe this," I say in a small, dull, tinny voice, like a suicidal robot. "It's like my entire past came back to haunt me, all in one day."

Taylor nods.

"Callum, plus Alison and Luce," she says soberly.

"Yeah. I feel so bad about them. Alison and Luce, I mean."

"Tomorrow you need to talk to them," Taylor advises.

"I sort of feel I should go and find them right now," I say.

38

"They'll be sharing a room. But I can't move." I try to wiggle my toes, and can't even manage that.

"When we get some free time, you can find them and go off by yourselves," Taylor says, "and basically apologize your ass off."

"Yep," I agree.

"I mean, you were completely in the wrong. You just have to fall on your sword and hope enough time's passed now that they'll forgive you."

"Yeah," I say more faintly.

"Of course, when people feel totally betrayed by their friends," Taylor continues, warming to her theme, "that's really hard to do. Forgive them, I mean. Because the trust is gone. They'll say lots of nasty things to you and you'll have to sit there and agree with everything."

"Not helping now," I mutter, but she's on a roll.

"You'll have to pretty much crawl on your hands and knees over broken glass," she says. "And even then, there's no guarantee—"

"Stop!" I snarl. "*Not* helping!"

I manage to drag myself up to sitting, and then catch the glint in Taylor's eyes.

"You did that deliberately," I accuse her.

She grins.

"You have to wash and get into your pj's," she says. "You were just lying there like a corpse in your stinky clothes. I had to do something."

"You could just have told me I ponged," I say, sliding off the bed and walking over to the far corner of the room.

The rooms here at Fetters are pretty basic compared to

what the Wakefield Hall girls get. Twin beds with mattresses that feel like they're stuffed with horsehair; two rickety old cupboards that smell, frankly, of trainers and jockstraps; and just one desk, over which I'm sure the two boys who share this room fight incessantly.

I pull off my hoodie, T-shirt, and bra and start running the water in the sink; I'm too tired and beaten down to feel like having a shower. When you're depressed, being completely naked under running water can be too much, too raw to cope with. Or maybe that's just me.

"It's weird that they have sinks in all the rooms," I say as I give myself a quick wipe-down with a soapy washcloth.

"Probably for the boys to wee in," Taylor says cynically. "Better that than out the window."

"Ugh!" I look down at the sink, scanning it for yellow marks. "That's disgusting!"

"You grow up with an older brother, you know just how gross and disgusting boys can be," she says, climbing into bed. "Honestly, it put me off them for years."

"I'm not surprised," I say, using my washcloth to turn off the taps, then remembering I have to brush my teeth. "Do you and Seth get on all right? You never talk about him much."

"That's the whole family situation," Taylor says, yawning. "It's just easier not to. But yeah, Seth's cool. He used to try to mess with me when I was younger, but I responded with maximum force." Even over the noise of my electric toothbrush, I can hear the grin in her voice. "He gave that up after a while. We're not, like, superclose, but we have each other's backs now."

"Sounds nice," I say a little wistfully, rinsing my mouth and pulling on my own pajamas (H&M flannel, and not half as nice and fluffy as Taylor's). "Shall I get the light?"

"Sure. I'm—uh, *knackered*," Taylor says, careful with her pronunciation of the English word.

I giggle.

"Very good," I say, yawning too, and turning off the light. I crawl into bed. "Ooh," I say. "Sheets and blankets instead of a duvet. Weird."

"I know," Taylor says. "Very old-school."

"Funny," I say appreciatively.

"So, Scarlett?" she asks, her voice sleepy now. "The Callum thing? What's up with that?"

I feel myself frown.

"There is no Callum thing," I say. "It was a total shock to see him again, but he was really nice about it. I mean, it was nice of him to want to say hi to me just by ourselves, after everything that's happened."

"Yup," Taylor says a little dryly. "Very nice of him."

I'm not an idiot. I know what she's pointing out. That I keep using the word *nice*, when it's not precisely what I mean.

"He's really handsome," I say frankly, "and he's pretty cool. I'd be blind if I didn't notice how handsome he is."

"And deaf," Taylor points out. "All those girls screaming his name after each song."

"Yeah." I grin, remembering the barely-teens with their high-pitched squeals. "But still, there is no Callum thing. When we kissed—"

I blush in the dark, thinking about it; maybe one day I'll

41

be sophisticated enough to be completely cool about kissing cute boys, but that's a long way off yet.

I clear my throat.

"Um, anyway, when that happened," I mumble, "I never thought I'd see him again. For, you know, obvious reasons. And then we went back to Wakefield, and Jase and I got together, and now . . ." I sigh. "Now I'm in love with Jase."

It should be such a happy thing to say. Because Jase loves me back. He told me so. I should be incredibly happy to be in love with a wonderful, gorgeous, caring guy who's in love with me.

The trouble is, Jase told me he loved me and promptly got on his motorbike and rode away. That was months ago. I haven't seen him since.

I remember seeing the red taillight of the bike fading into the dark. It sounds really romantic put like that, doesn't it? But what I'm learning, the very hard way, is that things that sound romantic in books or films are often horrendously painful in real life. And not pretty or rose-tinted at all.

So here I am, in love with a boy I might never see again. Nicely played, Scarlett.

"But you don't know where Jase is," Taylor says simply. "Or what he's doing. Or when you'll see him again."

I gulp.

"Sorry," she says, sounding repentant. "It's just that—"

"No, you're right," I say miserably. "Good friends tell you the truth, not just what you want to hear."

"I could try to be a bad friend," Taylor offers.

I sniffle in maudlin amusement.

"I'm in love with Jase," I say in a small voice. "I can't just turn that off like a tap."

"Of course not," Taylor says gently. "I was just asking."

"We never talk about who *you* like, Taylor," I say, and not just to distract myself from the enormous lump in my throat. "I mean, it's all about my messed-up love life, all the time."

"Yours is a lot more dramatic than mine," Taylor points out.

"Yes, but it shouldn't be all about me." I yawn, deeply now. "Tomorrow we'll talk about you . . . who you like . . . if you like anyone. . . . Oh God, I started talking about you and now I'm going to sleep. . . . I'm sorry. . . ."

But Taylor's already snoring heavily. I just have time to think *No! That's going to keep me awake all*— before I fall asleep myself as if someone hit me over the head with a brick.

· · ·

*My heart is pounding with excitement, because I'm about to meet Jase. I'm running down Lime Walk, the wide avenue lined on either side with tall linden trees that runs along the Great Lawn at Wakefield Hall and leads to the bottom of the stepped stone terraces rising to the old house. Where Jase is waiting for me.*

*My feet tangle in vines, and I kick them free. My trainer laces are working loose, but I keep running. I cut down across the Great Lawn to avoid the vines, but the grass is surprisingly high—why hasn't Jase cut it? It's at my ankles, but it's growing so fast I'm having to leap higher and higher to move through it—now it's almost up to my knees, slowing me down as if I'm wading through water. And the school bell's ringing, calling me back to the next lesson, which means I'll have no time with Jase at all.*

*But I might not even get to school. I might never see Jase. Because the grass is rising higher, up to my chest, my neck—I've got my hands up now, desperately pushing it away, trying not to choke, and the bell's ringing louder and louder—I'm going to be in such trouble if I miss class—*

I'm thrashing my head from side to side. I wake up gasping, the blankets and sheets caught in a tight twist around me as if someone tried to mummify me in my sleep. And that wasn't the only part of my dream that was real; the room is actually vibrating with the reverberations from the bell, which is pounding out in a long scream of emergency—

*Emergency. Alarm bell.*

"Taylor!" I scream, throwing the bedclothes off.

She's stirring, moaning in her sleep, and I dash over, grab her shoulders, and pull her up and out of bed.

"Fire alarm!" I yell. "Fire alarm!"

I hear voices outside the room now, footsteps pounding down the corridor. I know that sometimes you're not supposed to open the door when there's a fire, but I think that's when it's hot to the touch: I jam my palm against the wood and it feels okay. Plus, the door handle isn't burning. I drag the door open and turn to see Taylor stumbling out of bed, still half asleep.

"Come *on!*" I say, and then I do something I never thought I'd be reckless, or desperate, enough to do: I slap Taylor hard on the cheek, so hard that my palm stings.

"Aah!" Her eyes snap fully open and she shakes her head like a boxer recovering from a punch.

Sensibly, I nip behind her so that she can't hit me back, and start pushing her through the door. The corridor is full of smoke, and as we exit the room, it suddenly intensifies into a thick, blinding cloud. I cough. People are calling from the left, and we turn that way; I think I hear Miss Carter scream:

"Girls! *Girls!* Over here!"

We start down the corridor, feeling our way, trying not to stumble and trying not to panic; I can't believe how thick the billows of smoke are, settling around us like a heavy gray pall.

And then I hear it.

"Scarlett!" calls a faint voice behind me. "Scarlett! Help!"

I twist around, stopping in my tracks, squinting in a vain effort to see anything, anything at all. But I can't.

"Scarlett! *Help!*" comes the voice again.

There are rooms beyond ours down the corridor, at least four or five before the back staircase. Someone could still be in her room—someone who turned an ankle or something, getting out of bed in a panic. And—my brain flashes back to earlier this evening—the St. Tabby's girls are in the corridor above ours. One of them could have come down the stairs, running for the front door, tripped and fallen—

"Taylor?" I call, but she must have gone ahead without realizing that I wasn't hard on her heels.

I'm alone in the smoke.

It's a lightning-fast decision. I can't leave someone behind. Not when I'm the only person who knows there's a girl back there.

I turn and go as quickly as I can back down the corridor, yelling:

"Who's there? It's Scarlett! Are you okay?"

"Scarlett!" the voice comes, fainter now, as if she's being overwhelmed by the smoke. "On the stairs—"

*Alison? Luce?* I practically sprint for the fire door, dragging it open, choking as a fresh wave of smoke hits me. Doubling over, I'm overcome by long, racking coughs, and too late I think: *Wet hand towels—you're supposed to get something wet and put it over your mouth—I could have grabbed some and put them under the tap in our sink—ugh, why is it that you always forget what to do in an emergency, even though you've seen it in the films a hundred times—*

And just as I'm standing up again, drawing breath to yell once more for the girl who's been calling me for help, I feel two hands in the small of my back, and the next second they give me an enormous push that sends me hurtling forward.

It's such a shock that I can't get my footing. I'm catapulted ahead, tumbling over my feet, and another blow hits me, this time on the front of my body, a shockingly painful thwack across my hipbones. I double over again, but the momentum of that shove in the back means I'm still shooting forward.

*The stairs!* I think frantically, realizing what's happening much too late. *I slammed into the railing with my hips and when I doubled up, I went flying over it!*

I'll never know whether the person who pushed me came up behind me and gave me a final tip over the rail. I think they did. I couldn't possibly—even with the speed at which I was moving—have hit that balustrade fast enough for the impact to spin me and send me somersaulting over it into space.

Which is what happened. One moment I'm stumbling forward, in total shock at having been pushed so savagely; the next, I'm flying through the air headfirst, down a stairwell three stories high, with so much smoke in my lungs that I can't even scream.

# THERE'S ALWAYS A PLAN B

I'm spinning through the air, so dazed and stunned by what just happened that I don't even have time to be furious. I pivoted over that rail on my hips just as if I were doing the uneven bars in a gymnastics competition, but, having no control, I flipped head over heels. Thank God the stairwell's wide enough that I don't crack my legs on the far side and break something, but the lack of contact with anything solid means that I'm completely disoriented; I'm falling like Alice down the rabbit hole.

My back's arched, my hands are outstretched, my legs are flailing. Terror is screaming in my brain like a burst of white lightning, a firework exploding inside my head. If I don't do something fast—*really* fast—I'm going to crash to the hall floor far below. I'll be lucky if I just break a leg.

I could break my back.

I could die.

In a spasm of utter panic, I jackknife as if I were doing a flip between two bars. That gives me a little more momentum, a little more control, because as I come out of it my back is stretched to its full length, my arms reaching almost out of their sockets. It feels like Ricky, my old gymnastics coach, has his feet jammed into my upper thighs, and is leaning back, grabbing onto my wrists, pulling my back so long I have to bite my lip not to yell in pain.

My fingers are flexing frantically, reaching for anything they can find as I hurtle down the stairwell in an ugly, crooked swan dive. This is my one chance, this mad lunge across empty space, and if I don't make it, the consequences could be lethal—

Yes! My fingers slam into something and immediately, frantically, grip onto it as if I were drowning and it were a life preserver. The edge of the staircase. Has to be. It's a ninety-degree angle: my fingers are flat on the surface, my palms squeezing against the vertical face of the wall below, my hands clamping with everything I have as they take the weight of my entire body, which slams into the wall a second later.

*Owww!*—my *nose*—I brace my arms, desperately trying to hold myself far enough away so I don't smash it full force into the wall. The tip does smoosh against the wall, but I manage to jerk my chin up and lock my arms to give me a half inch or so. Barely adequate, but although I whack my nose, the cartilage doesn't break, thank God. I've seen girls break their noses before in gymnastics practice, taking headers onto the beam, and I know how bad it is. No way would I be able to keep clinging to the stair rung with that sort of pain in my face and pints of blood gushing out of my nostrils.

I'm flailing with my legs, but there's nothing below me;

49

the stair wall ends about midthigh. I can feel it cutting into me. I could try to swing my lower body enough to propel me forward onto the staircase below, but that's so high-risk the thought terrifies me immediately; if I don't make it, I'll land on my back or neck on the railing. And even if I do make it, I could still turn an ankle, break a leg, or worse, tumbling down the staircase.

*No. Can't do it.*

And my fingers are starting to slip.

*Okay. Stay calm. Find a Plan B. There's always a Plan B.*

Taylor and I have been doing a lot of oblique curl-ups recently. Trying to get into our waistlines, narrow them in. Neither of us has much in the way of a waist naturally, so this is something we've been working on hard: hanging off the bars at the school gym, pulling our knees to our chests, twisting from one side to the other.

Normally I would take a deep breath before I try this, but the heavy gray smoke surrounding me isn't going to help much with that. I cock my right hip, heaving it up as far as I can, using my abdominal muscles, curling into them to get my hip even higher so that my right leg can kick out sideways onto a stair edge.

My bare foot connects with two poles. *Banisters,* I think in triumph a second before I stub my toe painfully, unable to control how hard I sent my leg up and into them.

*Ow!* But I can't flinch. I need that banister to keep me alive. I push through the pain, driving my foot between the two banisters, jamming it there, my sole flat to the stair below, giving me enough purchase to take one hand off the stair it's on and reach for the stair rail above. I make it just as the other hand slips off, so sweaty by now it can't maintain its death clamp.

But I'm safe. One hand on a stair rail, one foot wedged between two banisters: that, to an ex-gymnast, is total security. My left foot snakes up to find the stair wall, walking up it vertically till my toes curl round the stair edge; my right hand comes up to grip the same banister as my left hand; like a monkey, I climb up it, swinging myself over the rail and landing on the concrete staircase.

I've never been more grateful to feel cold concrete beneath my feet in my life.

*Cold!* I think instantly, relief exploding in my brain. *If the fire were really dangerous, it'd be warm by now—which means it's okay to go downstairs—*

I dash down the stairs, smoke surrounding me, one hand on the stair rail to keep me oriented. I'm very aware that someone just pushed me—lured me into that stairwell and tried to kill me, or at least hurt me badly. I don't think she can have been watching my struggle to save myself, because the smoke is just too thick; but she could be lurking on the staircase, waiting in ambush.

She won't hear me though—bare feet make no sound on concrete. And I'd like to see her try to catch me. I'm down two flights in thirty seconds, flying on the pads of my feet, swinging round each turn of the stairs, pivoting round my hand on the stair rail like a dancer.

I usually hate fire doors; they're everywhere, they weigh a ton, you can't prop them open. But now I get the point of them for the first time in my life. Because at the bottom of the staircase is a fire door, and when I drag it open and dash through it, the smoke abates almost immediately.

*Oh my God! I can breathe!* And straightaway I start coughing in relief, the smoke that's been tearing at the lining of my lungs coming out now in a series of spasms as I stand for a moment, catching my breath, getting my bearings.

*Hooray for fire doors!* Ahead of me is a bright red Exit sign, and I lunge toward it, my hands slamming into the horizontal metal rail, pushing it down and away, an alarm wail going off as I slam the door open, adding an extra layer of cacophony to the siren of the fire alarm, which is still ringing madly overhead.

Fresh air. Cold white moonlight pouring through tree branches. Even colder stone beneath my feet.

And a group of screaming St. Tabby's and Wakefield Hall girls farther down the length of the school building, by the main entrance, clustered together on the grass.

More sirens are blaring in the distance. Still coughing, trying to catch my breath, I walk toward the girls, the damp night grass easier on my soles than the hard freezing stone, and as I get closer I see a struggle going on that resolves itself into Taylor at its center. She's wrestling to get free of Miss Carter, who's grabbing one of her arms while Jane, Miss Carter's girlfriend, holds on to the other. Taylor's in her red pajamas; Miss Carter is in pj's too, white with blue stripes, and Jane is wearing some sort of gray nightie with a lace trim. It's really weird to see teachers in their nightclothes. As if the universe got tipped on its head.

"You can't go back in there!" Aunt Gwen is shouting.

"Scarlett's in there!" Taylor yells. "I have to go! I thought she was right behind me!"

"Taylor"—Miss Carter sounds really distressed—"we can't let *anyone* back into the building—"

"I know where she was! I have to go back to find her!" Taylor's hair is falling in her face as she tries to shrug off the two women holding her.

Flashing lights, red and blue, appear suddenly as fire engines come past the high stone wall that encircles the Fetters grounds, turning in to the drive. The sirens' roar grows louder and louder, till everyone's screaming to be heard over it.

"Look, the firemen are here!" Miss Carter yells at Taylor. "They'll go in and find her! That's their job!"

"No! *I* have to! *I* have to go! She's my friend and I left her behind!"

I try to yell to Taylor that I'm okay, but my throat is still so sore I can't make a sound above a croak. Aunt Gwen, I see as I get closer, has her arms around Lizzie and Sophia, who are equally hysterical. I'd be amazed, if I had any time to process that sight. I've never seen Aunt Gwen willingly touch anyone. Emergencies obviously bring out sides of people's characters you never knew existed.

Just then, Taylor raises her arms and then wrenches them down so viciously that she loosens Miss Carter's and Jane's hold on her; they stagger back, crashing into Alison and Luce, who are in the group of St. Tabby's girls directly behind them. Shaking them free, Taylor takes off running. She's going straight for the front door. I can't shout, but I've got enough breath by now to take to my heels: I start running immediately, aiming to cut her off.

*I can't let her go back in there.*

Taylor's got better stamina than me, and she's much stronger. But gymnasts are sprinters. We have to be able to build up tons of momentum from a standing start. Also, we're used to taking really, really long strides to lengthen our bodies as much as possible.

She doesn't stand a chance. By the time I reach her I'm practically airborne. I lunge from my right foot and launch myself into what Ricky called Supergirl, almost horizontal in the air, my arms stretching out in front of me as if I'm flying, my legs stretching out behind me in parallel. Because this is how you go into a front handspring, my hands are intended to hit the ground first. And when you do floor work, you have to know exactly where your hands and feet are going to land—if you go outside the line, the judges deduct barrowfuls of points. It's been months and months since I did gymnastics, but my aim is still perfect.

My hands aren't aiming for the ground. They're targeted on Taylor's waist. A second later I barrel into her, my arms wrapping round her, my body rolling to the left, and there are huge "Ooofs!" of expelled air from both of us as we smash into the ground.

I was fast enough to grab her while she was still on the grass, thank goodness; otherwise the landing would have been even more painful. Red and blue lights flash across us as we roll over, elbows poking into each other. Taylor accidentally knees me in the tummy, and I groan.

"It's me! Scarlett!" I manage to pant.

*"Scarlett?"*

We've come to rest now, still tangled up in each other

on the damp grass. Taylor drags an arm out from under me and uses it to prop herself up enough to see my face.

"I thought you were back in there!" she yells at me angrily. "What *happened?*"

Firefighters are jumping down from the engines now, huge bulky bodies in their dark blue uniforms, unrolling gigantic hoses, the yellow reflective strips on their jackets and trousers catching the light and bouncing it back. They're shouting things to each other. I see two of them stride over to the group of girls and teachers.

"Someone tricked me!" I say, still panting. I wriggle free of Taylor and roll onto all fours; it's easier to breathe not lying flat on my back. "Some girl called my name, and when I went she pushed me down the back staircase—"

"*What?*"

I can't see Taylor's expression; the flashing lights are behind her, and they're layering red and blue over her face like something out of a music video. It's strangely hypnotic. I sink back to my heels, the shock of what just happened to me beginning to sink in, suddenly feeling totally drained.

"It's true," I say defensively, hearing the exhaustion in my voice. I know it sounds insane, like I have some sort of persecution mania. "She pushed me and I went over the stair rail."

"*Who?*"

"I don't know—I thought it was a girl, but the smoke was so thick—"

"Are you two all right?"

A fireman is bending over us, and we look up at him; he seems gigantic from this angle, larger than life, his voice distorted by his helmet. It's hard to believe there's a human being inside that shell.

"Yes," I say, as Taylor adds:

"She was in there longer than anyone—all that smoke—"

"I'm fine," I say as the fireman hooks one enormous yellow-gloved hand under my armpit and hauls me to my feet.

"Let's take a look at you, then, lassie," he says, pulling off his helmet, as behind him a loud voice yells authoritatively:

"Hold off, lads! Hold off!"

The sirens have stopped, though the lights are still flashing madly. The firefighters who were unrolling the hoses have stopped. The fireman is walking me over to the front steps, where he sits me down, yanks off one of his gloves, and checks my pulse. Two more firefighters pound heavily up the steps and in through the front doors, one of them saying to the other:

"I'm telling you, Stewart, sometimes there *is* smoke without fire—"

The fireman beside me hoists a huge yellow torch off his belt, turns it on, and points it into my face. I yelp feebly, raising one hand to shield my eyes.

"How's she doing?" asks another fireman, coming over.

"No facial burns, no singed nostril hairs," says the first one, directing the torch up my nose.

"Eeew!" I say indignantly, putting a hand up over it.

"You cough up any nasty black stuff, lassie?" the second one asks.

I shake my head.

"I've stopped coughing now, anyway," I say.

"No more coughing, no vomiting. Feel dizzy at all? Confused?" the first one asks.

I think this over.

"Just, you know, normal confusion," I say. "It's all been quite a shock."

*Nice understatement*, I think.

"Ach, she's fine. This is your chum, right?" He nods at Taylor, who's followed us and is standing behind him. "Keep an eye on her for the next hour or so, lassie. Ian, get me some water, will you?"

"Who's in charge here?" bellows one of the firefighters who entered the school building, emerging back outside, walking so heavily in his big boots that it looks as if he's wading through a river.

"I am!" Miss Carter, Aunt Gwen, and Ms. Burton-Race all chorus.

"Well, ladies," he says, waddling over to them, "I've got good news and bad news. The good news is that you never had much of a fire here. Just a lot of smoke. The bad news is that you've got some naughty girls playing silly buggers. Someone's been putting firelighters into those metal bins you have and setting them on fire."

He rolls his rs so heavily that *girls* comes out as *gurrrls*, and the word *fire* seems to last forever.

"Not just firelighters, Stew," says the other one, coming through the doors, waving a couple of long tubes in one yellow-gloved hand. "Some eejit's been playing around with smoke bombs."

"*What?*" Aunt Gwen and Miss Carter exclaim in shock.

"*Smoke bombs?*" Ms. Burton-Race echoes.

"They're smoke sticks," the second fireman informs us all. "Set off a few of these at once, you'll get a roomful of smoke. And if all the windows are closed, as they would be on a nasty damp night like this, you'll find that smoke hangs around for a long time."

"I can't *believe* this!" Ms. Burton-Race mutters furiously as the firefighter jumps down from the cab of one of the engines and comes over to me with a water bottle. I drink very gratefully; I hadn't realized how thirsty I was.

"You can all go back inside," says Stew, waving a huge yellow hand toward the front door. "And if I were you, ladies, I'd stage a major investigation, pronto, to find out which of these young women did something this stupid." He folds his arms over his chest. "Because playing with fire is verra, verra stupid, lassies. Someone could have got seriously hurt from smoke inhalation. Believe it or not, fifty to eighty percent of deaths from fires are down to smoke inhalation. Did you know that?"

We all shake our heads dutifully, eyes wide and fixed on Stewart; his voice is so booming and serious you can't help being impressed by him. Even Plum and Nadia, I notice, are focusing completely.

"And think about someone taking a nasty fall because they couldn't see where they were going!" he continues. "Think about someone going head over heels and breaking their neck! How would you feel if you'd played a silly trick like this and someone—one of your chums—got paralyzed for life? Or worse—died? Don't make me tell you how many corpses we've had to carry out of buildings! And what if one of those bins had overturned? You could have started a fire for real!"

Even though he pronounces *died* in a funny way, no one laughs. No one even sniggers. Stewart's manner is totally serious, and it makes us equally so. Looming over us, huge in his dark uniform, his shoulders looking wide as a house, the bright flashes of reflective strips gleaming, he's as imposing as the school building itself.

The lights in the hall come on. It's a shock, the harsh white fluorescent light flaming out into a long pale rectangle down the steps of Fetters like a theatrical effect; a couple of the girls yelp in surprise.

"All clear," says a firefighter, coming outside. "Safe for everyone to go back in now."

"We take what you just said *very* seriously, believe me, Officer," Miss Carter assures Stewart. "When we find out who did this, she will be very severely disciplined."

"Glad to hear it, miss," he says, standing aside as the teachers start shepherding the girls back into the school again.

Taylor helps me up; I'm surprisingly unsteady on my feet.

"Shock," the firefighter who looked after me says to us laconically. "Go slowly, lassie. And get some sleep."

"Thank you," I say, handing him back his water bottle.

It's so bright inside I find myself shading my eyes again with my hand. My throat's sore, even after drinking the water. Taylor's by my side as we follow the rest of the girls upstairs, one hand cupped under my elbow. Just in case.

"Ooh, look at Scarlett and Taylor," Plum coos, "all cozy and—"

"Shut *up*, Plum!" every single girl in earshot snaps simultaneously.

*Small mercies*, I think, managing to smile.

"Go to your rooms, all of you," Aunt Gwen says to us grimly. "We'll talk about this in the morning. And if I hear one peep out of any of you . . ."

She doesn't need to finish the sentence.

"I'm *so tired*," I say as I push open the door to our room. "I could sleep for a *week*."

There's a piece of paper on the floor. It must have fallen there, knocked off the desk when Taylor and I were evacuating the room, bleary-eyed and stumbling. Automatically, I bend over to pick it up.

"What is it?" Taylor asks, seeing me stare down at it, unable to believe what I'm reading.

Silently, I hand it to her. It's been torn from a notebook, white paper with faint gray lines making little boxes all over the background. Something about the paper's very familiar, but I can't access that memory right now, because I'm focusing on the thick black letters very carefully printed across the center of the page.

*No*, I realize. *Not printed; stenciled.*

*Clever. You can't trace handwriting from a stencil.*

And it reads, in capital letters:

YOU CAN'T RUN AWAY FROM THE PAST, SCARLETT.

# *five*

# "IN AUSTRIA THERE ARE MANY PRINCESSES"

We're all very, very subdued on the coach the next morning, for many reasons. Breakfast was delayed, to give us a chance to catch up on our sleep, but it turned out to be porridge, with a choice of raisins, golden syrup, jam, or stewed prunes. Very traditional and Scottish, and Miss Carter lectured us all about how porridge is the best way to start the day, but we're not used to eating that heavily in the morning (some of us aren't used to eating that many calories in a whole day), and now we're all slumped in our tartan-upholstered seats in a carbohydrate coma.

And, of course, that wasn't the only lecture we got this morning. Aunt Gwen, cold as an iceberg and much scarier, subjected us all to one of those "if the guilty party owns up now she will be dealt with leniently, but if she doesn't you will all undergo horrible punishment" speeches that never, *ever*, result in one girl standing up bravely, her hand on her heart, and saying:

"It was me, Miss Wakefield! I cannot see my fellow

students suffer for a crime I myself committed! Please—rain down whatever retribution you choose on me, but spare my innocent sisters!"

No one was idiot enough to confess to setting off the fire alarms and smoke bombs. So we're all waiting for the axe of punishment to descend on our necks, which is never a pleasant feeling.

But it does bring us nicely to Mary, Queen of Scots, who only reigned in Scotland for about five years before fleeing to England because lots of sexist old Scottish noblemen didn't like a woman being in charge of them and rose up against her. Then she was imprisoned by Elizabeth I and spent the next twenty years or so trying to escape, being moved around a series of castles, waiting for Elizabeth to decide she was too much trouble to keep alive, before having her head chopped off in 1587. With a sword, actually. Not an axe.

(We're doing the Tudors for history A-level. And we're on our way to Holyroodhouse, the Edinburgh royal palace, where poor old Mary lived most of the time when she was queen of Scotland.)

"I must say," I observe to Taylor, who naturally is sitting next to me, "being a princess isn't all it's cracked up to be."

Taylor raises an eyebrow.

"Who ever said it was?" she asks.

"Oh, I was desperate to be a princess when I was little!" I say, thinking of my obsession with the Little Mermaid and (God help me) Sleeping Beauty. "Isn't everyone? But look at Princess Diana. And Mary, Queen of Scots. And Elizabeth the First—I mean, she was a great queen, but she couldn't even get married because she didn't trust a guy not to try to take over her throne."

"I never wanted to be a princess," Taylor says flatly. "I wanted to be SpongeBob SquarePants." She considers for a moment. "Or Pippi Longstocking," she adds. "She was cool."

"I'm glad you identified with *one* girl," I say, not entirely sure whether Taylor's joking about SpongeBob. For an American, she has a really dry sense of humor.

"She was superstrong! And a pirate!" Taylor says. "Of course I liked her!"

"But they had fabulous dresses!" Lizzie's head pops up above the back of the seat in front. As usual, she's wearing a whole applicator pen's worth of eyeliner. It doesn't suit her, but it's fashionable, and that's all she cares about.

"SpongeBob SquarePants?" I ask, baffled. "Pippi Long-stocking?"

"*Princess Diana! Mary, Queen of Scots!*" Lizzie chants, her eyes bright. "And they had lots of lovers and they were really beautiful!"

"They had miserable lives and they died young," Taylor says flatly.

Lizzie pouts.

"You ruin everything, Taylor," she complains.

"In Austria," Sophia von und zu Whatsit observes, popping her head up next to Lizzie's, "there are many princesses, and some of them have very good lives."

As always when Sophia says something, I have absolutely no idea how to reply. She can kill a conversation dead at thirty paces.

Even Lizzie, Little Miss Chatterbox, is slightly flummoxed by this one.

"Do you know any princesses?" she asks eventually.

"Oh yes," Sophia says, her blue eyes opening wide like a really expensive doll's. She could be a china doll in almost every respect, I think: golden curls, round face, perfectly smooth white skin, brains made of hardened ceramic. "They are often guests at my parents' *schloss*," she continues.

"Your parents' *what?*" Taylor says incredulously.

"*Schloss!* It means 'castle' in German," Sophia informs her as I stifle a giggle. I know it's very immature of me to laugh at words in foreign languages, but there's no denying that *schloss* sounds pretty silly to English ears.

"Wow," Taylor says. "What's the plural of that?"

"*Schlosser*, of course!" Sophia says quite seriously.

I gulp as hard as I can, pressing my lips tightly together, and stare out the window. The coach has been chugging up one of the steep inclines that seem to characterize Edinburgh, and now it's diving down the other side, round a wide curve with a high, gracious crescent of houses on the right and a breathtaking view on the left: a drop that rises to rolling high hills beyond, grassy and green, the highest one peaked like a mountain, its top gray and craggy with stone outcroppings.

At least the talk about princesses and *schlosser* has distracted me for a little while from my speculation about who was behind last night's drama. That note just confirmed my suspicion that the entire thing was staged to lure me into the stairwell and give someone a chance to push me over the rail, making it look as if I were injured in a freak accident while I was trying to escape from what we all thought was a burning building.

I say "injured," but what I really mean is "killed." Because I don't know what my assailant meant to do to me—whether she really set out to kill me—but that was such a likely result of toppling me down the stairs that I shiver when I think about it. I have bruises on my arms where I whacked into the side of the staircase as a vivid reminder; not that I need one.

Someone has tried to kill me before. I've had a shotgun pointed at my face. But, weird though this sounds, that time it wasn't personal. I wasn't the intended target; I just got in the way.

This was personal. No question. That girl was calling my name. She knew exactly who she was shoving over that rail. And she wanted me to know she was nursing a huge grudge against me, a grudge that goes back into the past, because she left me a note to tell me so.

I shiver.

Alison? Luce? But this happened the very first night we found ourselves all staying at Fetters together. I refuse to believe that one of them has been traveling with firelighters and smoke bombs in her luggage for the past year, just in case she runs into me. Still, I suppose it's by no means impossible that someone could have overheard Ms. Burton-Race at St. Tabby's talking to another teacher about her plans to meet up with Miss Carter and the Wakefield Hall contingent in Edinburgh. . . .

Plum? I just don't see Plum, with her smooth hands and French manicure, painstakingly collecting metal rubbish bins and lighting firelighters in them. Or, strangely, being able to disguise her voice enough to trick me: Plum is always so much herself I don't believe she'd be capable of taking on another persona.

But I do believe that Plum would be able to talk or blackmail or bully someone else into doing it for her.

Then I wonder about Nadia. She's shown herself to be much sneakier than either Taylor or I thought she was. But I can't think of a motive for Nadia to go after me. Certainly nothing strong enough to make her want to see me badly injured. Or dead.

And so the spinning wheel of my thoughts returns to where it started: someone, last night, wanted to do me serious harm.

I just can't think of one thing I've ever done in my life that was bad enough for anyone to want to kill me.

"*It is a house of many memories. . . . Wars have been plotted, dancing has lasted deep into the night, murder has been done in its chambers,*" Ms. Burton-Race intones into the coach microphone, making us all jump. "Robert Louis Stevenson wrote those words about Holyrood in his 'Edinburgh: Picturesque Notes' in 1878. So now let's go and see the chamber where murder was committed for ourselves! *And* the bed slept in by Mary, Queen of Scots, plus the famous Darnley jewel!"

The coach is pulling up outside the golden-stone wall of what must be Holyroodhouse. And I have to give Ms. Burton-Race credit: I never had her for history at St. Tabby's, but she certainly knows how to grab your attention and get you interested. The porridge-induced carb coma is forgotten; the girls pile out almost before we've come to a stop, eager to see where a murder happened. Plus, of course, anything to do with Mary, Queen of Scots. And jewelry.

Famous jewelry. That's what's got us moving. Ms. Burton-Race really does know sixteen- and seventeen-year-old girls.

$\bullet$ $\bullet$ $\bullet$

"It's rather small for a palace, isn't it?" Plum says disdainfully as we walk through the high stone gateway into the central quadrangle of Holyroodhouse, a huge green grass square. High, symmetrical windows run all around the encircling golden-gray stone walls; it's beautiful, but you'd always feel watched. "I mean, I've *stayed* in ones that were much bigger."

A couple of women who work here, bustling past in their neat uniforms, shoot Plum killing looks at this insult. But she's oblivious, of course, as she is to pretty much anyone who has to work for a living.

"It is small, isn't it?" Nadia agrees, tilting her head back to look as Ms. Burton-Race points out the royal coat of arms carved on the part of the facade that hosts the royal apartments. "It's really more like a *stately home*."

"They're going to get stabbed," Taylor hisses to me as a tour group of Scottish people on the other side of the quadrangle stare across at Plum and Nadia and then start talking to each other with a lot of shaking heads and pursed mouths of disapproval. It's very unfortunate that both the girls have those high-pitched, clear, posh voices, which bounce around the stone walls, carrying their message of disdain to everyone within a hundred yards of them.

"'Murder has been done in its chambers,'" I quote to Taylor cheerfully. "And if someone *does* stab Plum, I for one am not investigating that."

"Jeez, no," Taylor agrees. "They'd be doing the world a service." She looks over at Plum and Nadia, who are rolling their eyes at each other, energized by having something to patronize. "Hey—did you know they were talking to each other again?" she asks me, frowning. "When did that happen?"

She's absolutely right.

"Good point," I say, thinking hard, as Ms. Burton-Race leads us inside the palace and immediately starts babbling enthusiastically about cantilevered stairs, fresco panels, and impressive plasterwork ceilings; there's a gigantic oak staircase, wide enough to ride a horse up, wrapping round the walls, rising three stories high to a ceiling that looks like wedding cake icing gone completely mad.

I tune out Ms. Burton-Race's commentary as we go up the stairs and into the royal apartments, that, of course, being the bit we're here to goggle at. Taylor's observation is bang-on: Plum and Nadia, as far as we know, are deadly enemies.

So why are they exchanging any kind of civil conversation, rather than scuttling around putting hair removal cream in each other's shampoo or—more likely—planting drugs on each other someplace where a teacher's bound to find it?

"This, of course, is the throne room," Ms. Burton-Race says, leading us into a large, red-carpeted room with shiny wood-paneled walls hung with portraits and chandeliers. We all draw in our breaths with excitement and then let them out again in disappointment. I've never seen a throne room, but I was expecting something really majestic: a carved golden seat high up on a dais, a bit like the ones in the film *The Slipper and the Rose* (a musical about Cinderella that is my all-time-favorite guilty pleasure. Taylor totally doesn't get it).

Instead, the thrones are smallish wooden seats, almost like folding chairs, upholstered in embroidered red velvet with golden tassels, low matching footstools placed in front of them. They're barely even elevated, just placed in a small alcove at the far end of the room, up a couple of red-carpeted steps.

"Scottish people," Taylor comments dryly, "aren't exactly show-offs."

"This is the official residence of the Queen when she comes to Scotland," Ms. Burton-Race says loudly, sensing our feelings of anticlimax. "She has an annual garden party here each July. And Prince Charles is resident here for a week every year too."

"Does that mean William and Harry have stayed here?" Lizzie says excitedly. "Oh my God! I *love* Harry!"

"How *can* you? He's a *ginge*!" Plum says disdainfully, slanting her eyes over at redheaded Alison.

"Plum!" Ms. Burton-Race says angrily. "That is a *very* discriminatory way to refer to redheads!"

And again, Taylor and I watch as Plum and Nadia roll their eyes and toss their hair back in unison, exchanging little superior smiles with each other.

"They've definitely made up," I say to Taylor. "Very interesting."

"It must have happened last night," Taylor says. "'Cause they didn't look at all friendly at the concert."

"No, they didn't," I agree. "Do you think Plum's lulling Nadia into a false sense of security so she can get some more stuff on her and have her revenge?"

"Or she's just going with 'If you can't beat 'em, join 'em,'" Taylor suggests.

"The thing is, together they're unstoppable," I comment, looking over at them as we move into the king's bedchamber, girls oohing and aahing at the state bed, canopied with red damask trimmed with gold, heavily frilled, its cornice and headboard painted red and gold too, looking as regal as you could imagine.

"If they were making friends again last night," Taylor adds, "they weren't running around setting smoke bombs or trying to push you downstairs."

"Unless that was their idea of bonding," I say jokingly.

But now I'm staring at Alison and Luce, who are absorbed in talk. Alison's fiddling with her long mane of hair, which I think she must have lightened in the last months; I remember it being more carroty. Now it's a strawberry blond, straightened out of its frizzy curls, and it looks really striking. She's wearing the unofficial St. Tabby's uniform this season—a rock-chick look, narrow jacket and T-shirt over leggings tucked into slouchy suede boots. For Alison, who used to live in exercise clothes, this is a really big deal. Equally so for Luce, who's in a variation of the same outfit, but with ballerina shoes. Clever—they keep her tiny little wiry body in proportion. In the boots everyone else is wearing, Luce would look as if she'd pulled on her mum's Wellingtons.

They look so smart now, Luce and Alison. Wearing makeup, trendy haircuts, scarves draped fashionably round their necks. Like they've had the kind of makeover I did, when I went to a fashionable boutique and threw myself on the mercy of a surprisingly nice salesgirl.

*So maybe*, I think hopefully, *they don't care about my betrayal of them anymore, now that they've turned into full-blown, head-to-toe St. Tabby's girls.*

And then Luce, sensing my gaze, swivels her head away from the hangings of the state bed to look directly at me. Our eyes meet.

The shock is huge. I feel like she punched me in the breastbone. It's the first time Luce and I have truly looked at each other since our awful breakup. For a brief, breath-holding moment, I have a blinding flash of hope that everything will magically be all right; that she'll manage a small smile for me, or even make a gesture that says I should come over and talk to her and Alison. . . .

And then she squinches up her eyes, crinkles her nose, and pokes her tongue out at me in an unmistakeable grimace of contempt. I've seen Luce pull this face at people before: a girl in one of our gymnastics competitions who tried to do what Taylor would have called trash talking, or a bus inspector who lectured us about having proper ID to prove we were under sixteen and entitled to free fares (as if any of us looked our ages back then).

But she's never done it to me.

It's achingly familiar, and it really hurts. I'm shocked at how painful it is. Luce looks really embarrassed that she did something so childish; she goes bright pink and whips away out of the room, dragging Alison with her, saying something to her urgently. Tears actually spring to my eyes at the sight of Luce and Alison scurrying away from me.

"She should be more careful," Sophia observes behind me, her tone serious. But since Sophia's tone is always serious—she has no discernible sense of humor—I pay little attention to this comment.

"What do you mean?" Lizzie, perpetually curious, instantly asks.

"Lucy," Sophia says, clicking her tongue in disapproval. "She was sent to therapy last term, for anger issues. She should be careful not to look angry in front of the teachers."

It takes me a moment to realize she's talking about Luce.

"*Really?*" Lizzie is immediately agog, and so am I; I sidle toward Lizzie and Sophia, ears pricked up, whipping open the Holyrood information leaflet that up till now has been scrunched up, ignored, in my hand.

"Yes," Sophia informs her. "After Dan died"—I sense Sophia and Lizzie look sideways at me, and I pretend to be utterly absorbed in the map showing Holyrood's layout— "Plum was very nasty with Alison and Lucy. You know, because they were Scarlett's friends. Not straight after the party: it started a few days later, after Scarlett was expelled. Plum never left them alone. They called Scarlett the Kiss of Death girl in the newspapers, of course, so Plum would get everyone to make kiss noises at Alison and Lucy."

"Well, that's not *so* bad," Lizzie starts hopefully, but Sophia's flat voice cuts right across her.

"Because Dan died of an allergy," she continues, "like a poisoning, Plum was pretending that Alison and Lucy might be poisonous too. No one would sit with them at meals, or near them in class. It was quite bad for them. All the younger girls copied it too—they would scream if they walked close to Alison and Lucy in the corridors. Only the teachers didn't know what was happening. Everyone else knew."

*That's so unfair!* I'm screaming in my head. *Alison and Luce didn't have anything to do with Dan dying! They weren't even there!* And then I'm struck by the timing—it started "after Scarlett was expelled." That would mean just after I went back to school to clear out my locker: once the inquest verdict on Dan (death by misadventure) had come in, the headmistress of St. Tabby's asked me to leave (I *wasn't* expelled, technically) because of all the press camped outside the school. Plum confronted me, with her posse behind her, and I humiliated her in front of them, slamming her into a locker, seeing naked fear in her eyes for the first time ever.

*She took it out on Alison and Luce,* I realize slowly. *I made her look weak in front of her sidekicks, and she took it out on my best friends. I went off with my stuff, free from her for a while, at least. And she promptly turned round and tortured Alison and Luce, until Luce snapped with "anger issues."*

"She pushed Plum down a flight of stairs," Sophia's telling Lizzie now. "Plum landed on Mam'selle Bouvier and twisted her ankle."

*Good for Luce!* I think, grinning from ear to ear, but still

73

pretending to be deep in concentration on the leaflet. *Bet Plum stopped giving you a hard time after that!* Plum's scared of physical confrontation: I saw that when I held her against that locker. And tiny though Luce is, gymnastics, with all the conditioning that we do, means that she punches far above her weight.

And then the penny drops. *She pushed Plum down a flight of stairs.*

My breath stops. My heart sinks.

"So they call in Lucy's parents and say she has anger issues and must go to see a therapist," Sophia says.

Lizzie snorts.

"Sounds more like she has Plum issues!" she comments.

"Hah! That is very good. Yes, she has Plum issues," Sophia says approvingly.

"Come on, girls," Miss Carter says, bustling up behind us, chivvying us along. "The best is still to come—don't you want to see Mary's private rooms?"

Sophia and Lizzie follow her, and as I walk slowly in their wake, Taylor falls in beside me.

"You hear all that?" she mutters.

I nod, not trusting my voice quite yet.

"She *pushed Plum downstairs*!" Taylor hisses. "I think that's *very* interesting!"

She's quite right. But I can't manage a response; I'm haunted by the wording of that note left in our room last night. Right now, it *does* feel exactly as if I can't outrun the past. My own past—my guilt about what I did to Alison and Luce. Not only abandoning them to go to a party; now, as it turns out, leaving them behind at St. Tabby's to be tormented by Plum as scapegoats for me. I couldn't help being sent away from St. Tabby's, but it's awful to know that Alison and Luce ended up paying for stuff I did. They were already furious with me for dumping them. It must have been real salt in the wound to be taunted by Plum in my name.

And then there's my family's past: my family's and Jase's, the Wakefields' and the Barneses'. Things our parents did years ago, awful things that Jase and I are paying for in the present. My mother, according to Aunt Gwen, might have had an affair with Jase's father, who, according to Jase's grandmother, deliberately ran down and killed both my parents. It's as bad as it could be. Really terrible, sad, miserable family drama.

It's not fair, not at all, but there's no point saying that things aren't fair. Jase and I are stuck with them, and we have to try to work them out. Or, the way I feel at the moment, be buried alive underneath their weight.

Even the excitement of seeing the tapestry-hung bedchamber where Mary, Queen of Scots slept, imagining her walking on this very floor, sleeping in this very bed, can't penetrate my misery. Weirdly, the only thing that helps is stepping into the tiny supper room where a brutal murder took place.

"Right here, one night, Mary was having a nice, quiet, cozy dinner with her attendant ladies and her secretary, David Rizzio," Ms. Burton-Race narrates dramatically, "when her estranged husband, Lord Darnley, burst in on them. Mary was pregnant with the baby who would be James the First, King of England and Scotland, but her pregnancy didn't stop her husband; he stormed in and dragged Rizzio from the table. Rizzio clung to Mary's skirts, begging for his life, but Darnley had no mercy. Together with a group of other men, Darnley stabbed his victim to death—*fifty-six times*. His blood soaked into the floor of the outer chamber and he bled to death in front of Mary."

We know this already, but only from reading about it in dry history books. Being in the place where it happened is infinitely more powerful. Gasps and squeaks of horror echo off the walls of the small turret room as we react to Ms. Burton-Race's words. I imagine Mary, watching helplessly, probably sobbing and screaming, as her husband and a gang of thugs haul her friend away and stab him to death.

This is a horrible admission, but that image actually makes me feel better. I mean, talk about putting things into perspective. It's like reading really gruesome mysteries, or watching horror movies. Atrocious things happening to other people—in fiction, or the distant past—are weirdly comforting. Catharsis, my classics teacher would call it. The ancient Greeks worked it out centuries ago. You watch gruesome stories onstage, you go down to the depths with the actors, and you emerge feeling lighter afterward.

I take a deep breath, feeling some of the weight lifted off me. And I manage a reassuring grin for Taylor. I must say, those ancient Greeks weren't completely stupid.

*   *   *

The Holyrood gift shop isn't that big, but it's very well stocked with products calculated to appeal to its visitors. One whole wall is dedicated to shiny, pretty objects with the word *princess* embroidered or printed or stamped onto every surface. China mugs. Teddy bears. Cushions. Jewelry. Perfect for girls who've just been worked into a royal frenzy by Mary, Queen of Scots, and the Darnley jewel. All the princess items are pink and gold, and all are adorable enough to have packs of girls cooing as they pick them up and show them to each other.

"My God, what *is* that?" Nadia says as we emerge from the gift shop, many girls clutching bags in which are resting their princess-themed purchases. Most of the purchasers mumbled excuses about buying presents for younger sisters; only Lizzie Livermore was brave enough to admit openly that the princess mug was for her own hot chocolate. I have to say, I admire her for that.

Nadia's not staring at any gift shop purchase, though; her gaze is fixed on the large building directly across the road.

"That," Ms. Burton-Race says with a thread of embarrassment in her voice, "is the new Scottish Parliament."

"My God," Plum drawls. "I thought it was a *leisure center*. With flats upstairs for aspiring yuppies."

She and Nadia giggle snobbishly in unison. But the thing is, Plum isn't wrong. The Scottish Parliament is a very odd building indeed. It stretches out at all kinds of odd curves and angles, with bits sticking out of it that don't seem to do anything at all. The front of it has a cantilevered metal-and-glass roof projecting out into space, which looks like an oversized bus shelter, and the roof is covered in what looks like enormous twigs, as if a giant bird had been building a nest, got bored halfway through, dumped a whole bundle of sticks, and flew away. There are more oversized twigs stuck to the front of the building in irregular clumps. We all stand and stare at it for a while, feeling that Plum has pretty much summed it up with her leisure-center comment. You expect to smell wafts of chlorine coming out from the vents.

"There *is* the option of a Parliament tour," Aunt Gwen starts, and next to me, Lizzie actually whimpers in fear. *"But,"* Aunt Gwen continues, looking at her reprovingly, "the word *option*, by its nature, indicates that the tour is not *compulsory*."

Aunt Gwen's eyes are bulging with satisfaction at having made a perfect grammatical point. This kind of triumph is meat and drink to her.

"Up there is the Royal Mile," Ms. Burton-Race says, pointing at the street that rises up the hill next to the Parliament. "Full of nice shops. Including lots of cashmere," she adds cheerfully, prompting murmurs of excitement from the St. Tabby's girls.

"I hope they have Brora," Nadia says excitedly to Plum. "I can't get *enough* Brora scarves."

"You have two hours, girls," Aunt Gwen announces. "Be back in the Holyrood car park at one. Then we'll go back to school for lunch."

"I think I can see a Starbucks up there," Sophia hisses to Lizzie. "We can get a wrap or something."

"I don't suppose there's a sushi place round here, is there?" Plum asks no one in particular. "I'd kill for a miso soup."

Only a couple of sad limp history freaks from (of course) Wakefield Hall follow Aunt Gwen and Ms. Burton-Race under the bus-shelter roof into the Parliament. The rest of us split immediately into our own little nuclei, not wanting to walk up the Royal Mile together in a solid mass. Luce and Alison, I notice, have already crossed the road and are making their way up the street. Taylor and I are hanging back to let Plum, Nadia, and Susan stroll off and put some distance between us; we're in no hurry.

"Hopefully, Plum'll say something rude about not finding any sushi in Edinburgh, and someone will punch her," Taylor speculates.

"Or head-butt her," I suggest. "That's called a Glasgow kiss, but maybe they do it in Edinburgh too. . . ."

"What are you two talking about?" asks a male voice beside us, full of laughter, and I spin round to see the distinctive dark red curls and freckled face of Ewan, the Mac Attack guitarist. "Did I hear you saying you wanted to give someone a Glasgae kiss?"

I blush, even more when I see Callum behind him, raising his eyebrows in amusement.

"Already planning mayhem?" he says. "Holyrood's made you both bloodthirsty."

"You're not wearing your kilts," Taylor says to them, and I feel my own eyebrows shoot up; coming from anyone but Taylor, I would have called that comment downright flirtatious.

"It's a wee bit chilly for that," Ewan says, grinning down at her.

"And more than a bit windy," Callum adds. "We don't want to be flashing half of the city, do we?"

Ewan mimes holding down a skirt, his mouth pursing into a shocked O, like a startled Marilyn Monroe in the famous photo of her in the white dress. I giggle stupidly, and hear Taylor following suit.

We actually sound like a pair of girls flirting with a pair of boys. Normal girls, who've never saved anyone's lives, or discovered dead bodies, or investigated murders. Or seen their boyfriend ride away from them on his motorbike, because he'd found out something so awful about his family that he couldn't bear to stay a moment longer.

I remember drinking champagne with Dan last summer, and how light and bubbly and happy it made me feel, as if my head were a balloon, floating up and lifting me away. That's the sensation swirling through me now. I feel delightfully giddy, as if nothing at all matters in the world but this moment, now, being silly and laughing and feeling, to be honest, hugely flattered that Ewan and Callum seem to have tracked us down somehow.

Because I don't think they regularly hang round on a cold March day outside Holyrood Palace, waiting to chat up girls emerging from the gift shop with princess items in their dark blue plastic bags. . . .

"Funny meeting you guys here," Taylor's already saying. She does have a way of getting straight to the point.

"Oh, we heard your teachers saying last night you were headed to Holyrood," Ewan said casually. "Thought we might drop by and try to rescue you from the Scottish Parliament tour."

"Man, it's *deadly*," Callum said seriously. "It goes on for hours, and by the end you feel like they've sucked your brains out through your nose."

"Like the Ancient Egyptians," Taylor says, turning to him. "They did that with crochet hooks. For embalming."

"Girls don't usually know that," Callum says, looking a little taken aback.

Ewan snorts with laughter.

"Callum!" Plum's voice cuts through our chatter like a high-pitched chain saw. "And, uh, your friend from the band!" She swirls past Taylor and me to embrace Callum as if she hasn't seen him for years. "What fun! Fancy seeing you here! So!" She tosses her mane of hair back over her shoulders and flashes him and Ewan her best, most dazzling smile. "We've got two hours to kill! What *shall* we do?"

Callum darts a look at Ewan, then at me and Taylor. It would take a braver man than him to tell Plum he didn't come here to meet her, and actually, I don't want him to. Not only would it provoke an awful scene, it would mean that, for the rest of our time in Edinburgh, at least, Plum would try to punish Taylor and me for her own humiliation. I can stand up to Plum, but it's exhausting: I'd much rather fly under her radar than be her target. Look what happened to poor Alison and Luce.

So when Callum yields to force majeure, points up to a nearby hill, and says something about maybe grabbing a sarnie and going to hang out up there, we know that everyone is now invited. Ewan, rolling his eyes at us expressively, is already pulling out his mobile and making a call as the boys turn to lead the way, Plum, Nadia, Susan, and Lizzie clustering along in their wake.

"Should we skip it?" I say to Taylor quietly. "I mean, I'd

rather have to wear a princess T-shirt to tea with my grand-mother than hang out with Plum. . . ."

"I kind of want to," Taylor says, and though she shrugs at the same time, I know her well enough to read her message and be aware that it's her words I should listen to, not her gesture.

*Right,* I think, watching Ewan, who's tall enough to see clear over everyone else's heads, swivel round with flattering interest to look for Taylor and me. Talking urgently into his phone, he jerks his head at us, indicating that we should join the group, and in response, Taylor starts to follow.

*Taylor likes Ewan,* I conclude. *Cool.* Ewan seems really nice and funny. I've never really thought about who would suit Taylor, but I can see that a comic like him, who loves to pull faces and entertain, would balance dour, tough Taylor very nicely.

And just then, Callum turns too, making sure we're part of the posse, and as his gray eyes meet mine, I have a sud-den flash of memory once more. Of our kiss at Glasgow airport. Totally surprised that it was happening; totally sur-prised that I was attracted to him. And totally surprised too that grumpy, gruff Callum could kiss that sweetly.

God. Now I'm really confused. Maybe it's not such a bad thing after all that Plum just elbowed her way into our little quartet. . . .

*six*

# "MISFORTUNE SOOTHED BY WISDOM"

The direction the boys are leading us in is so unpromising that I start to hope Plum will decide she doesn't want to join them after all, especially as they refuse to tell us where we're going. We're walking away from the Royal Mile and the shops, away from everything that looks at all appealing, up past a row of neat little modern houses, and under a nasty old railway bridge whose dripping girders elicit screams of disgust from Nadia, who covers her hair theatrically with her hands. We clamber up a flight of steep stone stairs cut into the cliffside and into a narrow little park where a couple of people are walking their dogs.

"This is *it*?" Nadia exclaims disparagingly, and I sort of take her point, especially as an Alsatian chooses that moment to squat down and poo on the grass, staring at us with orange eyes.

"Guid boy!" exclaims its owner, a shaved-headed young man bustling over with a plastic bag wrapped round his hand.

"Ugh, *foul*," Plum says, turning away pointedly as we reach the end of the park and promptly double back on ourselves, taking a couple of steps down a steep drop again—

And then I see what at first I think is another little park, green and lush, sloping away to a stunning view beyond. I gasp in appreciation of the sight, which is framed by two high stone pillars. Gateposts. A sign on the right-hand one says NO ACCESS TO LOWER CALTON ROAD, but someone— doubtless a boy—has scrawled over it in marker pen, CREEPY CORNER. A huge iron gate gapes open beyond the pillars, outlining a wide stone path that leads into—

"It's a cemetery!" Taylor breathes. "Oh *wow*!"

She's darted past Plum and the other girls, who have stopped to light up cigarettes, and is through the gate already, walking down the path, looking around in wonder.

"Scarlett!" she calls. "Come look at this!"

"She really likes cemeteries, right?" Ewan says, grinning at me as we follow Taylor inside.

I grin in response. There's something very charming about Ewan. He's definitely good-looking, with those dark red springy curls and that attractively bony face, but even if he weren't, the charm would still be there; it comes from his energy, which is bouncy and irrepressible and hugely positive.

"Taylor's not, like, a huge goth or anything," I say. "I think a lot of it's the history. You know what Americans are like. They go mental for anything that's a few hundred years old."

"They're like little houses!" Taylor exclaims, open-mouthed, staring at the tombs. The cemetery has plenty of burial stones, huge and imposing in carved gray granite, but it's also lined with tombs that really are like tiny one-room houses, with high walls and open doorways you can walk through. Just the sky above for a roof, and earth for a floor.

"The burying place of Alexander Henderson, Merchant, Edinburgh," Taylor reads, looking up at the lintel of one. She walks inside to study a stone plaque affixed to one of the walls. "And here's the names of the rest of his family. Where *are* they all?"

Ewan points to the ground we're standing on.

"Under here," he says cheerfully.

"Buried or cremated?" Taylor asks, looking at the packed earth with its loose topping of gravel.

"I dunno," he says. "Want to dig down and try to find out?"

She laughs at this.

"Sorry," she says. "I guess I ask a lot of questions."

"No worries," he says easily. "Hey, do you two like to climb stuff?"

Taylor and I exchange amused glances.

"You have *no idea* who you're talking to," I say.

The cemetery falls away in an almost sheer drop down the side of the hill; Edinburgh seems to be built on nothing but one hill after another. Stunning views of Holyrood, the Parliament, and the near-mountain beyond are spread out before us like a perfect postcard photo as Ewan leads us down the slope. We vault over tombstones, feet sinking into the lush green grass, jump up and down a series of stone steps that lead up to a whole array of tombs, one after the other, like a miniature terrace of houses. . . .

"It's like people could live here!" Taylor marvels, but I'm focused on our destination: a turret, three stories high, almost in the far corner of the walled cemetery, wide and fat with a castellated top. Tilting my head back, squinting into the clouded sunshine, I see that there's a metal staircase running round the top story, but it doesn't seem to reach down to the ground.

"You can sort of climb up onto that tomb next to it and jump over," Ewan's saying. "There's a trick we found. It's not too hard. I'll show you— Oh."

He's staring, mouth agape, at Taylor, who's already scaling the side of the turret, finding a series of hand- and footholds in the open brickwork.

"*Jesus,*" he says devoutly.

"She does a bit of rock climbing with her family," I say. "In the holidays."

I dart a glance sideways to see if he's put off by how good Taylor is; I know sometimes boys don't like it when you can do physical stuff really easily. Jase threw a fit when he heard I'd ridden his motorbike, even though he did say I was amazing afterward.

"Will you look at her go," Ewan marvels as Taylor swings one leg onto the top wall of the tomb beside the turret, hauls herself up, and climbs onto the metal staircase.

This is one of the reasons I love Taylor. It would never, in a million years, occur to her to pretend she couldn't manage something, or let a boy show her how to do it, just to get him to like her. It simply isn't in her DNA.

"Coming?" he says to me, already round the side of the tomb, where a big piece of projecting stone forms a sort of step we can climb onto. "Unless you're going to go all Spider-Man like her."

I grin.

"No, she's better at that stuff than me," I admit.

I can't help looking back toward the cemetery entrance, though, where the rest of them are still clustered. I'm seeing what Callum's doing . . . whether he knows we're over by the turret. . . .

"I called for reinforcements," Ewan says as I notice more boys milling around the group. "Callum gave me the nod. We thought we'd be swamped otherwise. Those glamour-girl friends of yours seem to need a lot of attention, eh?"

"They're not our friends," I say quickly. "Just in the same year as us."

He grins. "I can't exactly see them climbing up here. They wouldn't want to break their fingernails, right?"

"Are you two going to move your asses and get up here?" Taylor calls from the top of the turret. "The view is awesome!"

"Coming, hen!" Ewan says, winking at me, and we climb easily enough up onto the tomb, levering ourselves over onto the metal staircase. The turret door is locked, but, as Ewan said, it's easy enough to climb onto the staircase rail and pull yourself up onto the roof from there.

"Wow," I say, raising a hand to shield my eyes. Taylor's dark, shaggy hair is flapping in the breeze, blowing over her face in straight lines; it looks very striking, I think. Ewan seems to agree with me. He's staring at her in appreciation.

"So," he says, "you're some kind of Action Woman, eh?"

"Us marines don't like to boast," Taylor says, deadpan.

They're getting on so well, they don't need me. I take in the view instead, realizing that behind Holyrood there's a whole range of green hills rising and falling softly into the distance, peaking in that shale-topped mountain that towers over the city. The downs are green and lush, a much-needed contrast to the gray stone of the Edinburgh houses. It's not a pretty city by any means; it's a strong one. Hard stone, with nothing to soften it. I feel sorrier than ever for poor spoiled, indulged Mary, Queen of Scots, brought up in French luxury, sleeping on silks and velvets and goose down, thinking she would be cozy in France forever, and then wrested out of her pampered nest and sent across the steel-gray sea to this windy, hard country where her pretty face and her charm would do nothing but count against her with the grim, dour lords who ran her kingdom.

*No wonder Taylor seems to be taking to Edinburgh like a duck to water,* I think. If Taylor had been in Mary's shoes, the Scottish lords would be whimpering by now in fear.

Ewan is leaning on the castellations next to Taylor now, pointing out various landmarks, I imagine, answering the questions she's firing at him. I'm definitely a third wheel here. The sound of me swinging myself back down over the edge of the turret, finding the staircase rail with my feet, and maneuvering back down to the metal rungs again is covered by the whip of the wind; I don't think they even notice my departure. I drop to the ground thirty seconds later, dust myself off, and step out from the narrow niche between the turret and the tomb, into the main cemetery again.

And then I yelp loudly in surprise. I even jump back a step.

Because there's a corner tomb to my right, just along from the turret. It has a short flight of steps inside its doorway, leading up to something I can't see. And someone has just jumped down from there in one big leap, over the narrow stone lip below, arriving on the grass in a perfectly judged piece of drama that shocked the living daylights out of me.

It's Callum McAndrew.

"Did you think I was a ghost?" he asks, smiling at me.

"I don't know what I thought!" I say, cross with him. "I could have tripped and turned my ankle or something! You shouldn't startle people like that!"

"Nah, not you," he says. "I just watched you climb down that thing." He nods at the turret. "You're not going to fall over just because I jump out of a tomb and give you a wee surprise."

I narrow my eyes, but he's right.

"It *was* a shock," I say a little sullenly.

*But why am I being sullen?* I think. I'm glad to see Callum, after all; I was looking for him earlier.

*I can't help it. I'm feeling really weird around him all of a sudden.*

I take a deep breath and tell myself it's natural that I should feel strange, alone for even a few minutes with Callum McAndrew. Conflicting feelings are whirling round my brain. I remember how hostile he was to me for so long, when we met before. That awful, life-altering afternoon, in a ruined tower near his parents' estate, that ended in a death. Callum kissing me, and me kissing him back. A kiss that was supposed to be goodbye forever, because nothing could ever happen between us; not after his brother's death, not after what we'd been through.

Callum is running his hand over his short, almost shaved hair, in a way that I recall very vividly from last year, but he isn't saying a word. He's waiting. Waiting for all my tangled thoughts to untwist themselves.

And the fact that he's prepared to wait for me to work out what I think is strangely liberating. It means I blurt out the first thing that comes into my head.

"At Airlie," I say, naming his parents' castle, "you were always grumpy with me. And now I feel grumpy with you."

I don't know how he'll take this, but, unexpectedly, his face cracks into a beautiful smile.

"I *was* a grumpy bastard with you," he admits. "But not always. That's not quite fair."

His gaze is focused on my mouth now, and I know what he means; he's remembering our kiss.

"D'you think you could get over the bad temper a bit quicker than I did?" he's asking. "Like, maybe"—he pretends to look at an imaginary watch—"in the next couple of minutes?"

"I'll do my best," I say.

"Hey!" He throws his arms wide. He's wearing one of his oversized knitted Arran sweaters—dark gray like his eyes and unraveling at the wrists—over faded, ripped blue jeans. Callum's definitely not a dandy. "It's sunny! In Scotland! D'you *know* how rare that is? And we're in a cemetery! What could be more likely to bring a smile to a girl's face?"

That does make me smile. And just then, a gust of wind

brings Plum's high, carrying voice to our ears. We can't hear what she's saying, but the sound has Callum flinching.

"That girl brings me out in hives," he says, grimacing. "Come on."

He's dashing around the side of a row of tombs tall enough to hide us from anyone approaching. I follow him, the sun warming my face as we sprint downhill and come to a stop with our backs to a high obelisk. In front of us is a stone wall set with something genuinely unusual.

In keeping with the grim, unadorned style of the rest of the city, the other tombs and gravestones have no flourishes or decorations, just the chiseled names of their occupants. But this is a big stone panel set into the wall, beautifully carved with a tableau: a younger man kneeling to an older one, who's holding his hand gently. They're both wearing Greek robes. On either side of them is another panel, projecting farther from the wall to frame the central one, each depicting a naked figure leaning dejectedly on a staff. There are Greek urns carved underneath, and decorative curlicues running up the sides of the panel and over the top.

It's still quite austere by normal churchyard standards; no weeping women or guardian angels. But because it's not sentimental at all, that makes it even more moving. I stare at it for a while in silence, absorbing the images, feeling calmer as I do, though I don't know why.

"Look," Callum says eventually, leaning forward, indicating the words carved directly below the figures of the two men.

"Misfortune Soothed by Wisdom," I read.

"I like that a lot," he says quietly. "Don't you?"

I think about everything Callum and his family have gone through in the past year. Their losses. The secret Callum, Taylor, and I carry about the truth behind Dan's death. And I find myself reaching for his hand, wanting to give him some comfort. His fingers close around mine gratefully, warm and tight. We stand there, looking at the carving, its graceful lines and calm message soothing our raw spirits as the older man in the corner soothes the younger one. Just as it was intended to do.

**To the Memory of**
**Andrew Skene**

it reads underneath. And then:

**Born 26 Feb 1784**
**Died 2 April 1835**

"How are you doing?" I ask Callum eventually.

He shrugs, his hand dropping away from mine.

"Och, you know. It comes and goes," he says. "Good days and bad days. Misfortune soothed by wisdom." He gives a short, humorless laugh, shoving his hands into his pockets. "The music helps," he adds unexpectedly. "I don't think about anything but the music when I'm playing."

I nod, knowing what he means. It's like that for me when I'm working out.

"What about you?" he asks. "And Taylor?"

"Good days and bad days sort of sums it up," I agree.

And we smile at each other. The carving's done its work; for a little while, Callum McAndrew and I stand and grieve together for his brother, and for that other death, the one I don't imagine we'll ever talk about, because it was too horrible. All the jagged edges, the mutual suspicion and hostility, even the sexual tension, have gone; it's like we've come through a storm and out the other side to that calm place afterward.

Which complicates things a lot. Because there's more in our connection than just friendship. I know it, and Callum does too, without a word being said. In this new calm place, a lot of things might be possible.

Well, they might be. If I weren't in love with Jase.

"*Omigod!*" comes a squeak of excitement. "*Pink!* Look, Sophia! It's all *shiny*! And it's got *frills* round it! I *so* want a pink gravestone!"

Lizzie Livermore has erupted onto the scene, and I can't say, on balance, that I'm sorry to see her. Just like a golden retriever, she rushes up to her target, points at it, wriggling with excitement, and then rushes back to her human, her whole body vibrating with the urgent need to share her new discovery.

"*Look!*" she squeals, her hair bouncing, her bracelets jangling, as Sophia swims into view. If Lizzie's a retriever, Sophia is a tall white swan, as calm and collected as Lizzie is eternally overexcited. "*Pink!*"

Sophia halts in front of the pink granite gravestone Lizzie's indicating: three of them, actually, joined together, each one pointed at the top in a Gothic arch and decorated round the edges with more pink granite in a sort of carved ruffly trim that does, to give Lizzie credit, look exactly like a frill.

"Don't you think it's a little—*shiny*, Lizzie?" Sophia, descendant of generations of Austrian aristocracy, asks. The sunlight catching the pink granite is bouncing off it, bright as glass.

"No!" squeals Lizzie, whose father is a self-made billionaire. "I *love* it!"

I save this one up to tell Taylor. Old money likes everything a little shabby, a little fraying at the seams, to show that it's been in the family for countless generations. Even the silver shouldn't be too polished. But new money likes shiny, and plenty of it; since new money can't boast quietly about its centuries of history, it brags loudly about what it can afford instead.

"Hey!" Taylor calls, strolling down the stretch of grass, Ewan next to her. "Where did you sneak off to?"

Her swift, knowing glance from me to Callum answers her own question, and she smirks at me. I didn't actually slip away to find Callum, but I know that's what she assumes. I can scarcely tell her I thought I'd leave Ewan and her alone.

"I love your city," she says to Callum with surprising enthusiasm in her voice. "It was really cool seeing it from up there." She gestures to the turret with a fervent sweep of her arm. "It's so stark and beautiful."

"Good to hear," Callum says, flourishing a bow to her. "We're quite fond of it ourselves."

"It's cold, though. And windy," says Sophia, princess of

the obvious, wrapping her fur-lined jacket closer around her. "I think we should go to Starbucks now."

"Okay!" says Lizzie happily, darting off toward the entrance gate; Sophia's wish is clearly her command.

"Aww," Taylor drawls as the two girls walk away. "Lizzie's found a friend."

"I think she just wanted someone posh to tell her what to do," I comment.

"I zink ve should go to Shtarbucks now," Ewan hisses, exaggerating Sophia's very light Austrian accent and completely flat inflection: it makes us all giggle naughtily, safe in the knowledge that she's too far away to hear.

"Plum! *There* you are!" Lizzie's dashed into a tomb whose lintel proclaims it belongs to Andrew Fyfe, Surgeon, Edinburgh; down each side run lists of Andrew Fyfe's nearest and dearest, who are presumably crammed into the space with him. "We were *looking* for you *everywhere!*" Lizzie's complaining. "Didn't you hear me calling before?"

"I'd hide from her too," Callum mutters as Plum and Susan emerge from Andrew Fyfe's last resting place, flushed out by Lizzie's eagerness.

"We're going to Starbucks!" Lizzie announces.

"Oh, joy," Plum says dryly as Lizzie herds her and Susan up the path to where Nadia is holding court, three young men standing around her in a circle admiringly as she plays with her thick blue-black hair and flashes her dark eyes at them. I have to admit, Nadia certainly knows how to flirt; her gold jewelry glints enticingly with every movement of her head as she turns capriciously from one boy to the next, not looking for too long at any of them, making them compete for her attention.

Plum's reapplying lip gloss, presumably to look as fabulous for Starbucks as possible. Susan, pale and ethereal, catches the attention of more than one of Nadia's targets; long, almost colorless hair hanging down her back, her white skin nearly translucent, Susan looks like a beautiful ghost. I'm surprised all over again that Plum has chosen Susan as her Wakefield Hall best friend. Like Lizzie, Susan seems amenable to going along with whatever a stronger personality suggests. But I've seen Susan come to class with a stinking cold—red nose, swollen eyes—and still be more beautiful than the rest of us put together. I wouldn't have thought Plum would appreciate the constant competition.

*Maybe*, I think, *Plum's so confident that she assumes everyone's always looking at her.*

It's an enviable attitude. I watch Plum pass Susan her lip gloss so she can use it too, flash a smile at the group, and purr:

"Actually, a nice hot latte *would* be rather perfect. I'm *dying* of cold."

Beside me, Taylor's saying something to Callum. I look at her, thinking how lucky I am to have her as my best friend, a girl who'd run into a building she thought was burning to try to save me. I hope I'm as good a friend to her. But all I bring Taylor is danger, drama, and dead bodies.

Still, I notice that Ewan's looking down at her with open appreciation.

*Maybe being friends with me has brought Taylor something positive, for once*, I think, brightening up. *Who knows? Maybe I've accidentally introduced her to a Scottish boyfriend!*

## *seven*

## "YOU'VE ALWAYS HATED ME"

"So, Scarlett! What do you have to say for yourself?"

Aunt Gwen's staring at me severely. She's marched me into a small teacher's office, got me to sit down in the hard wooden chair in front of the desk, and then—very unfairly—not taken the seat behind the desk herself, which would at least maintain a decent, proper distance. No, instead she's propped her wide, tweed-skirted bottom against the desk, leaning against it just a couple of feet away, so she's not only too close but also towering over me, her bulbous green gobstopper eyes staring down at me with extreme disapproval.

That last part is only what I'm used to. Aunt Gwen always stares at me with extreme disapproval.

She also seems to be expecting something from me, but I have no idea what. I'm nervous; I shift restlessly in my chair. It feels like I've been sitting down for hours. After lunch (cold egg and cress sandwiches, limp in the middle and curling dryly at the edges; thank God we all grabbed panini and wraps from the coffee shops down the Royal

Mile) we were herded into the assembly hall and subjected to not one, but two lectures: Ms. Burton-Race on Mary, Queen of Scots, and her son James, who succeeded Elizabeth I as king of both England and Scotland. That was actually pretty interesting. Unfortunately, it was followed by Aunt Gwen on the geology of Scotland, which was just as leaden and soul-destroying as you'd imagine. There were a lot of photos of bits of stone that all seemed to look exactly the same. I think Taylor and I would have carried out a suicide pact if we could have worked out a way to kill each other simultaneously.

We staggered out, all of us girls mad-eyed and staring. I wouldn't have been surprised if our hair had turned white and our faces wrinkly; it felt as if Aunt Gwen's presentation had gone on for forty years. And then, just as Taylor and I were escaping to the grounds behind the school to do something physical to let off steam—anything: throw rocks at trees, jump up and down screaming—Aunt Gwen practically grabbed me by the scruff of my neck and dragged me into this office. The look of pity and sympathy in Taylor's eyes was awful to see. Like I'd just got out of prison, but at the last moment they'd decided that I wasn't pardoned after all, and I had to do ten more years in maximum security with Aunt Gwen as my personal jailer.

Eventually, I crack under pressure.

"So, um, what?" I ask, which sounds ruder than I meant to. Aunt Gwen stiffens visibly. Hastily, I add:

"I don't know what you mean, Aunt Gwen. Is this something about the geology lecture?"

I really hope she's not going to start questioning me

about the strata of Edinburgh limestone, or whatever it was she was banging on about before. That would be totally unfair.

"Last night!" Aunt Gwen snaps angrily. "I'm asking you about last night, of course! You were the last one out of the school building! You must, at the very least, have some idea who let off the smoke bombs!"

My mouth drops open. I never expected this.

It doesn't occur to me for a moment to tell Aunt Gwen the truth of what happened yesterday—or, rather, early this morning. I know perfectly well that she won't believe me; she's much more likely to accuse me of having delusions of grandeur, thinking I'm important enough for someone to want to take some sort of vengeance against me.

"I don't know anything about it, Aunt Gwen," I say weakly. "I really don't."

She clicks her tongue impatiently.

"I don't believe you, Scarlett," she says, looking down her nose at me. "I can tell you're keeping something back. Was Taylor McGovern in it with you? Are you protecting her?"

I shake my head so vehemently it hurts.

"You've had Taylor in your geography class for nearly a year, Aunt Gwen," I say. "You must know her well enough by now—she's much too responsible to do anything as stupid as letting off smoke bombs in a school building."

This is a really, really good point, and it holds Aunt Gwen for a good few seconds. She rocks back a little, her A-line skirt swishing around her sturdy calves.

"So she knew what you were up to!" she says eventually,

regrouping her forces. "And she tried to get back into the school to stop you!"

"Why would I *do* that?" I ask, getting cross now. Being defensive never works with Aunt Gwen; I should know that. I need to go on the attack myself. "I'm not that stupid either! And you know how much I like my sleep! I'm the last person in the world to get out of a nice warm bed in the middle of the night and run around playing practical jokes!"

This isn't a bad point either. Ever since my parents died, when I was four, I've lived—pretty miserably—with Aunt Gwen in the small gatehouse on the grounds of Wakefield Hall. The gatehouse isn't that big, and I grew up in much closer proximity to Aunt Gwen than either she or I liked, but that does mean that she knows perfectly well the truth of what I'm saying. If there were a Sleeping Like the Dead event at the Olympics, I'd definitely be on the British team. Apart from the events of the last year—a lot of climbing out of my room late at night to see Jase, and, one wonderful time, his climbing in to see me—I sleep through the night so soundly that it practically takes an alarm clock strapped to my ear to wake me up. Aunt Gwen has had to bang on my bedroom door more times than I can remember.

So she knows I'm not exactly a night owl, likely to flit around the corridors of Fetters in the early hours of the morning, doing my best to wake everyone else so they'll get up and play with me too.

"It's more likely to be someone from St. Tabby's," I continue, pressing my advantage. "No one from Wakefield plays practical jokes like that. We've never had something like this happen before."

100

We're all too subdued at Wakefield Hall, too beaten down by the harsh rule of the teachers, the atrocious food, and the prison-type conditions to have any energy for elaborate practical jokes. Besides, Wakefield is a very serious school. Its entrance exams are famously difficult to pass, its interview process grueling. My grandmother's aim was to create an intellectual powerhouse for the brightest girls, and she's succeeded; it's one of the top girls' schools in the country. But that means its pupils are much more likely to be studying in the evening, determined to pass their exams with flying colors and be admitted to the university of their choice (Oxford, Cambridge, or the LSE) than to cover the contents of each other's rooms in toilet paper or painstakingly balance flour-bomb traps for their enemies on their doorjambs.

Not, of course, that anyone at St. Tabby's does that either. Apart from the fact that it's not a boarding school, St. Tabby's girls are much too sophisticated for practical jokes. As Ewan pointed out earlier today in another context, it would completely mess up their fingernails.

Aunt Gwen is frowning deeply now. She's steepled her fingers together under her chin and is rocking back and forth. This makes her look completely bonkers, and I shrink back in my chair in fear, getting as far from her as I can.

"I can't trust you, Scarlett," she says finally. "You're always in some kind of trouble. Ever since that unfortunate young man died last year—"

"That wasn't my fault!" I say furiously.

"—and you were expelled from St. Tabby's—"

"I wasn't expelled! *Plum* was expelled! I was *asked to*

*leave* because of all the photographers and TV cameras outside school!"

"—you have been a thorn in my side," she continues coldly, as if she hadn't heard a word of my protests. "Sneaking around with *Jason Barnes*—the son of the *gardener*, for God's sake. Your judgment is simply appalling. That young man was arrested for killing his own—"

"*He didn't do it!* You know he didn't! They let him go!"

"Thank God at least he's had the decency to take himself away from Wakefield," Aunt Gwen says, "and I hope that will be an end to the whole sordid situation."

I'm so angry at her for using the word *sordid* that I actually can't speak; I know now what it means to be choked with rage.

"But your decision-making skills are so poor, and your capacity for getting into trouble is so high, that I can't believe a word you say." She sighs. "I will be keeping a very close eye on you from now on."

"How *dare* you!" I shove my chair back and stand up, my hands bunching into fists. "You've always hated me! You hated my mother, and you've always hated me! I didn't *ask* to come to live with you! I'd rather have gone anywhere else at all!"

"Which," Aunt Gwen snaps, "makes two of us."

"And those smoke bombs were set as a trap for *me*!" I blurt out, so furious now that I've completely forgotten my very sensible resolution not to breathe a word of this to Aunt Gwen. "Someone called me into the stairwell and tried to push me downstairs!"

"*Really*," Aunt Gwen says in an utterly incredulous tone. "And who was this person?"

"I don't know! I couldn't see anything in the smoke!"

"How very convenient. And why didn't you say anything about this last night?"

"Because I knew you wouldn't believe me! And I was right!"

I can't stay here another moment; I'm scared I might say something awful, something I'll regret. Honestly, the way I feel, I'm scared that I might even slap Aunt Gwen just to wipe that nasty smirk of disbelief off her face. I turn and storm out of the room, slamming the door behind me as hard as I can. Miss Carter, coming down the corridor, looks at me with concern and starts to say something, but I can't stop; I dash past her, out the main door, and round the side of the building, looking for Taylor. I know she'll be outside, and I know she'll be doing something physical.

I find her on one of the all-weather tennis courts, trying and failing to bounce a football as if it's a basketball.

"Stupid English sports," she says crossly when she sees me approaching. "At least at Wakefield there's a netball court, so I can shoot some hoops. Boys' schools don't even have *netball*, and these stupid balls don't work properly."

Then she takes in my expression, and she straightens up.

"Uh-oh," she says. "What happened with you and your aunt? You look like you just killed her!"

"I really, really want to," I say between clenched teeth as I walk onto the court. "She just accused me of setting off the smoke bombs last night. Because she says I can't stay out of trouble. *And* she was really rude about Jase being the gardener's son. All that awful class stuff she bangs on about."

"Oh, *crap*," Taylor says, knowing how furious that makes me.

"She said I have terrible judgment and that she can't believe a word I say."

Taylor's grimacing like a gargoyle.

"*And*," I finish, "she even suggested that you might have been in on the whole smoke bomb thing with me."

To my surprise, this doesn't make Taylor as angry as I expected; instead, her dark brows draw together into a straight line, which usually means she's thinking hard.

"Well, that's just stupid," she mutters.

"I know!"

"Huh."

The football's resting by Taylor's feet. She kicks it into the air, catches it, and drops it so hard to the asphalt of the court that it actually bounces back into her hands.

"Cool," she says abstractedly.

"Taylor!" I say crossly. "Did you hear what I just said?"

"Did you tell your aunt that someone pushed you?" she asks.

"Yes," I admit. "I didn't mean to, but she got me so angry it just came out. I didn't tell her about the note, though."

"Oh yeah, the note," Taylor says, bouncing the ball hard again, her arm muscles swelling with the effort. "I've hidden that in a book in the library here. The *Encyclopedia Britannica. H* to *J–K*. I think it'll be pretty safe there."

"Okay." I'm still cross and puzzled by her failure to be sympathetic about the Aunt Gwen situation. "But—"

"Let's go kick this around on the soccer field," she says, tossing me the ball. I stagger: it's really heavy. "I'll be in goal. You can try scoring."

"It's 'football pitch,'" I correct her. "And—"

"You can work off some steam," she says. "Plus, no one can do anything bad to you when you're running round trying to score goals. You'll be safe, and I can do some thinking."

"All you'll be thinking is how humiliated you feel that I'm scoring so much," I say snarkily as we walk off the tennis court.

"That's right," Taylor says, "trash-talk away, little girl—cheer yourself up, go ahead. . . ."

But I can tell she's not fully engaged with me. Even as we duel on the football pitch—and despite my boasts, I don't score much, as Taylor unsurprisingly turns out to be a fantastic goalie—I can see that, no matter how much she's throwing her body around to block the ball, her brain's somewhere else entirely.

It's particularly annoying because, even without her concentrating properly, she's much better than me at football. Sometimes I do wonder why on earth I was stupid enough to be best friends with a natural athlete.

*eight*

# AN UNKINDNESS OF RAVENS

"Waste not, want not!" Miss Carter says brightly from behind a long table set up in a corner of Fetters's dining room. "Come and get your water bottles, girls!"

Next to her is Jane, holding a marker pen. The Wakefield Hall girls, used to this routine on any school trip, are lining up already, each taking a bottle on which Jane has marked their name, carrying it over to the tap at the dining room sink to fill it up.

Well, almost all of the Wakefield Hall girls. Plum's sipping coffee with the St. Tabby's posse, Susan by her side; she's looking over, appalled, at the activity going on at the trestle table.

"What on *earth*—" she starts.

"We have a very strict environmental policy at Wakefield, Plum!" Miss Carter says, fixing Plum with a firm stare. "No bottled water, and names on all your water bottles so that you're all responsible for your own plastic."

"God! My AmEx is the only plastic *I* could give a damn

about," Plum drawls, "and I'm not exactly responsible with it. . . ."

Susan giggles appreciatively, which fires up Miss Carter.

"Right! You two are carrying everyone's water to the coach!" Miss Carter snaps. "Now get on your feet this instant and come over here for your bottles!"

Plum bites her lip and reluctantly pushes the bench back from the table so she can get up, Susan following on her heels. The other girls fall in line behind Plum, even the St. Tabby's ones. Miss Carter is the gym mistress, which means she's more than capable of making Plum run laps around the grounds or do tons of press-ups if Plum doesn't behave, and Plum can't afford to get chucked out of Wakefield Hall, as her parents will go ballistic and cut off her trust fund if she gets expelled from two schools in a row.

"This is a very good idea," Ms. Burton-Race says approvingly to Miss Carter. "Recycling bottles, using tap water . . ."

"Oh, Lady Wakefield's terribly opposed to bottled water—she's madly keen on waste-not-want-not," Miss Carter says, smiling. "It's the unofficial school motto."

It's true; my grandmother says she learned thrifty habits growing up in wartime. She recycles what she calls "kirby-grips," hair grips whose plastic tips have come off; she insists that all the canteen's leftover bread go to the Wakefield Hall hens; she even saves the last slippery oval of her Bronnley Royal Horticultural Society gardeners' soap and sticks it onto the new one, to avoid wasting any. She regularly lectures us at morning assembly on ways to make do and mend, and occasionally she takes it into her head to stroll through the dormitories, looking for wastebaskets in which some unfortunate girl has thrown an empty toiletry bottle rather than walk down the corridor to the proper plastic-disposal bins. Naked terror of my grandmother's spot checks has made us a school of nervous, obsessive recyclers, flinching at the mere idea of a teacher catching us coming back from Wakefield village with a newly bought bottle of Buxton water in our hands.

Miss Carter is supervising Plum and Susan as they load our water bottles into the plastic crate they came from. Plum is grumpy, but Susan reaches out to stroke her hair briefly, calming her down.

"Now carry them out to the coach," Miss Carter says briskly. "Get the keys from Miss Wakefield."

"My *nails*," Plum moans, but she takes one end of the plastic crate; Susan already has the other.

"I'll get the keys for you," Lizzie offers, bustling away, as Taylor and I lean against the wall, enjoying the sight of Plum doing manual labor.

"Use your wrists to take the weight more," Taylor says affably to Plum, who positively snarls at her as she staggers by.

"Everyone, grab your coats and scarves!" Miss Carter says. "And make sure you're all wearing sensible shoes."

"I don't even know what sensible shoes *look* like," Nadia says, tossing back her heavy mane of hair. Miss Carter glares at her.

"St. Tabby's versus Wakefield Hall," Taylor comments cheerfully. "Nice. It's sort of like a cage match."

But we have no idea how extreme the division's about to become. Our destination—described last night as a "bracing scenic walk" by Miss Carter—turns out to be a hike up the mountain we saw yesterday, towering over Holyrood. It's called Arthur's Seat. From Aunt Gwen's endless talk yesterday we know that's it's an extinct volcano, and it's very high indeed.

"I'm *not*!" Plum wails as we disembark from the coach and take our water bottles from the crate. "I'm *not* going up there! You can't make me!"

"Hill walking is very good for the quads, hamstrings, and glutes," Miss Carter says, beaming evilly. "If you're going to keep wearing miniskirts, Plum, you'll want to make sure your legs are toned."

Before us are the green grassy downs we looked over from the cemetery, soft, gentle rolling hills. Dogs are gamboling over them, off the leash, their owners jogging beside them or throwing balls for them to fetch. The grass is dotted here and there with tiny white daisies; a couple of young men on mountain bikes sweep dashingly past, turning their heads to check out our group, their T-shirts clinging to their lean frames.

And then we look up at the high peak of Arthur's Seat, stony, steep, and forbidding.

"Cool," Taylor says happily.

"No!" Plum pleads desperately. "My *asthma*!"

"Oh? Show me your inhaler," Miss Carter says smugly.

Plum glares at her as Ms. Burton-Race says:

"Right, St. Tabby's girls! Anyone who wants to climb Arthur's Seat is more than welcome. The rest of you can join me and Miss Wakefield for a wildflower-spotting walk over the downs."

"*All* Wakefield Hall girls, to me and Jane," Miss Carter says as a breeze begins to lift our hair.

"It's going to be windy up there," Taylor observes as our group heads off to the foot of Arthur's Seat, Plum staring longingly at the other girls, who have already stopped in their tracks as Ms. Burton-Race points down at something in the grass. Aunt Gwen leans over to check it out; I assume it's a wildflower rather than dog poo. Nadia looks over at our intrepid posse and waves her manicured fingers rather tauntingly at Plum, while Sophia mouths "Good luck!" at Lizzie.

I know which of them I'd pick as a friend.

"Oh, and if I hear anyone complain, they'll be helping the kitchen staff with the washing up tonight," Miss Carter tosses over her shoulder.

She and Jane, I know, go on hiking holidays together every year; their sports gear is slick and aerodynamically sleek, leggings under snugly fitting zipped gray jackets piped with reflective strips, water bottles strapped neatly onto hip loops. Miss Carter's bum, which we get a very good view of as she leads the way up the hill, is a miracle of taut, toned muscularity; it doesn't wobble at all, even as she's leaping and bounding up the shallow stone steps cut into the hillside. We're in more motley clothes—you can tell which girls work out enough to have their own proper outfits and which ones have just brought the brown regulation Wakefield Hall tracksuit trousers that we wear for PE in the winter months.

And then there are Alison and Luce, the only volunteers

from St. Tabby's, clearly determined to make the point that St. Tabby's girls can be tougher and sportier than anything Wakefield Hall can field.

"Race you up?" Luce says to Alison, loud enough so that she can be sure I've heard her.

"Great!" Alison says at the same volume. "I don't see any competition round here, do you?"

"*God*, no!" Luce says, giving a high-pitched, totally fake laugh.

I bristle and glance at Taylor, expecting her to be on the balls of her feet already, about to take them on. But she shakes her head at me, frowning.

"Leave it," she mouths as Alison and Luce take off, darting up the steps past Miss Carter and Jane.

"Good for you, girls!" Jane calls approvingly.

The steps are narrow and steep and we have to wait, often, for people coming down to pass us, or step aside, clambering over rocks to take shortcuts. Taylor and I take it in bursts, using the occasional forced stop to drink some water and do some quick calf stretches. Below us, Lizzie, Plum, and Susan toil up the hill, leaning on every railing and outcropping they can find, casting looks of agony at each other, but not daring to voice their misery out loud in case they get stuck with washing-up duty later on.

They've stopped on a bend almost directly below us, twenty feet down; Taylor uncaps her water bottle and leans over the edge of the rickety wooden railing, yelling:

"Hey! Want to freshen up a bit?"

She trickles a drop out, and with her excellent aim manages to land it on Lizzie's head. Lizzie squeals in shock.

"No, Taylor! My *hair*!" she wails, clapping her hands to her scalp. "Please! It takes *hours* to do!"

Plum and Susan crane their heads back to see what's happening, and promptly gape in horror.

"Taylor! *Please* don't!" Susan pleads, her pale, beautiful face upturned to us, her hands actually pressed together as if she's praying. Plum, of course, has ducked behind her, using her as a shield.

"Ah, I can't do it," Taylor sighs, recapping the bottle. "It'd be like stoning puppies."

I want to laugh at that, but I'm too dizzy. Which is weird. Maybe I leaned too far over the rail, sending blood rushing to my head, but that doesn't sound right. It's not like I'm not used to being upside down. So it's odd that, when I straighten up, I'm still feeling unsteady on my feet. I take a long drink of water, hoping that will help. The people we were waiting for have passed us by now, heading down, and Taylor and I set off again. I find myself reaching out to balance myself on rocks and the moss of the hillside, but Taylor's in the lead, so she doesn't notice, which I'm grateful for; she'd definitely take the piss.

We level out onto a mossy plain after ten more minutes, and I'm taken aback by how relieved I am that the climb is over. My muscles are working, my lungs pumping oxygen round my body just like they're supposed to, but it's as if I'm feeling everything from such a distance that my head might as well be floating a couple of feet above my body.

I look round, a little dazed. The view is breathtaking; straight ahead of me, across the plain, beyond the city, the sea stretches away, steely blue, rippling in the breeze. It's the harbor of Leith, the port of Edinburgh, and I can see the far shore, hills rising on the other side, but nothing as high as where we're standing. Clouds scud across the sky, and now that we're not sheltered by the hillside, the wind is knife sharp, slicing through my fleece jacket and wool sweater. It wakes me up, clears my head. I take another long pull of water. Okay, I'm not feeling brilliant for some reason, but I've managed the climb, and if I came up, I can go down again. I'll have a snooze in the bus on the way back to school till the dizziness passes.

"Come on!" Taylor's saying impatiently, bouncing from one foot to the other. "What are you waiting for?"

"What?" I blink at her, confused.

And then I see that she's pointing off to my left, where another steep hill rises sharply. It looks like it's entirely made of rocks piled on top of each other in a sheer, uninviting peak.

"Oh *no*," I mumble, but Taylor's already taken off.

Reluctantly I follow her, and promptly turn my foot. Looking down, I see that the grassy ground is thickly scattered with stones. I do an awkward, barefoot-on-coals dance across them on tiptoe, scared of falling, unsure of my balance; by the time I reach Taylor, waiting for me at the foot of the peak, she's snorting with laughter.

"That was the *best* imitation of Lizzie!" she says. "You looked *exactly* like her when Miss Carter's making her run laps!"

*God, I must be in even worse shape than I realized*, I think. I bite my lip, hard enough so that the pain gives me a much-needed shock. What I really want to do is slap my own face, but I don't want to look like a loony in front of Taylor. She's already turned to the rock face, and I see with huge relief that there's a cleft in it; a couple of people are already farther up it, clambering and using the sides for extra leverage to pull themselves to the top.

*I can hold on all the way*, I tell myself. *And then I'll sit down and clear my head properly. Maybe Miss Carter's got some sports drink or something with sugar in it. . . . That would help. . . .*

There's no point worrying about what's wrong with me right now. I just need to get to the top of Arthur's Seat and have a rest. Lizzie and Plum and Susan will be miles behind by now; that'll buy me plenty of time before the group descent. I'll have a good twenty minutes to sit—or even lie—down, close my eyes, and get hold of myself.

And whatever I do, I mustn't panic. Must not, must not, must not . . .

It's only the thought of being able to lie down that gets me to the top of the climb. My head's spinning by now, as wobbly as a balloon tied to a stick. My hands keep slipping off the rocks on either side of me; I'm leaning forward so the front of my body's almost grazing the slope, desperate to make sure I don't fall backward. My legs are moving like a robot's, carrying me up the hill as if someone else is pushing me. By the time my head rises over the last ridge, I feel as if I'm made of jelly.

I just manage to swing my legs up so I'm sitting on the rocks. Heaving myself on my bum a few feet away from the top of the cleft, so I don't block access to it, I wrap my arms around my knees and lean forward to rest my head. It's perishingly cold up here; wind gusts round the peak as loud as whip cracks. My teeth are chattering. I take long, slow breaths of ice-cold air through my mouth, pulling it deep down into my lungs, steam forming in front of my mouth as I exhale again.

A crow caws, gliding past on the wind, its black wings outstretched, one beady eye turned to the people clustered on the mountaintop. I half close my eyes and suddenly it turns into a whole group of crows, clustered together, their wings flapping in unison.

*I know a flock of ravens is called an unkindness of ravens,* I think, *because it's the title of a mystery book I read. But what do you call a group of crows? I'm sure I've heard the name for it. . . .*

I'm shivering from the inside out now, but at least I've come up with a reason for why I'm feeling so weird. I've remembered that my period's due in a few days. I don't usually get much period pain, just enough sometimes to make me take a couple of ibuprofen, but sometimes I do feel a bit dozy just beforehand, a bit sluggish. I sit around and stuff down carbs and drink hot chocolate for forty-eight hours; and then, when it does arrive, I get a burst of energy, as if in compensation, and find myself going for salads and fruit instead. I haven't hit the carb craving yet, but maybe the dizziness I'm feeling is because I'm actually hungry. . . .

This is such a good theory that it cheers me up hugely. The worst part of this dizziness is the panic that I'm losing control of my body and I don't know why. Managing to come up with a reason, a good, solid, logical reason, reassures me enough to get me hoisting myself to my feet, looking

115

around. Forget sports drinks; maybe someone'll have something to eat up here. A sandwich or something, a sports bar—

"Scarlett! Come over here!" Taylor's calling.

I scramble over to where she's standing, right on the top of the very tallest part of the peak, shading her eyes from the sun that's come out from behind the passing clouds. Beside her is a sundial—or I think it's a sundial. It's a huge, smooth metal disk like a table, set onto a rough stone base, lines radiating out from the center with writing along each one.

"Hey, we're two hundred and fifty meters high," Taylor says, reading off the disk. "These must be all the highest hills in the country or something. Allermuir . . . Lammer Law . . . Carberry Hill . . . Traprain Law . . . North Berwick Law . . . Wow, why are there so many Laws?"

"It means 'grave mound,' lassie," a nice older lady bundled up in a dark blue padded jacket and woolly scarf informs her. "We do have a lot of them in Scotland, I suppose."

"Cool! Grave mounds! That's so dark!" Taylor says, leaning farther over the disk.

"Your friend doesn't seem too well," says the lady, looking over at me. "Does she mebbe need to have a wee sit-down?"

Damn. I didn't think it was that obvious. I've got both palms of my hands flat on the disk now to steady myself, but maybe I'm rocking back and forth a little bit. I don't feel that the ground is a hundred percent stable beneath my feet.

"Crap!" Taylor says, staring at me hard. "Uh, excuse me," she says politely to the lady. Swiftly, she picks her way round the radius of the disk to my side. "Scarlett?" she says, right next to me; I can feel her breath on my ear. "What's up? You look really weird."

"I think I'm getting my period," I say, having a hard time making my lips work properly. "I feel all wobbly."

"You feel wobbly cause you're getting your period?" she says, frowning. "That's new."

"I think maybe I need to eat something," I manage to say.

She's still frowning, but she nods.

"Stay here," she says. "I'll see if anyone's got something to eat. Do you have any pain?"

"No—I'm not due for a few days—"

"I don't get this," Taylor mutters. "Look. Sit down, okay?"

She puts her hands on my shoulders, helping me to an outcropping, where I sink gratefully back to my bum again.

"Whoo," I hear myself say as Taylor disappears. I tilt my head and find myself looking down at Edinburgh, stretched out directly below me. Wide green velvety swathes of grass wrap around the base of Arthur's Seat, and beyond them the city rises away, the hills it's built on so steep that I can't see the streets, just the elegant lines of gray buildings. Blocks of them, stacked at weird angles because of the way they cling to the sides of the hills. The shapes they make look like train carriages piled up, crashed into each other. Children's toys, dropped from a great height.

I uncap my bottle and finish my water. It's freezing cold by now and feels great going down, so good that on a sudden whim I upend the bottle over my head, the last few drops dripping icily down the back of my neck. I gasp in shock: it's exactly the wake-up call I need. I heave myself to my feet, embarrassed that I'm making this fuss about something as silly as a bit of pre-period wobbliness. Walking past the disk, I start picking my way down the rocks to where most of the Wakefield Hall group is standing. Taylor's taken Miss Carter and Jane aside, tactfully, to explain to them what's going on with me; Jane's already riffling through her backpack.

I'm doing fine. I'm really pleased with myself. I can walk over to them like someone who may not be feeling at her very best, but isn't collapsed on a pile of rocks making a whiny fuss about something really minor. . . .

And then the crow swoops past me, cawing loudly, its sleek black body so close I think I could reach out and touch its wing. I jump in shock, my heart pounding so fast that my chest hurts with the effort of containing it.

"God, what's up with Scarlett?" I hear Plum comment. "She looks like she's been hitting the cocktails! Is there a *bar* up here?"

Lizzie titters with laughter, and so does Luce; my vision's blurred, but I'd recognize Luce's high, girlish laugh anywhere.

I want to retort, but my lips can't maneuver around the words. The icy water on my scalp is clammy; I'm sweating suddenly, hot and cold at the same time. The crow turns on the thermal it's riding, making another pass, and I panic, thinking it's coming straight for me. My vision blurs further as I put up a hand to try to block the crow, stumbling away from its path.

My foot turns under me, the molded rubber heel of my trainer catching on a rock and slipping sideways. I'm falling, the edge of the cliff coming up to meet me. And this isn't like it was in the stairwell, when my brain and my body snapped into action together to save my life. Now my brain and body are as fuzzy as they were alert two nights ago. I can't jump out of danger; I can't rely on my quick-fire reflexes. Below me the rocks are an open mouth full of sharp teeth, and though I've put out my hands to protect my face, I know that when I hit them I'll be tumbling down the side of the cliff.

I'll get torn to pieces. And though that knowledge should make me scream in panic, I can barely connect with it. My skull might as well be packed with cotton wool. Even as I fall, I'm passing out.

The crow caws again, a weird, high-pitched, screaming cry, and my last thought before everything goes dark is:

*It's a murder: that's what you call a group of crows. A murder of crows.*

# nine

## "THIS ISN'T A COINCIDENCE"

I'm shivering all over. There's water running down my face, and it's hard to open my eyes. I try to raise a hand, meaning to wipe them, but my arm's as heavy as a sandbag and I barely manage to lift it an inch.

Someone exclaims loudly:

"She's moving! Look! Miss Carter, she's moving!"

Inexpertly, they dab at my face with a wodge of cloth that momentarily blocks my nose. I gulp for breath, turn my head away, and knock it on a sharp edge.

"Ow!" I say, or mean to: it comes out as a moan.

"She said something!" the same voice cries, and I wince at how high it is. I start wriggling, trying to sit up.

*Oh. I'm lying down. I didn't even realize that, I was so spaced-out. . . .*

Hands in my back help me sit up, holding me as I open my eyes. The first thing I see, blinking, is Luce, leaning forward, staring at me intently.

"Her pupils look fine," she comments seriously. Holding up one finger, she asks: "Can you follow this, Scarlett?" as she moves it back and forth. I swivel my eyeballs obediently. Luce nods as she watches me.

"No concussion, Miss Carter," Luce announces.

"Well, I didn't think she'd be concussed," Miss Carter says, sounding amused, "because she didn't hit her head. But thank you—Lucy, is it? That was a very professional job of checking."

"It's from gymnastics," Luce informs her. "Lots of girls crack their heads on the beams."

I think I can sit up now without being held, and I turn my head to tell Taylor so. I get a real shock when I see that the person kneeling behind me, propping me up, is actually Alison. I start, my upper body jerking forward, away from her supporting hands, in a way that I realize, too late, could be misinterpreted. It's as if I'm telling her I don't want her to touch me.

Alison goes red and jumps to her feet. I start to mumble an explanation but it's too late, and I'm still pretty dazed; I barely get a word out before she snaps:

"I caught you! You'd have smashed your head in if it wasn't for me!"

My eyebrows shoot up so high it hurts. I look around for Taylor and see that she's standing next to Miss Carter and Jane, talking urgently to them.

"Alison could have been hurt herself," Luce adds coldly, pushing herself away from me and standing up too. "She did a whacking great jump to grab you before you went over face-first. You should thank her."

"Thanks," I start to say as best I can, but I don't think anyone hears me. It's very noisy up here with the wind whipping round us, snatching the words out of our mouths, and although I apparently didn't hit my head, I still feel as dizzy as ever. I'm at eye level with everyone's knees; they're all standing around me, perched on the rock outcroppings like—well, a murder of crows. I get a flash of memory of what it's like to be a child in a world of giant grown-ups.

Bizarrely, although this should make me feel vulnerable, I find it strangely reassuring. They're all discussing how to take care of me; for once, looking out for myself isn't a hundred percent my responsibility. I close my eyes so I can't see Alison and Luce glaring at me, and wait for a few minutes, teeth chattering with the cold, till Taylor ducks down next to me and says:

"Okay, Scarlett. Me and Jane are going to help you back down to the bottom of the hill, and then we'll find the coach and take you back to school to see the nurse and figure out what's going on with you."

She shoves one hand into my armpit and heaves me to my feet. I wobble dangerously, but Jane is right there on my other side, taking my elbow firmly.

"I'll ring Gwen," Miss Carter says, her phone in her hand. "She's Scarlett's aunt, after all. She'll want to take Scarlett back to Fetters."

I cast an agonized glance at Taylor.

"You come too!" I plead, and though my mouth still isn't working very well she understands completely what I'm saying and nods repeatedly.

"I'm *totally* not leaving you alone with your aunt while you're sick," she reassured me. "Don't worry."

Jane shoots Taylor a frown, but doesn't question this;

she's probably known Aunt Gwen long enough to guess that Aunt Gwen has the empathy and bedside manner of Hannibal Lecter.

"Does she have any allergies?" Jane asks Taylor as they start to walk me over to the cleft that's the first descent we have to make.

"Nope," Taylor says. "This is totally weird. I've never seen her like this before."

Jane clears her throat.

"I know young people"—she starts—"um, sometimes experiment with things . . . like cough mixture, or cold medication. . . . Is there any possibility that she was doing something like that this morning? I'll be discreet," she adds quickly. "It's just that the nurse should know if Scarlett's on anything."

"We're not that dumb," Taylor says flatly. "We're not like that anyway, and we're *especially* not dumb enough to do anything that would make us trippy before we come out to *climb* a *mountain*."

I feel Jane nod beside me.

"Fine," she says equably. "I know you're both sporty girls. It makes sense that you'd respect your bodies and wouldn't do something so stupid."

Even in my debilitated state, I wince at being called sporty: it gives me an instant picture of Sharon Persaud, school hockey star, with her grim expression and enormous muscly thighs.

"Scarlett," Taylor says to me, "we're going to take you down this narrow bit now. Remember it when we came up? I'm going to go in front of you. I'll have one hand out to brace you the whole time. Just take it super slowly and you'll be fine."

If anything, my dizziness is increasing, and I'm so busy concentrating on putting one foot in front of the other, flat to the ground so I don't trip, that I don't lift my head to look around me. I register that two guys, whippet thin, pass us coming up; they're actually running up the steep ascent, shiny and sweaty in tight black Lycra. For a moment I think I'm hallucinating, because they go by so fast, and my grip on Taylor tightens; then Jane says,

"Hill running is *terribly* hard on the knees," and I relax in the knowledge that they're real.

Miss Carter must have got hold of Aunt Gwen, because she's waiting at the base of the stone steps cut into the hillside, her hands on her hips, eyes bulging furiously. The first words out of her mouth are:

"So she's managed to get herself into trouble *again*! What on earth is it this time?"

I flinch back, cannoning into Jane. She says carefully:

"Miss Wakefield—Scarlett's had some sort of a turn. She's not well."

"*Really,*" Aunt Gwen says disbelievingly.

"She's just had a collapse," Jane says slowly, as if she's speaking to a child. "Did Clemency not tell you that when she rang you?"

Aunt Gwen shrugs.

"It's one thing after another with Scarlett," she mutters crossly. "I simply can't keep up."

I feel Jane take a deep breath.

"You know what?" she says overbrightly. "Taylor and I

will take Scarlett back to Fetters. Sorry to have bothered you, Miss Wakefield. Come on, Scarlett. It's not far now to the coach."

Aunt Gwen turns away without saying another word, striding back down a deep grassy slope, presumably to rejoin the St. Tabby's group. A pheasant's hopping across the slope, a cock pheasant, his head bright green and red, his chestnut-colored body shiny and plump; he takes one look at Aunt Gwen stamping toward him and rises into the air, his wings whirring, getting out of her way as fast as he can.

"Uh, Scarlett and her aunt don't get on too well," Taylor says.

"Yes, I'm rather picking that up," Jane mutters, pulling her phone out of her pocket. "Clemency, it's me," she says when her call's answered. "I'm taking Scarlett back myself. Her aunt was, er—yes—*yes*—my God, she's not exactly— yes, we'll talk about this later. Let's just say I think I should take Scarlett to the school nurse myself. Taylor McGovern will come with me. Can you get the other girls down all right? Those two—Alison and Lucy, is it?—seem very capable, I'm sure they'll help—good—all right, darling, I'll see you back at the school—my *goodness*, what a morning!"

I get to lie down on the backseat of the coach going back, and the warm upholstery and rumbling of the wheels lull me into a doze; Taylor has to shake me awake when we arrive at Fetters, and I uncurl my limbs from the happy ball I've been snuggled in. To my embarrassment, I need to hold on to the tops of the seats for balance as I walk down the central aisle, and I'm unsteady going into the school building. All I want to do is sleep.

125

Jane and Taylor get me to the nurse's office, and while we're waiting for her to come back from wherever she is, I lie down on the narrow, green-plastic-upholstered examination table against the wall and pass out. I literally can't keep my eyes open a moment longer. Not even the bright fluorescent light strips of the infirmary can stop me from going to sleep. I hear bustling around me. Someone prises open one of my eyelids and shines a light onto my eyeball, and I whine in protest. Fingers close around my wrist, taking my pulse. My sweater's unzipped, my T-shirt pulled up, and the metal circle of a stethoscope is pressed to my bare chest; I whimper, because it's cold, but soon it goes away, my clothes are pulled down again, and someone tucks a pillow under my head and a blanket around my body. The voices fade away, the lights go out. I turn my head in to the pillow and go out like the lights just did.

. . .

I don't know how long I was unconscious, but when I eventually wake up, I'm cramped, my muscles tight and painful. I assume it's because, in my sleep, I've been squashing myself up, automatically making sure I don't turn over and fall off the high, narrow table. The paper covering of the pillow is damp where I've been drooling on it with an open mouth.

*Nice, Scarlett. Very elegant.* Embarrassed, I rip off the paper pillowcase, ball it up, and throw it into the wastebasket. I pull off the blanket and lever myself off the table, stretching as high as I can with both arms, working out the cramps in my muscles. Then I roll my head from side to side. I'm myself again. Any lingering wisps of drowsiness are fading away like mist in the dawn, burning off with the adrenaline that's racing through me as I look back over the events of this morning and realize, with growing horror, that what happened to me was very bad indeed.

*That wasn't because I was getting my period.* I know it now that I have my clarity back. *And I would never even have assumed it was for two seconds, if I hadn't been so trippy I could barely put one foot in front of the other.*

Not only have I never felt anything like that before when my period's nearly due, I've never heard of *anyone* getting a reaction like that just from being premenstrual. Feeling so weak, fainting . . . it's like something out of a Charlotte Brontë novel. We're doing *Villette* for English A-level, and the heroine spends half her time thinking she's hallucinating visions of a nun who was murdered for having an affair, or wandering through the town completely spaced-out after the villainess has drugged her with opium.

As you can tell even from that short summary, it's a brilliant book. A bit mad, but completely brilliant. But frankly, you read books precisely because you want to go through experiences in them that you'd run a mile from if you met them in real life. And though Lucy Snowe, the heroine of *Villette*, found herself walking through a carnival tripping on laudanum (which is actually a mix of opium and booze— the Victorians drank it to help them go to sleep. Mad, eh?), at least if you fall over at a carnival, you'll probably just topple onto a nice patch of grass and maybe go to sleep.

Whereas I was up a very steep mountain with rocks in

every direction. My faint could have had really serious consequences.

I'm shying away from the truth. Which is that it could have killed me.

Which makes twice in forty-eight hours that I could have died from a fall. And both times, it would have seemed like an accident.

I sit back down on the table, feeling very cold indeed. Sweat pools at the small of my back. I shiver as if someone's dropped an ice cube down my shoulder blades. Even though, in the last year, a lot of truly awful things have happened to me, I've never been targeted like this. I've been caught up in other people's drama, and it's turned nasty and dangerous. But I've never been the intended victim. I've never felt that someone else had me in their sights.

I've never been this scared in my life.

The infirmary door opens and I jump almost off the table. Even when I see that it's Taylor coming in, I don't completely relax. And that's an even worse shock, because in that split second, I've realized that I don't quite trust anyone a hundred percent. Not even Taylor.

*Taylor wasn't there to catch me when I took that tumble earlier today. She'd gone off to get help from Miss Carter. And she did tell me to stay sitting down and to wait for her. But she called me up to a particularly steep place—by the sundial—and then she left me there.*

"How're you feeling?" she asks, shaking her hair out of her eyes, sitting down on the table next to me.

"Better," I say. "Well"— I find myself qualifying that

immediately—"I'm not feeling dizzy anymore. But now I'm freaking out about what happened to me."

"You should," Taylor says seriously. She hands me a mug of tea. "I made this for you. Lots of sugar. The nurse said I should wake you up and give you some tea."

"Is she coming back in?" I ask, taking the mug gingerly, as it's steaming.

Taylor makes a face.

"I don't think so. I heard her telling Jane she thought you were exaggerating to get attention."

"*What?*" I nearly drop the mug, I'm so cross.

"Yeah, Jane told her she was sure you weren't, but then the nurse said something snarky about teenage girls thinking periods are an excuse for lots of drama, and she and Jane got into an argument."

"I can see why she's working in an all-boys' school," I say, blowing on my tea to cool it down. "The nurse, I mean."

"Totally. But she said your vital signs were all fine when you came in here," Taylor adds reassuringly. "Apparently your pulse was a bit fast, but that's it."

"It wasn't the period thing, Taylor," I say, looking at her directly. "I only thought that because—"

"Because anything else would have been way worse, and you didn't want to go into a major panic up on top of a mountain," Taylor finishes. "I didn't think it was your period either. I mean, you're never like that. You haven't even got cramps yet this time around, have you?"

I shake my head and start to sip the tea. It's strong enough to stand a spoon in and sweet enough to rot my teeth. Exactly what I need. After just a few sips I'm already feeling better.

"This isn't a coincidence," Taylor continues. "Not after that whole fire thing, and someone pushing you. Plus the note. Someone's definitely out to get you." She looks around the room, then gets up, closes the door, and comes back, pulling up the nurse's chair so she can sit opposite me. "I think whatever it was, they put it in your water," she says in a lowered voice. "I've been thinking about this nonstop since we got back here. All the water bottles had names on them. Plum and Susan carried them to the coach, and Lizzie got the keys. One of them could easily have tampered with your water bottle then. And after that, who knows if they gave the keys back to your aunt, right? They probably just left them in the lock and wandered off to check their makeup. And there'd have been plenty of time after we finished breakfast, before we set off for Arthur's Seat, for someone else to go out to the coach and find your bottle and put something in it. . . ."

"Like what?" I ask, drinking more tea. The sugar's picking me up, but my brain's still not working as fast as usual. I'm perfectly happy to sit here and let Taylor run through the entire theory she's been formulating while I was unconscious.

"Well, I've got an idea about that, too," Taylor says, leaning forward. "Have you ever taken antihistamines? You don't have any allergies, so probably not."

I think this over, already halfway through the mug of tea. Eventually, I shake my head again.

"I don't think so."

"Well, they can really knock you out," Taylor says. "My brother took two of my mom's Claritin once and he was zonked for hours. It was pretty funny, actually. He was like a zombie; he could barely keep his eyes open. Seth totally hates being out of control—he doesn't drink or anything, so I'd never seen him like that before. I said I was going to shave his eyebrows and he ran away and locked himself in his bedroom 'cause he was scared he'd pass out and I'd prank him." She grins in reminiscence. "I wouldn't have. But it was really funny to watch him sweat for once."

"So you think—"

"I think that someone emptied out some capsules of antihistamines and dumped them into your water bottle," she says. "That would be much easier than crushing up tablets, and you probably wouldn't taste it so much. There's powder in the capsules and it would dissolve in the water if they shook it up a bit. Did your water taste funny at all?"

I pull a face. "I don't think so. But Edinburgh tap water tastes really different to London water anyway. We've all been saying so. There's more fluoride or something."

"Right." Taylor nods slowly. "Makes sense. Anyway, it was a perfect opportunity. Antihistamines hit you pretty fast. Whoever did it would be hoping that you'd start feeling pretty woozy before long, and then if you took a fall, they'd be far away when it happened, and not be remotely blamed for it. Like, someone who was coming uphill really slowly, miles behind you." She tilts her chair back a bit. "Or even someone in the St. Tabby's group. Not on Arthur's Seat at all."

"So does that rule out Alison and Luce?" I say, thinking

aloud. "Alison actually caught me when I was about to split my skull open. . . ."

"It could have been Luce," Taylor says unhelpfully. "Or maybe Alison put the stuff in your water to give you a bad time, but freaked out when she saw that you might actually get killed."

"No one who was worried about me actually getting killed would have pushed me over the staircase rail," I point out.

"True," Taylor agrees. "Scarlett, I'm really sorry I wasn't there when you fell this morning, okay?" Nontactile, non-cuddly Taylor actually tilts forward and puts a hand awkwardly on my knee for emphasis. "But I thought you'd stay sitting down till I came back for you," she says, grimacing. "How was I supposed to know you'd be dumb and stubborn enough to try to walk down a cliff on your own?"

"Um, it's not really an apology when you finish by blaming the victim," I say sarcastically, finishing the tea. "But what if I didn't react to the antihistamines? Not everyone gets knocked out like that by them."

Taylor shrugs.

"They'd just have tried again some other way," she says grimly.

I put the mug down next to me on the table and look at her.

"*She'd* just have tried again some other way," I correct her. "I mean, one thing we can be sure about is that it's a girl. Or a woman."

Taylor nods. I sit for a moment, absorbing everything she's said.

"I'm going to our room," I say slowly. "I need to be by myself for a bit. You should go back with Jane and join everyone else for the afternoon. I know you wanted to do the tour of Edinburgh Castle."

"I should stay with you," Taylor says, but she looks torn. She really does want to see the castle. Lots of battles happened there. And sieges. Taylor loves both battles and sieges with a passion.

"Whoever tried to hurt me," I point out, "has to be in that group. So if you go, I'll still be fine, because all the suspects will be somewhere else, and you'll be able to keep an eye on them."

"Worst-case scenario, if someone sneaks out, I can make an excuse and follow them," Taylor agrees. She stands up. "I'll see you up to our room," she says.

"It's okay, Taylor," I say, standing too. "I can get there myself. Go and find Jane. If she needs to see me before she takes you off, that's where I'll be."

I pick up my mug and follow her out of the infirmary. We pause outside for a moment, looking at each other; Taylor's expression is weird, unreadable. It's as if she's deliberately masking her feelings from me.

"Stay in our room till we all get back," she says.

I nod. "I'm just going to read my book."

Her lips part; she looks as if she's about to say something else. And then she shakes her head, frowning, turns, and heads off down the corridor in the direction of the staff room.

Something's definitely up with Taylor. I know her well enough to be aware that there's something she's not telling me.

Well, Taylor isn't the only person in my life I can lean on. My fingers are already closing around the phone in my pocket as if it were a tiny life preserver; I'm pulling it out as I climb the main stairs up to the dormitories.

His number is 2 on my speed dial. He'd have been 1 if that weren't tied to voice mail. (And no, Taylor doesn't know that she isn't number 2.)

I haven't rung him since he left; or, to be precise, I haven't initiated ringing him, though I've returned his calls if he's missed me and left a message. This is the first time since Jase rode away from Wakefield Hall that I've called him out of the blue.

But if there was ever a time I need to talk to my boy-friend, now is it.

Closing the door behind me, I flop down on my bed, hold down the 2 key, and wait, heart pounding, to hear if he'll pick up.

# Ten

## FALLING DOWN THE RABBIT HOLE

I swore I wouldn't cry. I don't like crying at the best of times, and I particularly hate it when I cry in front of Jase; it makes me feel like some pathetically weak girlie girl in a film, weeping in her boyfriend's strong, manly arms. Which is very much not the image I have of myself. I like to feel I'm tough enough to take care not only of myself, but also of the people around me, if necessary. And my own arms are strong enough to pull me up a rope or to the top of a wall, if necessary.

So it's especially annoying that when Jase picks up and says: "Scarlett!" I promptly burst into hysterical sobs. Obviously I'm much more wound up by recent events than I realized. Just the sound of his voice, so wonderfully familiar and comforting, has opened the floodgates. I howl like a banshee for a solid minute or so, Jase's voice in my ear getting increasingly concerned. There aren't any tissues in the room, but there's a dispenser of nasty cheap paper hand towels above the sink (which I'm sorry to say does have suspicious yellow stains running down the inside. Boys are foul). I grab a fistful of the towels and start to blot my face with them. They're so dry and corrugated it's like I'm exfoliating with sandpaper.

"What's *happened?*" Jase is bellowing down the line at me by now. "Scarlett, stop crying and tell me! I'm freaking out!"

I try to speak but by now I'm so congested I can't breathe. So I do the most enormous nose blow in history, trumpeting and bubbling out pints of snot, and take a long breath, crumpling up the sodden towels.

"That's nice," Jase observes, his voice full of laughter. "Really pretty."

I realize that I haven't said a word to him yet; all I've done is ring him up, burst into tears, and then blow my nose at him. Very attractive. I start to giggle, weakly, but enough to make me feel better.

"Sorry," I say feebly. "It's just been a really awful couple of days."

"Yeah, I sort of worked that out," Jase says. "What's been going on? Is it your aunt again?"

"She's being a total cow," I say, "but that's not it."

I heave a sigh and launch into a description of everything that's happened since we arrived in Scotland. I try to relate it all as flatly as I can: just the facts, as little emotion as possible, so it doesn't sound too crazy.

One of the weird things about my and Jase's relationship is that there's always been drama swirling around us. His dad hated us being together, and so did my aunt Gwen, who banned me from seeing him. We've always had to sneak around behind their backs, which, I can assure you, isn't half as romantic as it is when you read about it or see it on TV. And then something truly terrible happened: Jase found out that his dad was driving the van that killed my parents when I was four years old. He ran into them deliberately; he even stopped long enough to snatch my mother's necklace from her body.

It's as bleak as it could be. But at least it means that what I'm telling Jase now isn't the most shocking thing he's ever heard in his life.

And it also means that he knows I'm not the kind of girl who makes up psycho-sounding stories just to grab her boyfriend's attention.

"*Scarlett*," he says eventually, sounding shell-shocked. And though he's clearly really worried about me, every time Jase says my name, it melts me a little with pure pleasure. "I don't know what to say. This is really, really bad."

He takes a long breath.

"I hate that this is happening to you and I'm not there," he says hopelessly. "I feel like the worst boyfriend in the world."

"I wish you were here," I say sadly. "I wish I could hug you right now."

"Oh, baby—I wish I could hug you right now too," he says in a small, miserable voice.

"Where are you?" I ask, even though it feels as if I'm breaching a taboo, because Jase hasn't really wanted to talk about his travels. It's as if now that he's not with me, he's simply Away, with a capital A, and he doesn't want to specify exactly where that place is.

I'm not imagining it; there's a pause before he answers:

"Nottingham. Crashing on a friend's sofa. I've been doing a lot of couch surfing." He laughs dryly. "Well, sofas and floors. Sometimes I'm a bit tall for the sofas, so I pull the pillows off and sleep on them on the living room floor. I've got really good at sleeping anywhere."

"Remember when we pulled the mattress off my bed and we slept on the floor?" I ask.

"Of course I do," he says softly. "It was the best night of my life."

I gulp. I can hardly swallow, it hurts so much.

"If it was the best night of your life," I say in a tiny thread of voice, "why don't you want to see me anymore? I'm so scared right now. . . . I feel really alone, I don't know who I can trust. . . ."

"Baby"—Jase's voice is ragged now—"you *know* that's not true! You *know* I want to see you more than anything! I just can't get my head round everything that's happened—I feel like I've got demons chasing me. Every time I get on the bike it's like I'm trying to outrun them—"

"But maybe you can't run away from them!" I say passionately. "Maybe that's what you're doing wrong! It's been months now, Jase, and if you're not feeling any better, then maybe running away isn't going to work!" I'm almost gasping now in my effort to convince him. "I don't mean 'running away' like you're a coward," I add swiftly.

"I know," he says. "I know you don't mean it like that. I said it myself, didn't I? It's just—it's so hard, Scarlett. My dad—what he did. And it's not just my dad—look at my grandma! It's like my family's cursed or something—"

"But that's only one side of your family," I insist, because there's not a single positive thing to be said for the Barnes half of Jase's bloodline. "Your mum's very nice."

"She's just so . . ." Jase tries to find something positive to say about poor Dawn, his mum, who means well but has less backbone than an earthworm. "She's just so *wet*," he finishes gloomily.

Dawn is totally wet; it's true. I contemplate Jase's situation. On one side, the Barneses, who are all pretty sociopathic; on the other, Dawn, who couldn't say boo to a goose without apologizing immediately afterward.

"It's not about your family," I say firmly, deciding that this is the best line to take if I'm to have any success convincing him to put the past behind him. "It's about you and me, making something new."

"I wish it were that easy," Jase says sadly.

"It should be," I insist, but with less conviction, and when he agrees:

"Yeah. It should be," he sounds as if he's in mourning.

"This is so hard," I echo him, lying down on my bed. "I miss you so much. It's so unfair."

"It is," he says very quietly. "It is unfair."

And we go silent for a while, nothing left to say, listening to each other breathe.

"I'm worried about you, though," Jase says eventually. "All this stuff that's been going on. Do you think it's that Plum girl?"

"It might be," I say. "She definitely doesn't like me."

I haven't told Jase that I have something incriminating on Plum, which I'm holding as insurance for her behaving well with me and Taylor. Instinct tells me that boys don't want to hear that their girlfriends are involved—even for the best of reasons—in a complicated bargaining system that on some level could be described as blackmail. I don't have much experience with boys, but I have the strong feeling that they like to see us as nicer than we actually are, and I'm not about to start testing that theory by telling Jase that I have a near-naked, slightly pornograhic Polaroid of Plum that I have no intention of giving back to her anytime soon.

"I can't see her running round setting off smoke bombs in the middle of the night, though," Jase says. "This is . . ." He pauses. *"Bollocks,"* he finally says, in a really heartfelt voice. "I *hate* to think of someone doing this kind of stuff to you."

"I've got Taylor," I say dully. "I'll be okay."

"But all this is going on while Taylor's right there sharing a room with you!" Jase points out. "That's not exactly reassuring me!"

"What do you want me to say?" My temper flares, finally. "You're not here! You won't come and see me, even though I miss you so much. . . ." I sit up, my anger building. "I'm sorry I rang you, I'm sorry I worried you, okay?" I snap. "I should have known that there wasn't any point, because even though I'm really *upset* and *scared* and *lonely* and I really miss you, you *still* won't come to see me!"

Clutching the phone in a now-sweaty hand, I wait to see what he'll say. Holding my breath, praying that if my pleas haven't worked, maybe my all-too-genuine resentment will. The longer the silence continues, the more I dare to hope. *He's thinking about it. My words are sinking in. He's going to say he'll come up to Edinburgh—*

"I can't," he says in a voice so low it's almost a whisper.

"Then I can't be with you," I hear myself say, and I sound surprisingly clear, surprisingly sure of myself. Which is exactly the opposite to the way I feel. "I can't be with someone who isn't there when I need him."

I give him a few seconds to protest. *One, two, three,* I count in my head. And when he hasn't flared up in that time to say no, he loves me, he can't be without me, he won't let me break up with him, he'll come to see me . . . then I click the button with the red handset icon on it, ending the call.

My phone is hot to the touch. I sit still as a statue as it begins to cool down. And still Jase isn't ringing me back. Eventually, I fumble my thumb on the button that turns off the phone. I can't bear to sit here waiting every moment for it to ring, listening desperately for a sound that doesn't come.

I feel even trippier than I did that morning, as if I'm floating above my body, which is sitting there like a lump of wood on the narrow mattress. Strangely, I don't feel any real, physical pain; I'm bizarrely detached from everything.

*Did I do the right thing? I want to be with Jase so badly. When he said we were boyfriend and girlfriend it was one of the best moments I've ever had in my life. Maybe even the best. And only a couple of months ago I told him that I loved him, and he said he loved me too. . . .*

*And I just broke up with him in a phone call.*

I close my eyes. I'm completely and utterly overloaded. The image whirling in the darkness is the turning rainbow-colored circle my computer throws up when it's clogged up with stuff to process, a sign that says it's too busy to do what

I want then and there. That's exactly how my brain feels: too busy, too stressed, to be able to spit out an answer to a single question I'm asking.

The circle keeps turning, fuchsia-blue-green-yellow-orange whirling back into fuchsia again, on and on and on, round and round and round. And I slump back down on the bed and let myself fall into it.

. . .

*I'm Alice in Wonderland falling down the rabbit hole. Tumbling head over heels down a long, dark well, amazed at how endless it is, completely disoriented. I reach out my hands to try to touch the sides, but unlike Alice's rabbit hole, there are no sides, just cold black air. And then I'm clutching onto someone; he's below me, which shouldn't be possible.*

*It's Callum. He's looking up at me with that expression I remember all too well, desperate and pleading, shocked to the core at what's just happened to him. But before, when I was clinging to him, I had a gymnastics grip on him, my hands digging into his forearms, his into mine. It's like you're holding on four times, and it makes the lock really strong. This time, our hands are clasped, and it's too weak to last. My fingers are numb, as if I'm still drugged from this morning. I can't connect properly, I can't wrap them around his as tightly as I need to.*

*He's slipping away from me, and there's nothing I can do about it. Slowly, his fingers trail down mine, his face slips farther and farther away. I remember how I saw green and gold flashes in his gray eyes before. We were so close in those moments;*

we thought each other's face would be the last thing we'd ever see.

But now all I'm touching of Callum is his fingertips, a last final brush of skin on skin as he falls away into the dark. Turning, spinning, gone. And I keep tumbling down the well. It's not a terrifying, headlong fall, more like a feather spiraling over and over itself as it slowly comes down to earth. I close my eyes, dizzy with the constant revolving motion, and something big and solid bumps into me. I think I've landed, and then the next second I realize I haven't; I'm holding on to Jase, and we're falling together, arms wrapped round one another, my head resting in the hollow of his neck.

He's wearing his leather motorcycle jacket. The zip digs into me, but I don't care. I can smell the worn old leather, the apple aftershave he loves, and him, underneath the other scents—his skin, warm and musky and so instantly familiar that tears of happiness and relief spring to my eyes. My whole body feels as if it's dissolving with the sheer bliss of being close to Jase again, hugging him as I've been craving to do.

I tilt my head back to look up at him, wanting to kiss him, wanting to see my own happiness reflected back at me in his golden eyes. And that's where it all falls apart. As soon as I look at him, he's dragged away from me as if a giant hand in the small of his back pulled him off, sucking him into the dark as if he were a toy, as if he weighed nothing at all. He mouths "Scarlett!" desperately at me as he disappears. I watch his body become tiny, arms and legs thrown out like a starfish, shrinking to the size of my thumb, vanishing into blackness.

And then I know the ground's coming up to meet me, faster

*than I thought. It's the fall at Castle Airlie, or the one at Arthur's Seat. Rocks below me, sharp and unyielding. I brace myself, pointlessly, because there's nothing I can do to stop myself from smashing into them, breaking every bone in my body—*

I wake up panting for breath.

You can never actually die in dreams. I read that somewhere. Your mind won't let you have that kind of trauma. So just before the killer's about to break through the door, or the werewolf's about to rip out your throat, or you're about to crash into the rocks, you wake up, wild-eyed and covered in sweat.

So much for sleep being restful.

# eleven

## SCHRÖDINGER'S CAT

I gave up physics lessons at fourteen. Lucky me. Talking to Taylor about American schools versus English ones, I've learned with horror that over there they make you do all sorts of subjects till you're eighteen; maths, science—*algebra*, even. It sounds terrifying. In the UK, you get to pick about eight subjects you do exams in at sixteen (O-levels) and then three or four to specialize in after that (A-levels), which means you get to give up all the stuff you hate (because you're appalling at it) much earlier. I did have to do maths O-level, because it's pretty much mandatory for everything in life, apparently; the way our teachers bang on, you'd think they wouldn't even let you be a traffic warden unless you had maths O-level.

But honestly, I'm not a science person. I don't like it much, and I have a strong sense that the feeling is mutual. Wrapping my brain around physics was like trying to carry a lot of sharp objects in a flimsy sheet of clingfilm. It was awkward and uncomfortable, and, eventually, painful, as the sharp objects ripped through the thin plastic and fell heavily onto my feet.

Which makes it particularly weird that, right now, the only way I can properly express the way I'm feeling is with a couple of physics metaphors.

My body is walking by Taylor's side down a narrow street whose dark cobbles are shiny in the occasional flare of an orange streetlight; it must have rained earlier, when I was passed out having nightmares about falling down a rabbit hole. Taylor is absorbed in navigating our progress through a maze of turns on her iPhone Google Maps app, its screen glowing in her hand, so we're not talking. Which suits me perfectly, as my brain is equally occupied with working out my state of mind about what happened with me and Jase this afternoon.

There's this famous physics hypothesis—I think that's the right word—called Schrödinger's cat. Basically, a scientist called Schrödinger imagined he put a cat in a box with a radioactive device thingy (*Nice*. Clearly an animal lover) which would give it a fifty percent chance of survival. So, when he opened the box, the cat would be exactly as likely to be alive as it would be to be dead. But his question was: Before I open the box, what state is the cat in? Alive or dead? And his answer (as I understand it) was that the cat is both.

Physics seems to have a lot of those examples—neither one thing nor the other. Like waves and particles. You can see light as a wave or as a particle, depending on how you look at it. It's both things at the same time. There's no single, clear truth; it's entirely in the eye of the beholder.

That's how I feel about Jase and me. The cat in the box, the light that can be both wave and particle, is our relationship. I don't know if it's alive or dead: it's both things at the same time.

On the live side, I love Jase, and he loves me. Just thinking of him, let alone being with him, makes me feel wonderful, complete, and secure in a way I've never been before.

While on the dead side, he won't come to see me when I'm frantic to be with him. And I told him a few hours ago that I was breaking up with him.

I reach my hand down to my phone, a smooth, narrow rectangle snug in the hip pocket of my jeans. And I realize why the metaphor of Schrödinger's cat popped into my head: it's because of the phone, which I still haven't turned back on since my fight with Jase. When I do, it'll be exactly like opening the box. If Jase has rung me back, or texted me, the cat will still be alive. But if he hasn't—if he's decided that being with me is just too painful, and he needs to make a fresh start somewhere far away from Wakefield Hall and all the family memories—then my phone won't have any message icons flashing on it.

The cat will be dead.

I squeeze my eyes shut for a moment to make sure I don't cry. I have a lot of eye makeup on and I don't want to show up at our destination looking like a deranged panda.

"Are we nearly there?" I ask Taylor, narrowly avoiding turning my heel on a cobblestone. I've got my skinniest jeans on, tucked into slim leather boots, a fashion I always said I wouldn't wear (because Plum does, and I don't want to look like a Plum-bot). But when I tried it on this evening, I had to admit I looked good. Taylor and I have been working out a lot, and my legs are lean from all the running.

I want to dress up as much as I can this evening. It's like some sort of challenge to Jase—which is insane, of course, as the whole point is that he's not here to see me. But I feel a really strong need to go out looking fabulous, to prove that I'm not the kind of girl who crumples into a wet heap of misery just because she's had a fight with her boyfriend.

"Oughta be," she says, tilting the screen a little. "If this alley comes out where I think it does . . ."

And then we both gasp, because the narrow street we're walking down has led us to the curve of a little river, right in the center of town. Like a canal in Venice. Or at least, that's what it looks like in the dark. Edinburgh doesn't seem all that keen on streetlights; its attitude, apparently, is that if you don't know where you're going, that's your problem. Oh, and if you fall in the canal because we haven't put any railings round the edges, don't come crying to us. It's not a city for wimps.

As my eyes adjust, however, I can see that the stretch of water widens in the distance. The tall buildings surrounding it part to make room as the river swells into a basin, boats moored along one side, and then what looks like a lock beyond, opening into a wide mouth that leads to—

"That's the Irish Sea," Taylor says, pointing into the dark. "Over there. They told us today at the castle that Leith was the port for the whole of Edinburgh. This is called the Waters of Leith. These were all mills along here, and warehouses for unloading everything from the ships."

We stand and look around for a little while at the dark, imposing buildings looming over us, the Waters of Leith lapping gently at our feet. As I've noticed before, Edinburgh isn't cozy, and I'm realizing that it's a city built for cold weather, with thick walls and small windows to keep the chill out. That's why it can look as if the houses are almost turning their backs on you, unwelcoming; the warmth is all tucked away, not for public consumption. Along the right bank of the river is a series of restaurants and bars, and they, too, aren't as bright as the ones in London, the heavily leaded panes of windows glowing gently rather than lit up like beacons to show off the people inside. Even the Pizza Express, one of a chain you see everywhere, has a more discreet sign, its logo a subtler blue than it would be farther south.

There's a bridge to our left, and I want to cross it, or at least stand halfway over it and watch the water below, dark and heavy like oil. But Taylor's already heading down the pavement that borders the river, and I follow her reluctantly.

"You're off in your own world," she comments, turning her head to check me out. "Are you still feeling weird from this morning?"

"Sort of," I say. "I had funny dreams."

I haven't told her that I talked to Jase, or how disastrous the conversation was. Which is completely unusual; normally I would have thrown myself on her neck as soon as she got back from the Edinburgh Castle visit, spilling everything. But Taylor's keeping stuff from me. I know it as surely as I know my own name. And that makes me a lot less likely to confide in her.

The other completely unusual thing is that under normal circumstances, Taylor would hear the catch in my voice that I can't control, and would know that I was lying. But she doesn't. She just nods, her hair flopping, as she looks across the street at the pubs and restaurants, working out our destination.

"Yeah, I'm not surprised," she says, gesturing that we should cross the road, navigating us through black-painted bollards that must once have been used for tying up ships' ropes. A car approaches, but stops just short of us, its lights flashing as the driver indicates that they'll wait for us to walk in front of it.

"Blimey," I mutter as we nip across the road. "That would *never* happen in London. . . ."

The Shore bar, where we're headed, has a heavy wooden door that even Taylor, with her upper-body strength, has to muscle open; when she does, the flood of warmth and light and music inside is like a tonic to my soul. I hadn't realized till this moment how much I needed this. I'd have stayed curled up on my bed if Taylor hadn't insisted on dragging me out, saying that we had a free night and a ten o'clock curfew, and we'd be idiots not to make the most of it.

I catch sight of us in a tarnished old mirror set into the ancient wood paneling of the pub walls; for a moment I don't recognize us, me with my makeup and my hair piled up on top of my head, Taylor actually wearing some mascara, in her new leather jacket with a ton of zips and dull silver piping. It's fantastic on her; she looks sort of androgynous and, to be perfectly honest, very sexy. I know better than to tell Taylor she looks sexy, as she'd start heaving her guts up, but with the mascara emphasizing her green eyes and making her long lashes look endless, and even a little lip gloss (clear, but *still*, quite an achievement for me, who made her put it on), she's turning heads. I see guys glancing sideways at her, and I realize for the first time that her swaggering walk, her take-no-prisoners stare, is like a challenge to some boys. Two of them, sitting at a table, are looking at her and whispering to each other.

I'm not going to be outdone by my friend in the cool stakes. As she looks around the room, I shoulder my way to the bar and wait to be served, my feet tapping to the Celtic music playing on the sound system. Cutlery and glasses clink behind me and I look over to see a dining room off the main bar, white-covered tables and a roaring fire going, flames dancing in the hearth.

"What can I get you?" the barman asks me, easily, no hesitation about how old I am.

*Nice*. There's a guy and a girl serving, and luckily I've got him. I think a girl would be a lot more aware of another girl's age.

"Two halves of cider, please," I say, trying to sound like I order alcohol every evening, like it's no big deal to me.

He pauses for a moment, checking me out, making sure I'm over sixteen, which is the legal drinking age for cider; I know, because I've had it with Jase before.

"Who's the other one for, hen?" he says in a friendly voice.

"Her," I say, jerking my head toward Taylor, who's found a couple of barstools by the far wall, and is sitting on one, hands jammed in her jacket pockets, swinging her legs. I know that, like me, she's putting on a bit of a front, trying to seem like she comes to pubs all the time; she's aiming for cool, and actually it's coming across as sulky and bored, which is absolutely perfect. One glance at Taylor's world-weary demeanor, and the barman's flicking down the pump handle for two half-pints of cider without another word being said.

I've rarely felt so grown-up in my life as I do crossing the pub, my heels tapping on the ancient wooden floorboards, a brimming glass in each hand, wiggling through the rickety tables, trying not to blush as young men pull their legs aside for me and check me out as I pass. It's like this whole evening is a rite of passage: getting dressed up, coming out to a pub with my best friend, buying a drink without the humiliation of having to show my Tube photocard as proof of age.

I hand one of the glasses to Taylor, who takes a long thirsty pull at its contents. Her double-take is like a comedy routine: her eyes bulge in shock, and her cheeks puff out with an effort not to spit back what she's drinking as she claps her free hand over her mouth. Confused, I sip some cider myself in case it's off or something, but it tastes fine: sharp, bubbly, apple-sweet. I set the glass down on the little wooden shelf that runs round the wall, under the dappled old mirrors, where it glints pale orange in the light from the sconce above.

"What?" I ask, taking the glass from Taylor so she doesn't spill it.

"It's *alcohol*!" she blurts out, suddenly looking years younger than she did a moment ago.

"Well, yeah! It's cider!" I drink some of hers. "It isn't very strong."

"This is, like, in *public*!" Taylor says. "What if they ask for IDs and kick us out?"

"You're sixteen, Taylor," I point out. "Nearly seventeen. It's legal here."

Actually, technically I think it's only legal if we're with someone who's over eighteen. But no one's going to give us a hard time—not unless Taylor keeps shrieking loud enough so they notice. I jerk my head at her, telling her to keep it down.

"What did you think cider *was*?" I hiss, confused.

"Apple juice!" she says, eyes wide. "Cider's apple juice! They sell it in *Starbucks*!"

I start giggling, and slide Taylor's glass onto the shelf next to mine.

"Not over here they don't," I say. "Here we let the apple juice ferment a bit."

"Oh! Like *hard* cider," Taylor says, the penny visibly dropping. "I've heard of that." She reaches for her glass and sips a little more. "Wow. It's kind of nice."

I roll my eyes. "To think I thought you were the cool one tonight."

"I suppose you've been drinking at pubs since you were five," she says sarcastically.

"My grandmother started giving me a little bit of wine with dinner when I was fourteen," I say smugly. "Watered down. She says it stops you binge drinking when you're older."

"God," Taylor says. "Your grandma could get sued for that in the States."

But I'm not listening, because the pub door's opened again and I recognize the girls who've just come in. Alison has a cute woolly beret tilted sideways on her head, but the long, straightened strawberry-blond hair spilling down her back is unmistakable. The final confirmation is Luce's tiny frame just behind her. She's wearing a padded coat for warmth, but she's skinny enough to belt the coat at her waist, a look that would make most of us resemble a duvet with a string tied round the middle.

"Oh *no!*" I say, nudging Taylor and making her almost spill her cider. She glances sideways, takes in the sight with one swift glance and turns away just as fast.

"Don't look at them," she says urgently, "people always know when you're looking at them. . . ."

But unfortunately, I find myself staring at them in the mirror instead. It's hard for me not to look; I'm fascinated by them, these girls I was such close friends with for so many years, looking so smart now. And Taylor's quite right. Alison's taking in the room, undoing her jacket, but Luce, always the sharper one of the two, has sensed my eyes on her and swivels to catch my reflection in the mirror. She tugs Alison's sleeve, saying something to her, and Alison glances over at me too.

"Did they follow us?" I say to Taylor, but she shakes her head.

"Nope. I'd have known if someone was following us," she says with absolute assurance. "And anyway, why would they? If it was one of them who set the fire and put the anti-histamines or whatever it was in your water, they're being really careful to do stuff that can't be traced back to them.

Whoever it was even used a stencil for that note so we couldn't try to work out whose handwriting it was."

"I don't—"

"They—or she—planned it out in advance," Taylor clarifies, talking to me now as if I'm six years old, or a moron. Or both. "That's the *opposite* of following you and me, when she doesn't know where we're going, or if she'll have any opportunity to do anything, and she certainly won't be able to plan anything in advance. Even if it's the two of them—"

"Or maybe just Luce, because Alison saved me this morning," I chip in.

"Okay, if it's the two of them, or just Luce, I think it's totally unlikely that they're here because of us. They wouldn't have come in after us where we could see them, would they? Nah—I bet they saw the listing for the show on MySpace."

"Oh," I say, hugely relieved. "You think . . ."

"Yeah," she says as Alison and Luce find a table by the small raised stage. "They're fans."

I take another pull of my cider, warmth and apple bubbles coursing through my veins. Dutch courage, it's called, when you have a drink and it makes you feel braver. I stand up, burping lightly, say "Back in a sec," and cross the room to Alison and Luce's table.

"Hey," I say, looking down at Alison, who's pulling off her beret and rearranging her hair to fall sleekly over one shoulder. "I wanted to say thank you for catching me today."

She shrugs, not meeting my eyes.

"Whatever," she says dismissively.

"She'd have done it for anyone," Luce chimes in, looking

at me directly; Luce was always easier with confrontation than Alison. The pixie haircut sets off her high cheekbones and sharp jawline. She looks elfin and delicately sophisticated.

I'm tempted to turn on my heel and storm back to Taylor's side. But instead I swallow hard and sit down so I'm not standing over them, propping my bum on the edge of the wooden stage.

"Look," I say, trying to keep my voice level. "You've got a really good reason to be pissed off with me. And I've apologized for that over and over again. I emailed you, I texted you, I left messages on both your phones. I honestly don't know what more I can do. But I can say sorry again right now, if that's what you want." I lean forward, elbows on my knees. "I'm really sorry for dumping you two to go to Plum's party. And I'm even sorrier that Plum took what happened out on you afterward. Sophia told me that she was a total bitch to you after I left St. Tabby's."

Luce is poker-faced, still registering no emotion. But Alison shifts on her chair, the wood creaking, and when I glance at her I see that her mouth is dragged down at the corners, her eyes sad.

"I know she didn't have anything against you two," I continue. "You were scapegoats for me—Plum was furious with me, but I wasn't around, and so she went for you instead. I'm really sorry that happened. I had no idea it was going on. I only just found out."

Luce nods; only once, and very abruptly. But at least it's an acknowledgment of what I'm saying.

"It's been okay at St. Tabby's since she's gone," Alison says quietly.

"Yeah," Luce says. "You've got the pleasure of her company now."

"Trapped with Plum at Wakefield Hall High-Security Prison," I say, grimacing. "And living with my Aunt Gwen full-time."

Alison and Luce wince at that; they've both met Aunt Gwen, and know exactly what living with her entails. Though you don't even need to meet Aunt Gwen in the flesh to be able to imagine it vividly; you just have to make the mistake of ringing the house to talk to me, have the phone answered by her instead, and reel back, trying not to cry, and mumbling "I didn't *mean* to treat you like an answering machine" as she subjects you to a stream of invective.

"So I really think I've been punished enough," I continue. "But if you want to have a go at me, tell me how you feel—go ahead. I deserve it. I know how badly I behaved."

Alison bites her lip. Luce glances swiftly at her, and then back at me.

"It's okay," Luce says, shrugging in her turn. "I mean, we're over it now."

*Right*, I think sarcastically, but don't say. *That's why you've been giving me the cold shoulder ever since we realized we were on the same school trip.*

"And living with your aunt must be really awful," Alison says, shuddering.

I nod.

"Are you okay now?" Luce asks. "I mean, after this morning?"

"You looked really bad," Alison agrees. "You were all white and sweaty. Miss Carter said you were getting your period, but you never used to look like that when you got it before."

"It wasn't my period," I confirm. "I don't know what it was."

I'm staring at them both narrowly, trying to read their expressions, see if there's any guilt written on their faces. You'd think I would know immediately: these are my oldest friends. Girls who were practically sisters to me from the time we started gymnastics classes together, girls who've seen me fall off beams, win competitions, land on my bum or my face, freak about my flat chest and then, eventually, the fact that my chest wasn't flat anymore. Girls whose own falls and triumphs and body worries I've shared in turn.

But since the events of last summer, we've all changed. I've seen two people die; I've found a dead body; I've found, and maybe lost, a boyfriend. I've learned that I can survive more than I ever thought possible. I don't know what Alison and Luce have been through in that time, though I hope it's nothing remotely like what I've experienced. But I can see that they've changed too. They're poised, elegant, glossy as the other St. Tabby's girls.

And I can't read them anymore.

"You look better now," Luce comments, and then her head tilts back, her eyes brighten, and her lips pinch together as if she's doing her best not to squeal with excitement. She's looking at something over my head. I'm already swinging around when a hand comes down on my shoulder, and a familiar voice says:

"Scarlett! You came! Cool! I didn't hear back from you, so I wasn't sure if you'd show. . . ."

His light Scottish accent is as attractive as ever. And his touch, I must admit, has pretty much the same effect on me as the sight of him had on Luce. He's dropped to his bare knees on the stage, his kilt brushing over them, and I can't help noticing his muscled calves under the heavy green wool socks with their incongruous touch of red ribbon.

Now I'm sure I'm blushing. Thank goodness the lighting in here is low and diffuse, shaded sconces glinting into tarnished mirrors, glowing subtly off the paneled walls; no one could tell there's more color in my cheeks than there was a moment before.

"Hey, Callum," I say, smiling up at him.

# Twelve

## "WHAT IF I'M NOT THE HEROINE?"

Before we all went our separate ways after our visit to the cemetery, Callum took my mobile number, and Ewan must have taken Taylor's. They texted us today to let us know that Mac Attack was doing a gig in a pub within walking distance of our school, hoping we could come. I never saw the text, of course, because I haven't switched on my phone again, but Taylor got hers and was very keen for us to go.

Whereas Alison and Luce, as Taylor deduced, checked out the Mac Attack page on MySpace and saw there that the band was playing tonight, opening for someone called Nuala Kennedy. I introduce them both to Callum and Ewan, and watch with amusement as they babble compliments to the boys and say how much they liked their playing at Celtic Connections.

"Well, thanks!" Ewan says, beaming cheerfully and jumping down from the stage to shake their hands in a way that should be silly, because it's a bit formal, but is actually charming. "What did you think of the MySpace page? I'm still tinkering with it—you got any suggestions?"

He couldn't have asked a better question. Luce, who's always been a computer whiz, dives into her bag, bringing out an iPad, which she turns on, logging on to MySpace to brainstorm with Ewan. Their heads meet as they scan down the Mac Attack page, Ewan enthusiastically narrating what he's done with it so far.

*He may not be the front man of the band,* I think, *but he's got the personality for it. He loves meeting new people, chatting them up—unlike Callum, who's more the strong and silent type.*

I look at Callum, who's doing a final tuning up of his violin, his chin squashed into it, an expression of serious concentration on his handsome face. He has the photogenic looks; there's a reason why, on the CD jewel case, Callum's in the center of the group, looking brooding and mysterious. But Ewan's the one who'll be great in interviews and for working the fans, who'll send out chatty MySpace bulletins and project an infectious enthusiasm that will keep them coming back.

*They're a great team,* I reflect. *Like me and Taylor.*

As if he's read my mind, Ewan's looking round for her now.

"Hey! Taylor!" he calls across the bar, waving at her, a big smile on his face, completely unembarrassed about yelling a girl's name across a crowded space.

Taylor grins back at him, even raising a hand to wave, calling a degree of attention to herself that she would usually very much dislike. But it's impossible to resist Ewan.

He's like a big friendly dog—not the brainless retriever that I've compared Lizzie to in the past, but a sheepdog who wants to round everyone up, collect us all into one big party together.

"Catch you later!" he calls, jumping up onto the stage and going over to grab his guitar.

I nod at Alison and Luce, and they actually smile back at me.

"See you after the gig," I say, noticing that they've softened considerably toward me. Alison even says:

"Great!"

Luce is bending down to slide her iPad back into her bag. And as she does so, I can't help noticing something else in there. It's a notebook, looking very old-fashioned next to the iPad, its cover battered and half torn off with wear, so that I can see the page beneath it, covered in Luce's small, neat writing. White paper, printed with a faint pale-gray grid of tiny boxes.

*That's why the paper of the note left in my and Taylor's room looked so familiar, I realize. Luce has always had notebooks like that, all the years I've known her.*

I turn away, processing this information, my brain racing. I'm suddenly aware of how very much I don't want Alison and Luce to have been behind the attacks on me. There's a real, physical pain in imagining friends to whom I've been so close turning on me so aggressively, playing tricks on me that could quite easily have led to my being seriously injured, or worse. I'm refusing to believe it, thinking up reasons instead that absolve them of guilt.

*Lots of people have notebooks like that, I tell myself.*

"So it went well?" Taylor asks as the members of Mac Attack—squashed together on the very small stage—raise their instruments.

"Really well," I say, hopping back up onto my stool. "I said sorry a lot, but what mostly swung it was knowing Callum and Ewan. Alison and Luce were really excited to meet them."

"Hmm, it's actually pretty neat," Taylor says, considering this. "You dumped them for a cool party, but then you make up for it by introducing them to some cool musicians. Sounds fair to me."

It *is* neat. I think Taylor meant that more in the American way, where "neat" seems to be a general term of approval; but it's neat in the English sense too, which means that everything has turned out tidily, tit for tat, no loose ends hanging.

"The only thing is," I say slowly, "I just saw a notebook in Luce's bag that's exactly like the paper from the note that was left in our room after the smoke bombs went off."

"Huh." Taylor digests this. "You didn't see a stencil, did you?"

I shake my head.

"Nah, that'd be too easy," she says dryly. "Whoever did it, if they have any sense, that stencil's in the bottom of the trash by now." She looks thoughtful. "All I'm going to say right now," she adds, "is that there are tons of notebooks like that. Lots of girls at school have them. On its own, it doesn't prove a thing."

I nod, feeling relief at her words that's disproportionate to what she's actually said, because she hasn't truly acquitted Alison and Luce of suspicion. I really, really don't want it to have been them; I'd give a great deal to have it proved, here and now, that they're innocent of everything but being snotty to me. Mercifully, just then Mac Attack launch into their first song, and the music's loud and tuneful enough to distract me from the complicated tangle of my thoughts.

I sit back on my stool, propping my back against the wall, retrieving my glass of cider and watching the band, feeling the tension in my body dissipate as they play. It's not just that they're really good, or that, in their kilts and tight black T-shirts, the muscles in their arms working as they play their instruments, they're also very easy on the eye. Being in a crowded room, everyone listening to the music, their attention completely focused on the boys onstage, is more of a relief to my sore heart than I could possibly have imagined. I'm in company, but no one's talking to me. No one wants anything from me. I can just be myself, let my thoughts wander, be soothed by the music, happily anonymous.

I let out a long, quiet sigh as the violin swirls high above the other instruments, winding a sweet, piercing tune around us, drawing everyone into an enchantment, smoothing out any rough edges. Across the roomful of people seated at the tables I see Alison and Luce tilting their heads back, staring up at Callum as he leads the group, the violin and bow like a conductor's baton. And I see the leather bag slung over the back of Luce's chair, the bag that contains the notebook that's sent me spinning into awful speculations.

*It's just a notebook in a bag,* I tell myself. *It proves nothing. No way could Alison and Luce be vindictive enough to put me in that much danger—not once, but twice.*

*Vindictive.* Of course, when that word pops into my brain, Plum's name is the first one that immediately follows it. And no, I can't see Plum running around getting her own hands dirty lighting smoke bombs. But I can easily picture her getting someone else to do that part while she shoves me over a stair rail and slips a nasty note into my room for me to find.

And out of everyone on the school trip, Plum is the sneakiest. Her twisted, conniving brain is more than capable of coming up with something as clever and cunning as composing a hate note with a stencil.

I think about Plum and Nadia, heads together, walking round Holyrood Palace, laughing at their own jokes, looking at the world with identical expressions of superiority and disdain. Examining their nails, heads cocked to the side, as if their fingertips were the most important things in the world.

If Plum and Nadia have teamed up again, we could all be in a lot of trouble. They ran St. Tabby's like their own personal kingdom, with Plum as the princess and Nadia her head lady-in-waiting. No detail escaped them; they spotted, and ruthlessly trampled on, every tiny attempt by a girl to step out of the sphere to which Plum and Nadia had assigned her. It's no wonder that Luce and Alison are flourishing now that Plum has left St. Tabby's, enough to experiment with smart clothes and new hairstyles without fear of ridicule. Clearly Nadia on her own isn't strong enough to crack the whip over everyone's backs at once.

Their feuding brought them both down. It got Plum expelled from St. Tabby's, and saw Nadia's powers weakened without Plum's authority to back her up. But if they've reunited—realized that they're much stronger together than they are as deadly rivals—they'll be more dangerous than ever.

And who but me would they decide to target first? Plum hates me, and though I have dirt on her, she knows that I play fairer than she does. Which means I wouldn't use that photo I have of her unless I have solid proof that she's behind the attacks. And Nadia has used me and Taylor in the past. She's very well aware how resourceful we can be. It would be very easy for Plum to talk Nadia into launching a preemptive strike.

*And who would they get to do their dirty work?* I ask myself.

The answer comes immediately: *Lizzie. Who's now new best friends with Sophia.*

Between them, Lizzie and Sophia have the brains of a ginger tomcat (a notoriously stupid animal). But they're both born followers. They'll wear what Plum says, go where Plum goes, laugh when Plum says something mean, jump when she snaps her fingers. Plum probably has plenty of embarrassing information on both of them: that's how she operates. Enough to make them do her dirty work, certainly. I don't think they'd stoop to pushing me over a stair rail for Plum, but they'd certainly let off smoke bombs, as long as they were given clear, detailed instructions. And they'd lie to protect her with the straightest of faces. Lizzie and Sophia would swear up and down that black was white if Plum told them to do it.

Perhaps that's why Lizzie and Sophia are hanging out together on this trip. The sidekicks are bonding: partners in crime.

I've been so absorbed in speculation that I haven't noticed the music changing as songs end, or the audience applauding after each one. But that must have happened; Mac Attack's set must be over, because the people around me are pounding their feet on the boards and yelling "More! More!" as Callum, Ewan, and the other boys bow at the waist, faces flushed. Then Callum says into the mike:

"And now we're really lucky—Nuala Kennedy is going to join us for our encore before she plays her own set, so put your hands together for her, 'cause she's a really big deal—"

Callum's pronounced it "Noola," but I know it's written *Nuala*, because her name is in big letters on the posters for tonight that are stuck up on the walls. She walks onto the tiny stage carrying a flute, a slender woman in a floral dress with what I think of as classic Irish prettiness—white skin, dark hair, and small, delicate features. She smiles at the audience, raises the flute to her mouth, and starts to play, the sound of the flute sweet and throaty and so beautiful that I hear people in the audience sigh with pleasure. Mac Attack join in, and after a little while I realize that the tune is really familiar: it's the song Callum sang at Celtic Connections, "The Blooming Bright Star of Belle Isle." Sure enough, Nuala Kennedy takes the flute from her mouth and starts to sing the chorus in an exquisite clear soprano, Callum chiming in with the harmony. I can tell from his concentrated expression how hard he's focusing on his singing, and when the song finally winds to an end, he's pink in the face and frowning with the effort.

"Let's hear it for Callum, eh?" Nuala Kennedy says into the mike, over the wild applause. "We're all trying to get him to sing more, and he's not too shabby, is he?"

Alison and Luce, I see with amusement, actually scream at this, as if they were twelve-year-olds at a Disney teeny-bopper gig. And they're not the only ones. Other female cries of appreciation turn Callum's face from pink to red now.

"He's gonna have to get used to it," Taylor yells in my ear, grinning. "All the girls squealing for him."

Callum's blush is fading, but still present, by the time he and the rest of Mac Attack have packed away their instruments, clearing the stage for Nuala Kennedy's band, who are setting up now. He and Ewan cross the room to where Taylor and I are sitting, pausing to slap a couple of boys' hands in high fives. Although Callum and Ewan texted us asking us to come, it's still hugely flattering to watch them walking toward us; there's no denying that having boys play really good music, then jump down off the stage and come to find you, is one of the coolest things that can happen. I wriggle on my barstool with excitement. Even Taylor, I see, glancing at her, is holding on to her seat with both hands to stop herself jumping down, to avoid looking too eager: her eyes are sparkling and she's smiling with anticipation.

"You were great!" she exclaims to them. "And she was right, Callum—you should sing more."

"We've all been saying that," Ewan says, smiling at her. "He's the one with the voice. And a band needs a singer to really make it."

"I always thought Dan was the one with the voice," Callum says, looking down. "You know, Ewan. He could charm the birds off the trees."

Ewan looks sober at this mention of Callum's dead twin, and I hear myself say:

"No reason you both couldn't have good voices, is there? I mean, you looked just like each other—why couldn't you both be good singers too?"

Callum's gray eyes meet mine, genuinely shocked, though it seems that what I've said is the most obvious thing in the world. He looks lost for words. Luckily, just then Alison and Luce come up, shyly handing Ewan and Callum CDs of theirs bought at the Celtic Connections concert that they want the boys to personalize, and that's enough distraction for Callum to get himself together, swallow down the tears that I had the feeling were prickling at the back of his throat.

"I hate to say this," Taylor announces, "but it's, like, nine-thirty, and I have to allow for getting us a little bit lost walking home."

"You have to go?" Ewan says, looking so dejected that I hope Taylor is over the moon at how obviously keen he is on her. "Oh, no! We were hoping you could hang out for Nuala's set—she's amazing."

"We could walk you back to your school afterwards," Callum says hopefully. "It's Fetters, right? We know the way."

"We have a ten o'clock curfew," I say regretfully.

"Really?" Ewan's eyes widen. He has incredibly long, curling eyelashes, I notice. Like his long, curly red hair, but darker. "Can't you, I dunno, sneak in later or something?"

"The Wakefield Hall teachers are really strict," Luce pipes up, determined to be part of the conversation. She's as tenacious as a Chihuahua. And wow—now I look at her, standing next to Callum, she's noticeably taller. Surreptitiously, I tilt my head sideways and down; yup, Luce's must-have, this-year-everyone-at-St.-Tabby's-is-wearing suede slouchy boots end in what must be four-inch stiletto heels. Blimey. Luckily, Luce is skinny enough that they look nicely in proportion to her body; her legs are pin-thin. I'm always worried that I'll look a bit like a pig on stilts if I wear stilettos at all, let alone ones that high.

"Yeah, our gym teacher and Scarlett's aunt are waiting by the front door of the school with a big clipboard and a horsewhip," Taylor drawls.

"Your *aunt?*" Callum says to me.

"She's a teacher at my school," I say glumly. "Geography. I have to live with her, too."

"*Man,*" Callum says respectfully. "I thought *my* life was bad."

This is really black humor, because, more than anyone, I know a lot of pretty bad things that have happened in Callum's life; but somehow, it makes both of us smile, and in that moment, it's as if the whole room fades away, and it's just Callum and me, smiling at each other.

"Right!" Taylor says a bit too loudly. "Time to go!"

It's cold outside, and very dark. As the door of the Shore closes behind us, we all involuntarily turn to look back at the bar with a sigh of regret. Nuala Kennedy's started to play, and the sound of her flute is so beautiful and haunting that it's like a spell to pull us all back inside, into the warmth and the light, the clinking of glasses, the music—and, to be perfectly honest, the boys. Everything we want right now is inside the Shore, and as we start to walk away down the riverside, hugging our coats and jackets tight around us against the wind from the sea, we're all silent and gloomy for a while; it's pretty miserable to be leaving a place where several handsome boys want you to stay.

The pavement's too narrow for us all to walk together. Luce and Taylor, both natural organizers, have pulled a little ahead, consulting Taylor's iPhone, Luce's piping voice describing the route she and Alison took coming to the Shore. I shove my hands in my pockets and glance at Alison, who's tugging her beret down to cover her ears.

Sensing my eyes on her, she looks over at me.

"I didn't know you knew Callum that well," she says. "I mean, I saw you talking to him at the concert, but I thought he was more a friend of Plum's."

I huff out a laugh.

"No, he's definitely not a friend of Plum's," I say. "I know him because of—well, because of his brother. Dan."

Alison nods; she remembers Dan very well, from all those times we used to stare longingly at him, the best-looking boy in Plum and Nadia's whole carefully selected group of beautiful people, with his floppy fringe and his easy smile. It's true, as Callum says, that Dan could charm the birds from the trees. But, as their sister Catriona once said, Callum's worth twice of Dan.

I hope Callum comes out from Dan's shadow one day.

"He's really cool," Alison says wistfully. "And I do think he's got a good voice. He should definitely sing more."

171

"You should post that to his MySpace page," I suggest. "I'm sure he'd love to read that."

"Yeah, I could!" Alison perks up at having found a way to contact Callum, on whom she clearly has a massive crush. "That's a great idea!" She smiles at me. "He's got his own page as well as the band's one. I friended him on both of them."

I can't help feeling smug that I knew Callum before he and Mac Attack started to take off. It means that he'll never think of me as a fan, but as a friend, which is a huge difference. It wasn't exactly news to me that a good-looking boy who gets up onstage and plays in a band, let alone one who sings songs about beautiful maidens he's madly in love with, is like catnip to girls. But knowing it and seeing it in action are very different things. I remember the girls surrounding Mac Attack at Celtic Connections, how frenzied they were, and I'm really glad that Callum will never see me as one of them.

We're just passing the little bridge again. I turn my head, wanting a last glance at the Waters of Leith before we branch away from them; I'm hypnotized by how calm and beautiful the dark water is by night, with just a faint reflection of the moon through clouds.

And then I jump in shock and stumble on the pavement. Because I think I see a figure slipping over the road across the bridge, into the shadows cast by the building on the far side. I'm not surprised that someone else is out at this time of night; there are a few other people on the street, coming out of restaurants or bars, commenting on the cold to each other in quiet voices, waiting at the bus stop. But there was something surreptitious about the way that person moved that raised all the hairs on the back of my neck.

"Did you see that?" I ask Alison, my voice sounding higher and more panicked than I mean it to.

"What?" she says blankly.

"Oh . . . nothing . . ."

I don't want to seem like a paranoid idiot, seeing menace everywhere. I may be out late, or late-ish, but I've got three other girls with me; nothing bad's going to happen to me in this much company.

As we turn up a dark street, Taylor looks back to check we're following.

"What's up?" she asks.

"Scarlett thought she saw something," Alison says, which makes me sound like a total idiot.

"It was probably a seagull," I say quickly—there are a couple of gulls hopping round some rubbish bins farther down the street, looking for food to scavenge.

But I know it wasn't.

"You okay?" Taylor asks, dropping back and slinging an arm over my shoulder. This is so unlike her that she must feel that I'm really in need of reassurance. And it's definitely comforting to have an arm around me; but that immediately makes me think of Jase, how well we fit together when we walk, my arm round his waist, his round my shoulders, and I feel incredibly confused. All the feelings of missing him, of anger that he's not here, roar back into my mind, filling it up so much that I forget to answer Taylor.

Alison's caught up with Luce, and they've just turned a corner down another narrow, cobbled street. As they

173

disappear momentarily from view, straight ahead of Taylor and me I spot the figure again, pressed back against the shuttered doorway of a shop front. As if he's trying not to be seen.

It's only because my senses are hyperalert that I see him at all. I'm sure it's a him now—the height and the width of the shoulders make it very unlikely that it's a woman. He's medium height for a man, not as tall as Jase. Stockier, with a build like Callum's.

"Taylor!" I grab at the hand she's clasped on my shoulder. "Look—there *is* someone! Over there!"

"We go down here," Taylor says a split second after I start to talk, the pressure of her arm turning me down the side street.

"No! Back there!" I pull at her, trying to make her go back. "Didn't you see someone standing in that doorway?"

It seems to take ages to turn Taylor around, and by the time we swivel back the shape in the shop front is long gone.

"Nothing there," Taylor says unnecessarily. "Come on, we need to hurry to make it back to the school before ten."

Our feet sound very loud on the cobbles as we walk faster to catch up with Alison and Luce.

"I can't be seeing things," I say, "not after half a pint of cider. . . ."

"You're just wound up," Taylor says reassuringly, her arm still pulling me along. "You've had a really weird day."

"Yes, but . . ." I pause. "I'm sure I saw someone. A guy. I mean, I could tell you what his build was like, even."

"Scarlett, there are shadows *everywhere*," Taylor says

firmly. "I mean, look around you! Plus, Edinburgh's a really creepy city. There's a reason *Dr. Jekyll and Mr. Hyde* and tons of ghost stories were set here, you know."

"I suppose so," I say doubtfully, because it's beginning to seem like Taylor's trying to talk me out of what I'm pretty sure I saw with my own eyes. Which isn't like Taylor. One of the crucial things about our friendship is that we trust each other's instincts; I couldn't imagine telling Taylor she hadn't seen something she was sure she had.

"I just—" I start, and then I'm sure I hear something off to our right. There's another street running parallel to the one we're hurrying down, quite close, as this part of Leith is a warren of little alleys, and I could have sworn I heard light, muffled footsteps tracking ours. "Did you hear that?" I ask, my voice rising nervously again.

"Scarlett! You're freaking me out!" Taylor snaps. "That's leaves blowing on the pavement! We're not suddenly in a horror film, okay? 'Cause that's exactly what you're sounding like!"

I snuffle a laugh at this, because I do sound exactly like the whiny heroine of one of those endless *Scream* or *Final Destination* films, running around insisting she hears a monster while all her friends tell her she's being an idiot.

"Nearly there!" Luce calls from up ahead, and she's right; we emerge suddenly onto a wide road, the stone wall that borders Fetters's grounds right opposite us.

"Nice work," Taylor calls back approvingly.

"We should step it up—it's nearly ten," Luce says, and we start to jog as a taxi ticks past us, turning in to the drive. We reach the main door on the dot of ten, Plum, Nadia,

Susan, and Lizzie tumbling out of the taxi, giggling at having just made curfew.

"Here you go," Plum says, throwing some notes through the window at the cab driver. "And an extra twenty for getting us here on time."

I'm ridiculously relieved to be out of that shadowy maze of streets and back in the brightly lit hallway of Fetters, even with Aunt Gwen glowering at me as she crosses my name off her list, even with Plum and Nadia showing off by talking loudly, once the teachers are out of earshot, about the *divine* cocktails they just sank at the bar on the fourth floor of Harvey Nichols's department store—"*and* they have a wraparound terrace you can smoke on, it's *fabulous*, and the views are really quite nice, considering we're in bloody *Scotland.* . . ."

Back in our room, Taylor and I shove the chest of drawers in front of the door.

"Just to be safe," Taylor says, with such elaborate casualness that I know she's actually taking this quite seriously.

Having the door blocked should make me feel absolutely secure. Still, when we turn out the light and curl up in the narrow twin beds, I lie in the dark room, listening to Taylor's slow, steady breathing, unable to turn my brain off. Maybe it's because I had an extra nap when I passed out this afternoon that I can't fall asleep as easily as Taylor. But one unpleasant thought after another is cascading through my mind.

Am I making too much of my impression that Taylor seemed to be dragging me along just now, stopping me from seeing the guy who might have been there, might have been following us? Is it just a weird coincidence that he looked a bit like Callum—who must, surely, have been back at the Shore, listening to Nuala Kennedy's set? And why would someone want to follow me at all? Is there *anyone* I can trust a hundred percent?

Tonight, pulling me along the cobbled street, Taylor mocked me out of my panic, telling me I sounded like some nervy victim from a horror film. *But,* it occurs to me now, *the girl in horror films who no one takes seriously is usually right. There is a monster out there that wants to kill her.*

I take deep breaths to calm myself down. *The heroine always survives,* I tell myself. *Even if she has to run around for hours making an idiot of herself and screaming her head off, she fights back in the end. She always survives.*

But then I have an even worse thought.

*What if I'm not the heroine?*

# *Thirteen*

## I MIGHT AS WELL JUST FALL

"Oh, come on, Scarlett! What else are we going to do tonight? Sit around here and play Ping-Pong in the rec room?"

"I do like table tennis," I say a little feebly.

"We already played it for *two hours* before dinner!" Taylor points out. She's striding up and down our room between the beds, her shaggy fringe flopping over her face, her voice raised vehemently. "I'm *so* bored!"

After yesterday, which was packed with excursions, the coach drivers are having a day off; today, our schedule consisted of a series of historical and literary lectures focusing on Scotland (*Macbeth* and *Dr. Jekyll and Mr. Hyde* being A-level set texts), punctuated by a revolting lunch and an even nastier tea with dry biscuits. The table tennis was a much-needed release from all that sitting down being talked at, but Taylor's still popping with energy.

"I want to go *out!*" she exclaims, so loudly now that I hold my finger up to my mouth, shushing her; what she's proposing is definitely not allowed under the rules of our curfew.

Callum and Ewan have been texting us a lot today, disappointed that we had to head off early last night from the Shore. Tonight is Saturday, and apparently there's what they call a quarry party in the country outside Edinburgh, a huge group of teenagers who get together every weekend to play music, hang out, dance . . . it sounds amazing, and I'd really, really like to go.

Taylor is even keener than me; she's got it all worked out—how we'll sneak out of Fetters, where Callum and Ewan can meet us. I'm embarrassed that I'm holding back, being the boring one in the friendship.

I'm just remembering last night, and how spooky that figure was, slipping along the dark streets, following me. It's a totally cowardly reaction, and nothing's happened today at all to scare me or make me feel unsafe. But maybe that's why a warm, if not very cozy, bedroom with a door we can shove a chest of drawers in front of seems, right now, much more appealing than going out into the night, where that figure might be waiting for me again. . . .

*Oh my God! I'm being utterly and completely pathetic!*

"Are you freaking about someone being out to get you?" Taylor asks in a quieter tone, sitting down next to me on the bed. "'Cause I'm sure you'll be totally safe tonight, okay? I mean, you'll be with Callum and Ewan. And me, of course," she adds, doing a comedy flex of her arm muscles that has me giggling. "I'm tougher than two boys put together."

"I know you are," I agree.

Taylor didn't believe me about seeing the guy following us last night. So there's no point telling her that his shape looked very much like Callum's, or that, in my more paranoid moments, I can imagine why Callum might conceivably have a grudge against me. On the plus side, I did save his life. On the minus side, he might have brooded over the awful sequence of events that happened when I visited Castle Airlie, his home, and ended up blaming me for them. Callum's certainly capable of brooding more deeply than anyone else I know.

And no, it wouldn't be fair of him to come to the conclusion that it was all my fault. But one thing I've learned, as I get older, is that people are capable of making you a scapegoat for all sorts of things. Look at Plum with Alison and Luce, for instance.

I set my jaw. What kind of a person would I be if I turned down what sounded like a really cool invitation just because I was scared by the possibility that someone who looked very much like Callum was following us last night? Taylor was probably right all along: there wasn't anyone trailing us through Leith, and I let myself get idiotically worked into a freak-out for nothing at all.

Besides, I still haven't heard from Jase. And maybe I never will. If I stay here tonight, I'll start thinking about that even more than I am now, and that'll plunge me into a pit of depression as dark and deep as a well. Better to go out and find whatever distraction I can; and if there's some risk involved—well, I'm used to that by now.

And at least when I'm freaking out about being followed, I don't have time to remember how sad I am that

Jase hasn't rung me. The expression *out of the frying pan into the fire* is beginning to sum up my entire life.

*But I should be careful not to find myself alone with Callum,* I resolve. *Just in case it was him last night.*

"Right," I say, jumping up from the bed, whose horsehair mattress is so old that it promptly sags around Taylor, dropping her into a deep V. "We should put on lots of clothes, because it'll be cold out there, but not so many that we'll be so padded up we can't climb out the window."

"Or look like we weigh two tons," Taylor adds, levering herself out of the saggy mattress. "My shoulders already make me look big. I don't like wearing stuff that bulks me out too much."

My eyebrows shoot up to my hairline, but I turn away quickly so that Taylor can't see my expression. I whine about my boobs and hips all the time, and how I have to pick clothes that don't make them look too big; but this is the first time I've heard Taylor mention similar concerns. More than ever, I'm getting convinced that she and Ewan have something going. No wonder she's so determined to drag me out with her tonight.

Curfew comes and goes; Ms. Burton-Race, who's on duty this evening, pops her head into our room, finds us lying on our beds reading, and wishes us goodnight. Lights-out isn't till eleven, but we both answer her sleepily, and she closes the door again, satisfied that we're accounted for and ready to settle down for the night.

We give it ten minutes, to be sure, and then spring off our beds and into action. We've both got tights on under our jeans, and now we pull on the sweaters and jackets we picked out before, zipping and buttoning everything up snugly, hoods over our heads.

Then Taylor looks at me, flashes a huge grin, and bends down to heave up the sash of the old frame window.

I go through first, one leg after the other till I'm sitting on the windowsill, shifting along with my bum to the far edge. I reach out in the dark, letting my eyes accustom themselves to the darkness, my fingers closing around the metal top handrail of the fire escape, stretching out the closer leg to find the fire escape with my booted foot. Easy—for Taylor and me, anyway. We tested the heavy window first, and realized that it would be too dangerous to try to close it behind us, let alone open it again; the force we'd need might send us slipping off the windowsill and down three stories to the pavement below. So Taylor's opened it the minimum necessary for us to squeeze out, and I just stuffed a rolled-up towel along the bottom of the bedroom door so the cold night air won't blow under and cause a draft in the corridor that might seem suspicious to a teacher walking past.

"Okay?" Taylor whispers.

"No prob," I hiss back. Gripping the rail with both hands, digging both feet into the fire escape, I boost my bottom off the safety of the windowsill, swinging myself through the air for one dizzying moment until I'm standing flat against the outside of the fire escape. I lift my right leg in a wide semicircle—it's the leg I always lead with, plus it's my more flexible hip—straddling the top rail for a second before touching my foot to the iron floor of the fire escape.

Safety. And now the other leg can follow. I prop my hips against the rail and lean over it, stretching out my hands so that Taylor, now on the windowsill herself, can grab them and shorten the distance she has to cross. We've planned the whole maneuver beforehand, in detail, so we didn't have to exchange a word, and I'm proud of us; it goes as smoothly as if we've executed it hundreds of times before. Once Taylor's scissored her own legs over the rail, we exchange a swift high five, our palms barely meeting to avoid making noise, before making our way down the open stairs, wincing at every tiny creak and whine of tired old metal that could potentially give us away.

There's a lighted window up ahead, giving out onto the fire escape. *If ours did that, it would have been even easier to sneak out*, I think ruefully as I realize it's the room that Plum and Susan are sharing. I squint sideways, and see them, plus Nadia, Lizzie, and Sophia, a positive gaggle of long, shiny hair and long, skinny legs. Plum's got a bottle of white wine and she's filling plastic glasses from it, handing them round, giggling naughtily. They're all tipsy already, from what I can see—the result of another evening out at the Harvey Nichols bar drinking chocolate-strawberry martinis, no doubt.

And then Nadia comes toward the window, and I lurch back in panic, thinking she's spotted me. I gesture frantically at Taylor, who freezes on the steps above me as if we're playing a game of Musical Statues, while I press myself against the brickwork of the building, back flat to the wall, trying not to breathe. Nadia's shadow is cast onto the section of the fire escape directly outside the window lit up by the light from the bedroom; she leans forward and starts to lift the window sash.

*Oh no . . . she's spotted me, and now we're totally in their power. . . . If they think fast, they could race up to our room and shut the window, so we'd be trapped out here to be caught by a teacher—by Aunt Gwen—oh God, we're in such trouble. . . .*

I'm rigid, as stiff as a board. Nadia fumbles with the window.

"God, it's bloody *stuck*! And I'm dying for a fag!" she complains. "Sophia, you have a go. You're the biggest. And your nails aren't as nice as mine."

Her shadow retreats, and I signal Taylor with a big loop of my arm to make a move; ducking even more, we scuttle under the windowsill and down the next flight of stairs, just in time. As we make it round the corner, Sophia has dragged the window up, and Nadia is propping herself on the sill. I hear the click of her lighter as she fires up a cigarette.

Taylor and I exchange a speaking glance, hugely relieved. This fire escape is our only safe exit route, and with Nadia sitting in the window frame, smoking, there was no way we'd have been able to get past without being observed. Five minutes later and we wouldn't have been able to leave Fetters, wouldn't have been able to drop to the ground from the last rung of the fire escape and tear across the lawn, to vault over the stone wall and land on the pavement on the other side, breathless, excited, looking around for Ewan's car.

Headlights flash from a parked car across the street, and we run over, our hearts pounding.

"That was so lucky!" Taylor gasps as we drag open the back doors of the car—after checking that Ewan and Callum are in the front, of course; we're not complete idiots—and fall in. The boys swivel round to greet us, and in their eagerness, they bump heads; it's like a comedy double act. We both giggle, and Callum pantomimes rubbing his shaved skull.

"It's all right for him," he complains. "His hair's like a thatch of pubes—you could hit him with a sledgehammer and he wouldn't feel a thing."

"*Dude*," Ewan mutters, shocked. "Mixed company, as my mum would say."

"Oh—sorry!"

Callum sounds mortified at having blurted out what's probably a private boys' joke in front of a couple of girls. Taylor leans forward and says:

"My brother knows this guy he's at college with who has a double skull. It's like a throwback to the Neanderthals or something. This guy can head-butt a brick wall and not feel anything. Well, apart from getting a bruise, I suppose," she adds, scrupulously fair.

"You're joking!" Callum says as Ewan starts up the car and pulls away.

"No, it's true!" She's laughing. "I couldn't make that up! He only found out when he bumped heads with this other guy at basketball practice, and the second guy went flying across the court. Neanderthal Guy didn't feel a thing. So the coach thought that was weird and sent him for tests."

"That's like having a superpower," Ewan marvels as Callum says to her:

"But is his head bigger than normal?"

"Hah!" Taylor's really laughing now. "That's exactly what my brother said! No, it isn't! So he has—"

"A smaller brain," Callum finishes.

"But they can't mess with him about it," she says, "'cause he threatens to head-butt them."

"Does he have, like, a really low forehead, and eyebrows that stick out, and tiny little eyes?" Callum asks.

We're all laughing now, partly because it's funny, and partly out of relief that Taylor has rescued us from the embarrassment of Callum's having said "pubes" in front of us. I must say, she's very lucky to have grown up with an older brother; she knows just how to talk to boys. The ice is broken. We chatter away for the whole of the drive. Ewan heads out of Edinburgh; used to the size of London, I'm surprised at how soon the city falls away and we're surrounded by fields rising away on either side of the road. It would probably be very beautiful by daylight, but I can't see much at all now, just lines of hedgerows marching away over the fields. Ewan turns off the main highway and onto a couple of side roads with the ease of someone who's done this drive very often; soon the car wheels are crunching over an uneven, gravelly surface as tarmac gives way to something a lot more rural, and, as he turns a corner, we see that the narrow lane is suddenly lined with tightly parked cars.

Ewan whistles.

"Busy tonight, eh?" he says, slowing down to a crawl and driving past them, down a long stretch, till we come to the gated driveway to a farm. The gates are hung with placards advertising PICK YOUR OWN FRUIT and FARM PRODUCE SHOP, but the gates are padlocked shut, the farm buildings dark and silent. Ewan reverses the car in the short driveway and turns back the way we've come.

"Always turn the car *before* the party," he says cheerfully. "My dad told me that. Best advice he ever gave me."

He manages to maneuver the car up a bank, its right two wheels half a foot higher than the left, then cranks up the hand brake with an audible ratcheting sound and leaves the car in gear.

"Should be okay," he says with the ease of a boy used to country driving. "Climb out on the high side so it doesn't tip."

I'm pretty impressed at his confidence, especially when I see how high the car's slanted up onto the bank; but no one else seems to think there's anything dodgy about how Ewan's parked, and he's managed to get us right in the center of the cars, next to a ruined house that serves as a marker for where we head into the woods to find the party. Other groups are converging to where we're standing as Callum pulls a six-pack of beer out of the front seat and swings it up onto his shoulder, together with his violin case slung on a strap. Ewan's pulling stuff out from the boot. I glance at the old stone house as we pass it; the back's all crumbling, shored up with rusted steel struts.

"Wow," Taylor says as we walk down a dirt track wide enough to accommodate us all, side by side. Trees cluster densely around us, ancient oaks with trunks as thick as the width of Ewan's car, silver birches with spindly dark branches silhouetted against the sky. The moon's coming out from behind a cloud, and its light shines ghostly silver-gray. In the distance, I can hear the rhythmic thump of drums, the faint sweet wail of a saxophone, and my heart starts to beat with excitement, as fast as it used to before a gymnastics competition.

A real party. A real teenage party. Not like Plum and Nadia's parties, where they're so busy pretending they're twentysomething sophisticates, listening to jazz and drinking martinis, that everyone gets really insecure because they're trying to act like people they're not.

Here, we're all down-to-earth. Literally. As we get farther down the path, I gasp, because the trees fall away, the area widens out, and I see why this is called a quarry party; we're in a bowl, trees to our left, but a sweeping semicircle of high stone to our right, tall as a ten-story building, craggy and rugged. A huge bonfire is burning in the center of the bowl, and people are sitting all around it; up on the sides of the quarry, people are perched, the occasional small fire glinting high up on the stone rocks, incredibly dramatic. Music rises with the flames; someone must have rigged up a basic sound system with a generator. I hear it humming quietly under the amplified strum of the guitars and drums. Nothing loud, no rock tunes; this is a much more tribal kind of gathering, I can tell already from the atmosphere. It's mellow and very chilled, people talking quietly, making their own music in their own small groups, cooking marshmallows on the fire.

"It's kind of postapocalyptic," Taylor observes. "Very cool. My brother Seth would love this."

"We usually go over there," Callum says, leading us round the bonfire to a sheltered spot at the base of the quarry cliff. A big dog bounds across the path, followed by another, panting, two mutts playing happily in the dark.

Ewan has an old blanket, which he lays out on the ground, revealing a pair of bongo drums wrapped inside it.

"We brought some wine, too," Callum says a little shyly, setting down what he's carrying. "Girls don't always like beer, do they?"

"*I* like beer," Taylor says, plopping down on the blanket, popping a can of beer, and reaching for one of the bongos. She looks over at me and winks. "Now, *this* I'm used to," she says. "Sneaking beers when the adults aren't around."

"Man," Ewan says respectfully, sitting down next to her. "You're hard-core."

"Better believe it!" Taylor says as Ewan pulls the other bongo in front of him and crosses his legs around it.

Callum and I sit down too. I'm glad I have tights on under my jeans; the ground's hard and cold, and they give a much-needed extra layer of warmth. He unscrews the cap of the wine bottle and hands it to me. I tilt it to my mouth, misjudge the angle, and get a mouthful of warmish cheap white wine. I choke and swallow simultaneously, and end up having a coughing fit.

Callum's undoing the locks on his violin case, but he stops to pound me on the back. *God, how obvious could I make it that I'm not used to drinking?* I think, embarrassed, but it's surprisingly nice to feel Callum touching me, and I relax almost immediately. And he doesn't try to put his arm around me; when I stop coughing, he goes back to taking his violin and bow out, and I sit there, the wine burning its way down my esophagus, my head spinning, trying to work out how I'm feeling about this situation. Taylor and Ewan are already drumming their fingers on the bongos, setting up a light, steady rhythm. I had no idea Taylor could play the bongo, but that's Taylor for you: she loves being a dark horse.

Callum's tuning his violin, beginning to coax a sweet, soft, melancholy tune from it. Perfect. I wriggle back a bit till I feel the rock face against my back so I can lean into it, and close my eyes.

*Well, this is sort of unexpected*, I think. *It feels like we've paired off, Taylor with Ewan, me with Callum.* There's a subtle shift that happened as soon as we sat down, positioning ourselves on the blanket. *Did the boys do it deliberately, or was it just by chance?* Instinct tells me it's the former; there's something self-consciously aware about the way both Ewan and Callum are sitting, their bodies turned toward Taylor and me, blocking off the other pair. Transforming us into two couples rather than four friends.

I would have seen this coming if I hadn't been so absorbed in the tangle of my situation with Jase. When Callum and I stood in the cemetery together, looking at that tombstone, I knew that we were both remembering that kiss at the airport, the moment when our mutual resentment and suspicion finally melted away like clouds burning off in the sun. Leaving the truth in clear sight: that we're very attracted to each other.

I love Jase. But Jase isn't here. I don't know where he is, and I don't know if he'll ever contact me again. Maybe not. It's quite likely that I'll never see Jase again, that he'll never come back to Wakefield Hall; that we've broken up for good.

I swallow hard and tell myself to be strong. I'm not passive in this situation: I have choices. I can wallow in misery, or I can focus on whatever positives I can find. Like telling myself that if I'm alone and boyfriendless, that also means that I'm free to do what I want. Kiss who I want. And no one can blame me for it.

I explore the idea, tentatively, feeling the shape of it. Just for now—while we're up in Scotland—how would I feel if Callum tries to get closer to me this evening? I really doubt that he and I could have any kind of long-term thing, not with Dan's death, and its aftermath, lying between us. But goodness knows, I can't even imagine a long-term thing with another boy now, not with the breakup with Jase so raw and fresh.

And if I ever do manage to find another boy I want to get serious with, I reflect with a sudden, welcome flash of humor, I'll do my best to pick someone whose family and mine aren't tangled up in a horrible mess of murder and grieving.

*Yeah, why don't you try that, Scarlett?* I think, my mouth beginning to twist into a wry smile. *Try going out with a boy who doesn't have a single ghastly family skeleton rattling in the closet—just for a change?* I'm smiling full-on now, even though no one can see in the dark, cracking myself up with my own black humor. *Oh, I don't know if I possibly could. I mean, what would we have to talk about if someone in his family hadn't killed someone in mine?*

Callum shifts, stretching out his legs, and the movement brings him fractionally nearer to me, his calf almost brushing mine. I look over and meet his eyes; he's staring at me, and I'm blushing, though, again, it's mercifully hidden by the night around us.

*How would I feel if he tried to kiss me tonight?*

The idea sends a warm flood of excitement into the pit of my stomach. I draw up my knees and hug them, feeling suddenly very exposed and vulnerable.

*But not in a bad way*, I realize, surprised. *Not in a bad way at all.*

It's weird, looking back, to see how much my life has changed. This time last year, if you told me I'd have two hot boys interested in me, I'd have slapped you round the face and told you to pull yourself together. But back then, I would have thought it was the absolute summit of my dreams to have kissed boys like Callum and Jase: like standing on the top of Arthur's Seat with the wind blowing round me.

And now, exciting though it is, it's also unexpectedly painful, because the fact that I'm sitting here contemplating kissing Callum again means that Jase and I truly are no longer together. How can I help but see that the whole situation with our families is just too hard for him? The worst part is that, though I struggle with it, I can't even blame him for the way he feels. If I were in his shoes, I don't know how I'd react. Being fair, I have to admit that if I were Jase's friend, rather than his ex-girlfriend, I might well tell him to put the past behind him, leave Wakefield Hall and all its awful memories for good. And if that means leaving the

Wakefield girl behind too . . . well, there's always a price to pay.

So I don't have a boyfriend anymore. There's no point hiding from the truth.

I look at Callum's wide shoulders, his head tilted to one side on his violin as he plays; he's glancing at Taylor and Ewan, his tune melting into their rhythmic beat, the poignant, minor-key song he's playing perfect for my mood. As if he's read my mind; as if he's playing the sound track to this moment of my life.

It's so beautiful and sad that I have to shut my eyes so I don't cry. I lose myself in the tune, the bright gold flames of the bonfire flickering through my closed eyelids, and I drift off into a haze that must be sort of what meditation feels like; when I come to with a start, the music's over, Taylor's laughing happily, and Ewan is pushing the wine bottle against my hand.

"Did you nod off?" he says. "Were we that bad?"

"Oh no, it was great!" I take the bottle and swig at it, more carefully this time, just a small mouthful. "I actually went into a sort of trance," I confess.

"Cool," says happy hippy Ewan. "That's exactly what we were going for. Enchantment." He says this last word in a trippy voice, and flickers his fingers at me in a spell-casting, fake-magician way that has Taylor honking.

"Idiot," she says, shoving him playfully.

"Jeez, you're strong," he says, rubbing his upper arm. "Hey! Want to do the circuit?" He jumps to his feet. "Walk around the bonfire, maybe take the bongos, see if there's a jam session we can join?"

"Cool!" Taylor jumps up too. She ducks down to grab the bongos. "Let's head over there." She points to the other side of the bonfire, where a large group has gathered around the amplifier.

*I didn't know Taylor was so confident with boys*, I think. *Or at parties. Or, come to that, with bongo drums.* But we're so sheltered at Wakefield Hall, so cut off from the world, that I just haven't had the opportunity to see what she's like in a normal setting. And I forget that she has a brother, a pretty cool, jet-setting brother capable of passing himself off as a playboy at smart parties in Venice, no less. It makes complete sense that with an older brother like that, Taylor would be much more comfortable hanging out with boys than I am.

"We should really stay here," Callum says, laying his violin in its case. "To, you know, watch our stuff."

"Yeah," Ewan agrees, voice artificially serious. "That stuff won't watch itself."

He takes one of the bongos from Taylor, who says something to him as they walk away that makes him snuffle with laughter.

"They get on really well," I observe to Callum.

"Yeah," he says thoughtfully, looking after their figures as they disappear into the dark. I was implying that I thought Taylor and Ewan were getting together—hooking up, as Taylor says, though I'm never sure what that means, exactly, how far hooking up goes. But that's not how Callum sounded. He doesn't seem convinced, and I wonder why.

Silence descends, and I fidget awkwardly. I've been

alone with boys a few times now, and even that limited experience has taught me that silence is necessary, essential, even, so that the mood can shift into something different; something charged with excitement and possibility.

And then I feel that shift happen between us. It's palpable, and I realize I've forgotten to breathe; my rib cage is tight, my stomach feels hollow. I look at Callum, which is maybe a mistake, because even though I can barely see his face, with the fire flickering behind him, I know that we've made eye contact. It's like an electric shock.

I reach for the bottle of wine, and simultaneously, Callum leans over to pull a can of beer off the six-pack, our movements almost synchronized. He moves the beers that are left to the edge of the blanket, propping them against his violin case, using that as a way to end up sitting next to me, his leg now firmly touching mine. Clearing his throat, he pops his beer can open.

"So, um, I was right," he says, drinking a little.

"Right?" My voice comes out higher and squeakier than I would like.

"About girls not liking beer," he says, turning to look at me.

I have the bottle uncapped, but there's no way I'm tilting a nearly full bottle of wine to my mouth in front of him when he's this close to me. I'll look ridiculous, like an alcoholic. So I hold it clumsily beside me, and say:

"I've never tried beer, only cider. So I don't know."

"Want to try?" He holds the can out to me, so close now that he hardly needs to move much. I twist the cap back on the wine and take the can from him, our fingers brushing against each other, my heart jumping as we make that contact.

I lift the can to my lips, bubbles rushing out at me, the taste sour and sharp and yeasty.

"Ugh!" I grimace, and Callum, seeing my reaction, laughs and takes the can back from me.

"It does taste weird the first time," he admits. "I should've told you." He pauses. "You've got froth all over your mouth."

He reaches out and smooths some of it away with his thumb. Testing my reaction, seeing if I'll pull back, say something quickly, turn away to grab the wine instead.

But I don't. I turn my face up to him, and wait.

He lowers his face toward me, slowly. I close my eyes, my heart beating almost louder than the drums that are pounding by the bonfire, making the ground below us throb with their rhythm. I smell the beer on his breath as his mouth comes down on mine, taste it on his lips, and I must admit it does put me off for a moment.

Callum senses that, and pulls back.

"Oh shit," he says quickly, "I taste of beer, don't I? Sorry!" He grabs the bottle of wine and takes a swig from it, almost gargling it around his mouth. It should be funny, but I'm too wound up now, too nervous, to be able to make a laughing comment or reassure him; I just sit there, feeling glued to the spot, as he kisses me again, with less hesitation this time.

"That better?" he says against my mouth, and I nod and mumble "Uh-huh," because it is. It's lovely. He's warm, and the wine's intoxicating as I kiss him back, first with small, delicate nips, finding each other, finding the connection; then, leaning against each other with more weight, Callum's body heavy and solid, my hands coming up to wrap around his neck, feeling him wind his arms round my waist to pull me closer.

My head tips to the side, and Callum follows me eagerly, urgent now. *God, I love kissing,* I think, my heart surging, my body flooding with the thrill of it, as Callum's tongue meets mine and I let myself go completely. Everything I have is going into this kiss. I want nothing more than to forget about Jase, forget about Dan, forget about anything that's ever gone wrong for me, just lose myself in kissing Callum McAndrew, right here, right now, on a blanket in front of a bonfire, drums pounding, music swirling around us, his mouth tasting of wine, his tongue sliding past my open lips. . . .

My eyes snap open. My hands, even though they're around his neck, touching his warm skin, are suddenly clammy and cold.

Something doesn't feel right.

I pull back, unwrapping my arms from him, rubbing my hands together, mumbling awkwardly:

"Sorry—my hands were freezing—"

"Yeah, it's pretty chilly," Callum agrees. "Like, um, the wind got up all of a sudden."

"I know," I agree instantly, though I haven't felt even a breeze and I don't think he has either.

"Do you want me to warm them?" he asks, awkwardly, but he doesn't make a move to reach out to take my hands between his, and when I shake my head, he doesn't insist. I make a big show of rubbing my hands together, even putting them into my armpits under my jacket and pantomiming shivering, as if I were a really talentless children's TV presenter, miming being cold so obviously that even a two-year-old would understand what I was trying to convey.

Thank God for the music, the rise and fall of voices around the bonfire and up on the quarry ledges, the crackle of flames from the fires. Without them, our silence would be even more obvious. And it's embarrassing enough as it is.

Callum shuffles his legs nervously. I can't sit there any longer with my hands in my armpits. I'm beginning to feel like I'm not miming cold anymore, but imitating a gorilla instead, again at a two-year-old level: I have a crazy impulse to squat and start going 'Ooh-ooh! Ooh-ooh!' Pulling my hands out from under my jacket, I rest them in my lap and look down at them.

"Better?" Callum asks.

"Yes," I mumble.

Callum shifts uncomfortably. I pull my legs up to my side, unable to sit still. I'm twitching as if my skin is crawling off my body. I open my mouth, needing to say something, anything, to break the silence, and what comes out is:

"Um . . . I really need to go to the loo."

*Nice, Scarlett. Really nice. First you do a gorilla impersonation and then you talk about going to the toilet.*

"Everyone goes in the bushes," Callum offers. "Over there, usually."

He turns, extending an arm, pointing to the thick undergrowth bordering the access path to the quarry.

"You just have to be careful not to get scratched up," he adds. "Um—do you want me to come with you?"

"No!" I almost scream, jumping to my feet as if I'd just been stung by fire ants. "I'll be fine! Thanks! But I'll be fine!"

I take off in the direction of the bushes in such a hurry that I stumble over a hillock of stubbly dirt and turn my left foot over on the plastic flange on the heel of my trainer. Ow. I bite my tongue to avoid gasping in pain, and don't even break stride, hobbling along as Callum calls:

"You all right?"

I raise one hand to reassure him and keep going grimly, ignoring the stabbing pain in my ankle. Not till I reach the undergrowth and can bury myself safely inside its shelter do I stop, grab a branch, and balance on my right foot while circling my left one way and then the other, easing out the ankle strain.

I think I must be in shock. I can't believe what just happened.

Kissing Callum was lovely, just as lovely as it was last year. Until—and I can't think of a nicer way to put this— until his tongue slid into my mouth.

And then all I wanted to do was scream at him to get it out.

It's not Callum's fault, not in any way. I wanted him to kiss me, and I wanted to kiss him back just as much. I opened my mouth, I tightened my arms around him, I met his own tongue with the tip of mine. Up until that moment, I was yearning to press my whole body against his, to lie down next to him on the blanket, kissing and touching till we worked each other up into as high a state of excitement as we could manage.

*So what just went so badly wrong that I scarpered away as if my trainers were on fire?*

My brain's spinning. The only two logical conclusions I can come to are:

A) I don't actually fancy Callum after all,

or:

B) I'm so in love with Jase that I can't even French-kiss a boy without feeling so guilty that I have to stop.

Neither of these theories is remotely consoling.

I set my left foot back to the ground and start pushing my way farther into the bushes. I'm so wound up by now with conflicting emotions that I feel really vulnerable: no way am I peeling down my jeans and tights and squatting to wee on the ground without making sure I'm safely in deep cover. Thank goodness at least that I don't actually need to go to the loo that badly. It was mostly an excuse to get away from that nightmare situation, Callum and I just sitting there, riven with embarrassment.

*Oh.* Another thought hits me. If it had been just me pulling away from him—if he still wanted to kiss me—he'd have tried harder to get me back in his arms. He'd have kissed me again, tried to convince me that I really wanted to keep kissing him back. That's how boys behave; once they've started, they hate to stop. And they'll say, and do, a lot to keep you there.

But Callum didn't do a thing. He acted like he wanted to stop as much as I did. He didn't try to hold on to me, and when he offered to warm my hands or walk me to the bushes, he was just being polite. I could tell he didn't really mean it.

It seemed as if he felt exactly the same as me.

Which leads me to option A: I don't actually fancy Callum after all. I found that out as soon as our kissing got serious. And it was just the same for him. For some alchemical reason, we just didn't kiss the way the other person liked. And after that, there's no going back.

I've never heard of this kind of situation before. I really need some girls to talk to, girls who've kissed a lot of boys and maybe have had this same kind of experience. Because it's utterly confusing to me. Unfortunately, all the girls I know who've kissed a lot of boys are total cows who'd lie to me just to mess up my head, so I can't rely on any of them to tell me the truth.

I'm racking my brains to think about anyone at all I could ask, and not coming up with a single name. I've been weaving my way through the bushes for a while now; they're not as dense as they look from the path, and it's been easy enough to keep walking at a steady pace, lost in thought. But now that I've hit a dead end, mentally, my feet stop too.

And now that I'm not making any noise myself, I hear a heavy rustling in the bushes behind me.

*The dogs*, I tell myself immediately, over the instant

terror that surges through me. *It's just those big dogs I saw playing before, chasing each other through the forest.*

Nothing to freak me out there: I like dogs. But as I stand, not moving a muscle, my ears practically pricked into points to listen to the sound that seems to be coming closer by the second, it doesn't seem like a dog, or even two. It's too steady. Too even.

Too much like footsteps.

And no matter how calm I tell myself to be, the memory of that male figure I saw yesterday evening, following us through the dark streets of Leith, swamps my reason. I'm convinced, suddenly, that it's Callum behind me in the woods. That it was Callum last night stalking us, and that, though he seemed totally calm and fine about me taking off just now with a rather feeble excuse about needing the loo, he's a much better actor than I realize, and in fact, he wasn't calm and fine at all.

After all, that wouldn't make him the only good actor in his family.

Is Callum playing some weird double game? Is he angry with me because of Dan's death and everything that happened at Castle Airlie afterward? Or is he following me now—making enough noise so I can't help but be aware there's someone else in the woods—to scare me because I pulled away from kissing him?

Wild speculations spin through my mind, speeding up into a whir of panic, and my feet speed up too. I take off, crashing into the bushes, cannoning off branches, my breath coming in panting gasps, stumbling over roots and debris on the forest floor. Acting, in other words, like the kind of pathetic, ridiculous victim that I totally despise when I watch them in horror films.

When I watch those films, I'm always shouting advice to the girls in them. *Don't open the door without a weapon in your hand! Hit him over the head with the frying pan till he falls down—not just once, you moron, keep hitting him till he can't move!* Or, when she's being followed in a gloomy dark forest: *Duck down behind a big tree stump, hide till he's past you, and then double back!*

And of course, when it actually happens to me, I don't follow my own suggestions. Instead of hiding in the dark, I flail around like a madwoman; if someone didn't notice I was there before, they certainly do now as I tear through the bushes in a raptus of fear. But it's stronger than me. I can't stop. I physically can't. I'm a running machine, fueled by pure terror. All the events of the last few days—the smoke, the fire alarm, the push over the stair rail, the drugging of my water, the possibility that someone was following me last night—all sweep together in one sharp stabbing scream inside my head, a conviction that the person behind me—Callum, it must be!—is out to kill me.

The bushes part and close behind me. I'm racing out onto some scrub land, moonlight glinting down on the gray, almost lunar landscape in front of me. Loose shingle underfoot makes it hard to keep my balance. I slip and slide, carried forward down a shallow slope, still going at full pelt.

And suddenly, I see a drop in front of me. Darkness below, a steep fall. I realize in a split second what it is: another quarry.

Because the bowl of stone in which everyone's partying

reaches up to high cliffs around us, I assumed there wouldn't be any lower ground. But that bowl must once have been hollowed from the earth, cut out over years to quarry the stone to build the city. And the stoneworkers kept digging down, looking for more. Opening up at my feet is a huge, gaping maw, like a mouth about to swallow me.

My momentum is unstoppable. I try to dig my feet in, to turn them sideways to brake my body, but that sends me off balance, and I skid sideways, finding no purchase on the shale. I'm being carried inexorably toward the rim of the quarry. In a matter of seconds, I'll slide over the edge.

And in that moment I don't care. I shut my eyes and let go. It's the first time in my life that I've ever given up, and it feels better than I thought it would. I'm so tired. I'm so tired of all this drama, the miserable break with Jase, the weirdness with Callum, the fear that someone's seriously trying to hurt me, maybe even kill me.

I can't fight anymore: I've got nothing left.

So I might as well just fall.

## fourteen

## "I LOVE YOU, SCARLETT"

A split second later, I realize what an idiot I'm being. An idiot drama queen, getting carried away by the wine I've drunk and the nonstop craziness that's been my life ever since we reached Edinburgh. Of *course* I don't want to fall! Of *course* I have more fight in me! Of *course* I don't want to be found with a broken neck or a broken back at the bottom of a quarry when a search party eventually comes out looking for me!

With every ounce of strength I have, I throw myself backward, aiming to land on my bum. Even though I'm bound to take a tumble, I'll do much better sliding down the slope on my bottom than I will pitching headfirst into nothingness. My arms flail wildly, pushing away as if through water, a huge paddling motion that, though awkward, does help to tip me backward. I brace myself for a painful landing, for getting scraped and dragged along the rough shale beneath.

And then I'm jerked back with such force that I go flying through the air. Something's grabbed me by the scruff of the neck and pulled me as if I were a dog being hauled by its collar. The zip of my jacket cuts into the soft skin of my throat, and I scrabble with my fingers, trying to work them under the metal to stop myself from choking.

I fall back like a dead weight, landing with an impact that smacks the breath from my body. Gasping, shocked, I realize that I haven't hit ground; there's no sharp shale below me, but a hard, warm body. Nothing soft about it, no yielding flesh, just solid muscle.

*Taylor?* I think. *But Taylor isn't this big, this wide....*

"Scarlett!" gasps a voice above my head.

I wriggle off him onto my knees in one rush of movement, unable to believe what I think I just heard.

"*Jase?*" I exclaim, looking down at him. Moonlight is glowing on us, sparking flashes of light off the sharp edges of the gravel. But even if we weren't so well illuminated, I would recognize Jase anywhere. His touch, his scent, his voice, his shape.

I can't believe he's here. But I know it's him.

"Hey," he says weakly, still winded by the fall.

"Oh, *Jase*—"

I throw myself on top of him again, wrapping my arms around as much of his body as I can manage. Breathing him in, taking huge comfort in pressing myself against as much of him as I can possibly manage. And, of course, I'm showering his face with burning kisses, to quote a P. G. Wodehouse novel I recently read in which the hero did that to the heroine.

"What are you *doing* here?" I exclaim, between bouts of burning-kiss showering. "How did you know where I was?

206

Where did you *come* from? Why are you— Oh, Jase, you saved me! Jase, I missed you *so* much!"

"Scarlett—" He's kissing me back, his hands on my face, but not with the mad enthusiasm I'm showing. "Look, let me sit up—Scarlett, let go a sec—"

But I can't. I'm gripping him so tightly he has to put his hands behind him on the ground and lever himself up, carrying me with him like a monkey clinging to a tree for dear life.

"What are you *doing* here?" I ask again, like a CD stuck in a scratch. "I don't understand—why are you—"

"Stop! Scarlett, stop!" He prises my hands off him and holds them tightly. "Let me get a word in, Scarlett, *please!*"

I squeeze his hands back, staring at him in amazement. His hair's grown a little, his curls more of a short, trendy Afro now; his golden eyes are glinting at me. And he isn't smiling.

"I saw you," he blurts out. "I saw you back there. With that guy."

"Back where?" I ask stupidly, before I realize what he means.

"I saw you kissing him," Jase says quietly.

"Jase . . ." I gulp and catch my breath, mustering my thoughts. Knowing how important it is that I say the right words, find a way to tell him the truth without offending or blaming him. "You went away. I haven't seen you for months. And when I told you on the phone that I couldn't be with someone who wasn't there when I needed him . . . you didn't say anything."

Thank God. I've said the right thing. Jase's expression

shifts from accusatory to embarrassed; he bites his full lower lip.

"I *was* there for you," he insists. "Just now. You'd've taken a header down that quarry if it weren't for me."

"Yes." I tighten my grip on his hands as he tries to pull away. "You were. Thank you." I look sideways at the slope, tilting to the sheer drop into black nothingness, and shiver: I could be down there right now, badly injured or worse. And it would be completely my own fault; no one to blame this time but myself.

"I thought you'd broken up with me," I say, looking down at our hands. "When you never rang me back."

"I thought you'd broken up with *me*," he says instantly.

"No, I didn't!" I drag in a deep breath. "But I missed you so much, and it isn't enough just to talk to you on the phone every so often. I need you closer than that. I need to be with you, Jase. I really do. I missed you so badly, I couldn't bear it."

We're hugging now, Jase pulling me onto his lap, his arms wrapping around my back.

"I missed you too!" he mumbles into my neck, his breath deliciously tickly on my bare skin. "I was so messed up . . . but when you said that about me not being there for you, it really did my head in. I felt so bad, I can't tell you. And I didn't know what to say." He pauses. "No, that's not right. I thought there wasn't anything I *could* say. I went around and around in circles. And then I decided I was being completely stupid. You rang me 'cause you were in trouble, and I wasn't there. And I *should* be there if you're in trouble. That's what a boyfriend's for. So I got on my bike and came straight up to Edinburgh to find you."

"Oh, *Jase* . . . ," I say idiotically, my heart too full to manage another word. I'm determined not to cry.

"I found the school easy enough, first thing this morning," he goes on. "But I wasn't sure what to do next. I thought, they'll never let me in to see you, and what could I do in a girls' school anyway?"

"It's actually a boys' school," I mumble, "but never mind. . . ."

"So I got a bunk in a hostel and just hung around outside all day, waiting for you. But no one came out."

"They had us doing lectures all day," I explain.

"And then I saw someone climbing down a fire escape," he says, "and I knew it had to be you and Taylor, because who else would do something like that—"

"You were waiting outside all day and all evening?" I practically coo. "Oh, *Jase*, that's so *sweet* of you. . . ."

"—I was getting off my bike to come and talk to you, but you raced across the road like someone was chasing you, and jumped into that car," he continues. "So when it took off, I thought I might as well follow you. I mean," he adds dryly, "I didn't have anything else to do this evening."

We're getting to the dodgy bit now. I wince.

"It's a nice party, isn't it?" I mutter feebly. "The music's pretty good."

"I parked my bike near that old heap of a car," Jase says, "and walked in after you. You didn't even look back, you were much too busy having a laugh with those boys." He clears his throat. "I wasn't spying on you," he says quickly. "I just wanted to make sure you were okay. I mean, I didn't know that boy from Adam. It might not have been safe for you to be alone with him."

*Well, alone in the middle of a crowd of people,* I think. *But Jase is right—having people around doesn't make you safe.*

"And you kissed him!" Jase concludes accusingly. "I saw you kissing him!"

"I'm sorry you saw that," I say slowly.

"And that made me think that maybe you broke up with me because you wanted to be with him," he says in a much smaller voice. "Not because I wasn't around. I thought maybe you were just making an excuse because there was someone else you liked better."

"No!" I pull his head down, stare straight into his eyes, crying now, but unable to help it. "There isn't *anyone* I like better in the whole *world*! Jase, you have to believe me! I was feeling so lonely, and scared, and I thought kissing him would make me feel better, but it just made me feel worse— it was weird and wrong and it just made me miss you more . . . that's why I took off and came into the bushes by myself, because I felt so awful and strange and lonely. . . ."

"Really?" he says, his arms tightening around me, and just by the tone of his voice, I know that he's forgiven me for kissing another boy. Not that, technically, I did anything wrong, I note to myself. We were broken up, or I thought we were. And I was careful not to apologize for kissing Callum— I said I was sorry Jase saw it, but that's different. Instinct tells me not to say that I'm sorry just to get back with my boyfriend. This way I can be happy that I told nothing but the truth.

"Yes," I say, winding my fingers as best I can through his ridiculously thick curls, causing him to yelp and wince because they're so tightly knit. "Sorry," I say guiltily. "I like your hair longer, by the way. It's really cool."

"I do too. But I can't have it too long," he says. "'Cause of the bike helmet."

"Right," I say.

And then we stop talking and look at each other, a long, serious stare right into each other's eyes. Silence falls, a calm, all-encompassing silence, in which we're not saying anything because there's nothing left to say. And I learn that sometimes, having nothing left to say can be the most wonderfully peaceful thing you ever feel.

I'm smiling with this realization as Jase lowers his head to kiss me and I tilt mine up to his. For a moment I have a flash of déjà vu, an image of Callum and me doing exactly the same thing only half an hour before. God, I was just thinking that I needed to find a girl with more experience than me to ask her about what happened with Callum—and now I'm kissing two boys in one night! How did my life get to be this mad?

And then Jase's lips come down on mine, and a flood of happy recognition sweeps through me, the softness of his full lips so familiar and wonderful that it's like coming home—if coming home were the most exciting thing that you could possibly imagine.

"I love you," I say against his mouth, and I feel, more

than hear, him say it back to me as my eyes close in sheer, perfect happiness at being back with Jase again, being able to touch him, run my hands up and down his arms, feel him pressing tightly against me, knowing this is where we belong. I know we're back together now, back to being a couple; that Jase has fought his demons and discovered that what he feels about me is more important than what our families did in the past.

And I make a silent promise to him: that I'll never bring it up, never reproach him with it. What his father did is not his fault, and if we're going to have a chance of staying together, I have to show him that I truly believe that.

Jase is kissing my neck now, and I'm stroking his hair, making the sort of noises that would really embarrass me if I heard them coming from someone else. But I don't care. There's no one around; we're alone here, in this strange, bare landscape, clinging to each other as if we'd die if we weren't touching. And I'm letting go. It feels almost as it did when I thought I was plummeting down the ragged stone quarry, arms outstretched frantically, knowing nothing would break my fall.

I'm falling now just as hard. Just as fast, just as deep. Letting go just as much. Falling into Jase, as he's falling into me.

"Do you realize"—I gasp against his head—"this is the first time we've ever been really alone like this? I mean, without having to worry about my aunt or your dad catching us?"

Jase bites my neck lightly and looks up at me, his eyes now gleaming gold with happiness and excitement.

"Yeah," he says dryly. "Typical of us that it's in the middle of a freezing stone quarry with half the gravel in Scotland sticking into my bum! Couldn't we have picked some cozy place with, I dunno, comfy seats and central heating?"

It's true: Jase and I do seem doomed to make out in uncomfortable locations. Even when he and I spent a night together in my bedroom back at Wakefield Hall, we were squashed together on my single mattress, pulled off the bed onto the floor, having to keep very quiet because of Aunt Gwen sleeping next door, and Jase had to climb out the window at dawn.

"There's been much too much drama," I say, squishing down in his lap so I can kiss his neck in return. "You know what I'd love? A really boring, normal, bog-standard life."

"No chance of that, babe," Jase says, sighing in pleasure as I slip my hands under his jacket and sweater, pulling up his T-shirt to touch his bare skin. "I think drama's always going to follow you round."

"It never used to," I say, running my hands up his chest. "I was Little Miss Boring for sixteen whole years."

"Well"—Jase starts to pull up my own layers of clothing, sending pulses of electricity up and down my spine—"I'd say you're definitely making up for that now. . . ."

And then he yelps with surprise as my jacket buzzes under his eager fingers.

"It's my phone—sorry." I drag it out of my jacket pocket and answer it, my conscience suddenly poking me with sharp sticks. "Taylor!" I start apologetically, but she's far ahead of me.

"Scarlett! I was *freaking out!*" she yells. "Where *are* you? Callum said you went for a pee and never came back, but he's acting sort of weird so I thought there was more to it, but he said no, you really did just go for a pee, so I said why wasn't he worried that you hadn't come back, and he said maybe you went off to listen to some music or came to find us, which sounded *totally* lame—like, why wouldn't he have worried? And I—"

You can tell that Taylor's in amazing shape; she's got such good lung capacity that she doesn't even pause for breath during that rant.

"I'm with Jase!" I say loudly, cutting through her stream of consciousness by main force.

She actually stops dead at that, as if I'd slammed the wind out of her.

"*What?*" she says eventually, sounding stunned.

"He came up to Edinburgh to see me," I explain, in a voice that would be beaming if that were possible.

"Huh." Taylor processes this and launches into another stream of words. "How did he know where you were? Did you call him? You didn't tell me you called him! And are you by the bonfire? I walked all around it looking for you, but it's so dark!"

"I'm sorry," I say, genuinely remorseful at having worried her. "No, we're off by this other quarry. Like a huge hole in the ground."

"Wow, sounds majorly romantic," she drawls. "Hanging out by a huge hole in the ground. Well, I'll fill the guys in on what you're up to, and let you get back to whatever you were doing, okay? Sorry I broke the flow."

214

*We didn't actually stop*, I think, blushing; Jase has pulled up my sweater and T-shirt and I'm writhing with pleasure at what he's doing right now.

"I'll call you when we're getting ready to go," she concludes.

"Great," I squeak as Jase's fingers find a particularly sensitive spot.

"Eew, you're at it while I'm on the phone with you? *Gross*," Taylor says, and hangs up.

"Don't stop," I say to Jase, shoving the phone back at my pocket, missing, and hearing it fall to the ground without even caring. "Just don't stop. . . ."

And later on, it's him begging me not to stop, neither of us caring how much the gravel digs into us through our jeans, how cold it is wherever we're not touching each other, how eerie it is out here in the pale gray moonlight; we're barely aware of anything but each other's bodies, how wonderful it is to be back together, how totally and completely right everything feels, how amazing it is that we can drive each other this crazy and, even while we let go and fall, know that we're completely safe, that our landings will be soft and sweet, cushioned in each other's arms.

"I love you, Scarlett," Jase says when we swim back to consciousness, taking the hand that's lying across his chest and kissing its palm. "I know it's not going to be easy, being together. I can't promise it's not going to get to me, this crap with my dad and your parents. I can't promise I won't get my head messed up with it and that it might come between us sometimes. But I love you, and I won't just disappear on you anymore."

215

"Good," I say fervently, ducking my head to kiss his arm. "Because I don't think I could bear it if you ever did that again."

"I won't," he says quietly. "I promise."

Dawn's almost breaking as we walk slowly back through the bushes, hand in hand, Jase navigating our way and holding back branches for me in a very gentlemanly fashion. Boys, I've noticed, act very protectively when they like you, as if you couldn't manage to open doors or find your own way through a wood without falling over and smacking your head open. I bite my tongue, because I've worked out by now that this behavior doesn't mean that Jase thinks I'm a silly girl who couldn't cope for two seconds out in the world by myself. He wants to show how much he cares about me, and this is one of the ways boys do it.

When we reach the main path, we join the steady flow of people walking back to their cars carrying instruments, rolled-up rugs propped over their shoulders, and black bin liners clanking with empty cans and bottles. A tall, skinny white boy with a head of dreadlocks that look like they weigh more than he does is dragging a small generator on a trolley, its wheels bouncing over the ruts in the path. Everyone's yawning and happy, totally chilled, people walking in groups, holding hands, or with their arms round each other's shoulders.

I think back to my only other teenage party, Nadia's chic penthouse soiree, rich kids clinking champagne glasses, and how mean and cliquey the atmosphere was. This is the complete opposite; I'm exchanging smiles with people we pass, shared, weary grins of pure happiness at having had an amazing, magical night.

"Brilliant party," people mumble to each other cheerfully. A girl splits off from a trio walking up ahead to give the dreadlocked boy a hand pulling the trolley, as someone else dives into a bush to retrieve some empty plastic bottles.

*I only ever want parties to be like this from now on,* I think, blissfully exhausted, as we reach the ruined old stone house and I guide Jase around it to where Ewan parked the car up on the bank. Taylor, Callum, and Ewan are already gathered there, the boys loading their stuff into the boot, Taylor leaning against the side of the car. She's obviously had a brilliant time at the party: she looks as relaxed as if she's had a full-body massage, her hands tucked into her pockets, her mouth tilting upward at the corners even before she spots us.

"I think over here they'd call you a dirty stopout," she drawls as we walk up to her. "Isn't that the expression?" She grins at Jase. "Nice to see you again," she adds.

"You too," Jase says, returning her grin. He's always liked Taylor.

"Are you coming back to Wakefield?" she asks.

Jase heaves a sigh. "I dunno," he says, not letting go of my hand. "I dunno if I can. But Scarlett and I are going to make it work, whatever happens."

I squeeze his hand, choked up by this public declaration.

"Um, this is Jase," Taylor says to Callum and Ewan as they slam the car boot shut, making the car wobble precipitately on the slope. "Scarlett's boyfriend. You know."

Wow, this is awkward. I've been so caught up in my overwhelming excitement at seeing Jase that I haven't had a moment to think about what meeting up with Callum again will be like. It'd be cringe-worthy enough even without Jase on my arm; with him, it's positively nuclear. *Hi, you know how I kissed you and then shot off like I'd been fired out of a cannon as soon as you put your tongue in my mouth? Well, this is my boyfriend. Taylor filled you in on him, right? I didn't say a word about him before, but I'm madly in love with him. Whoops!*

If I were Callum, I'd be livid. Even though I'm as sure as I can be that Callum didn't feel any chemistry between us either, I'd still be furious if he'd kissed me, legged it, and turned up hours later, beaming from ear to ear, wrapped around a total stranger and announcing that she was his girlfriend. I'd feel pretty used.

Jase stiffens as Callum walks toward us, and I look at Callum nervously. It's not that I'm expecting a major scene, with insults or even punches thrown, but I wouldn't blame Callum at all for being miffed and making that clear—or trying to embarrass me in front of Jase.

But Callum doesn't meet my eyes, which is good, I suppose. Better than an angry stare. He mutters a brief "All right" of acknowledgment at the two of us as he passes, and turns away to where Taylor's standing by the car. He unlocks the driver's door as Ewan strides round the other side of the car; Ewan glances at me and Jase over the slant of the roof, a harder expression in his hazel eyes than I've ever seen.

*He's cross with me because he thinks I led Callum on,* I realize, wincing. *And I can't blame him either.*

There's no way I can launch into a long explanation of the circumstances behind my apparent jump from one boy to another tonight. Not now, anyway, when everyone's exhausted and we need to get going. Ewan reaches out and grabs the keys from Callum abruptly, as if he's got a bone to pick with him too. Probably he's just knackered, but the atmosphere's so heavy with tension you could cut it with a butter knife. I feel really guilty for having precipitated this, especially when I ended up having such a wonderful time while both Callum and Ewan, who had all the bother of bringing us to the party, are visibly cross and tired. It doesn't feel fair.

"We should hit the road," Callum mutters as Ewan levers himself into the driver's seat, the car creaking with his weight. "The girls have to sneak back into school before it's full daylight."

"Yeah, I know," Jase says, with an edge to his voice, wrapping his arm round me.

Wow, I think. Tonight I ran away from Callum and ended up with Jase, and Jase is the one who's acting aggressively. How does that work?

Streaks of pale pink are beginning to flood gently into the pale gray sky. A bright dot of sun stretches into a clear white line of light on the horizon, the pale pink darkening to rose, infusing the dawn, as Jase and I stand side by side and watch the sun peek into view.

"I'll let you get back," he says, bending to kiss me, taking his time, making the point to Callum that he might have kissed me at the start of the evening, but Jase is the one who's ended up with me. "Call me later, okay?"

"Okay," I say, really happy that he's kissed me, but awkward that it's happened in front of Callum. I just peck him back, and then dive into the car after Taylor, landing almost on top of her because of the angle at which it's parked.

"You on your bike, Jase?" Taylor calls.

"Yeah." Jase tilts his thumb at it, pulled up on the far side of the road. "Scarlett, maybe I can see you this evening?"

"I should be able to get out for an hour or two, at least," I say eagerly through the window, filled with happiness at this sudden shift from not knowing when I'll see him next to planning meetings on a daily basis. "I'll text you as soon as I know our schedule, okay?"

Callum opens the glove compartment, pulls out a can of something, and pops it open, handing it to Ewan.

"Emergency driving rations," he says shortly.

Taylor and I crane our heads: *It can't be beer,* I think nervously. *If it is, and Jase spots it—*

But it's Irn-Bru, that weird Scottish orange sort-of-energy-drink. Ewan mutters thanks and tilts his head back, glugging it down as he starts the car. I swivel in the backseat as Ewan bumps the car down the bank and onto the dirt road again; I'm watching Jase pull out his helmet and straddle his bike, and I raise my hand to him, waving through the back window. He looks up, sees me, and waves back, his hand now encased in its heavy gauntlet. I subside back into the seat, grinning from ear to ear with happiness. To my amazement, Taylor, smiling widely, wraps an arm around me and pulls me against her, something she's never, ever done before, her whole body loose and relaxed.

220

*Wow, Taylor's actually being physically affectionate. She and Ewan must have done more than just play bongos together,* I think, closing my eyes. It's odd; we're in the back, curled up against each other, smiling as we relive our happy memories of the night we've just spent, while in the front the two boys' backs are as stiff and straight as if they'd been taking tips in posture from my grandmother's etiquette guide for students. I assume that Callum's pissed off that Ewan managed to have a nice time with Taylor, while Callum was left in the cold, and that Ewan's embarrassed about the situation, but, really, what do I know? I'm scarcely an expert on boys. I only really know one of them.

*And that's more than enough for me,* I think happily as the motion of the car and the cozy hug with Taylor rock me to sleep.

Taylor crashes out too: Callum and Ewan have to wake us both up when we arrive back at Fetters. I blink, yawning deeply, as Ewan says shortly:

"You'd better leg it—it's getting bright."

I expect Taylor to acknowledge him in some way: touch his shoulder, maybe, or even kiss him through the open window. But she's out of the car before me, tossing a goodbye over her shoulder, crossing the street without looking back. Even in my exhausted state, I'm taken aback by this. Maybe she's being sensitive to the fact that Ewan and she got on well while Callum was left spinning, the third wheel, but even so, it seems a bit curt. I assume she's going to text him as soon as we're back in our room.

I echo her goodbye and add a thank you for good measure as I tear out of the car too, so relieved to be away from the deep awkwardness of the situation that, despite my tiredness, I'm positively sprinting as I vault over the wall and run back across the lawn to the fire escape. We chin ourselves up, swing our legs onto the stairs, and dash up as fast as we can without making the metal framework creak too loudly. Taylor puts her finger to her lips as we reach Plum and Susan's bedroom window, which we passed on our way down. I nod to show I remember, but the litter of cigarette butts on the sill would have identified it for me even without her reminder.

The curtains are half open, and I can't help peering in as we reach it, wondering if everyone crashed in Plum's room after their impromptu party. But what I see is not at all what I expect.

The layout of the bedroom is just the same as mine and Taylor's: a single bed on each side, a patterned strip of carpet running down the center. The difference between our bedroom and this one is that here, one of the beds is unoccupied. And the other one has two girls in it, lying very close together to fit onto the narrow mattress.

Susan seems fast asleep, her fair hair drifting over Plum's chest, her head cradled on Plum's narrow chest. There's a blanket drawn up over the two girls, but I can see them clearly in the pale morning light; Plum's head is on the pillow, one arm around Susan's waist, the other cradling her head. Gently, she's stroking Susan's hair, looking down at the top of Susan's head with a softness in her gaze that, in anyone else, I wouldn't hesitate to call love.

I shouldn't be staring. This isn't any business of mine. But I'm paralyzed by the sight. I honestly don't know what's more of a shock: realizing that Plum and Susan are a couple—or seeing Plum behave this tenderly to another person.

*My God,* I think. *She's actually human after all.*

Taylor is pulling at my arm to move me on; and then, over my shoulder, she sees what I'm looking at, and she freezes too. That must have caught Plum's attention, because she looks up. And before I can duck, her eyes meet mine.

It feels like that moment lasts forever. Plum's hand has stilled on Susan's hair; we're all as motionless as statues. Plum's green eyes are wide now with sheer panic. I've never seen her look this scared.

I'm almost hypnotized.

"Come on!" Taylor hisses, and we turn away from the window, though not before I dart a final glance back at Plum. She still looks stricken with fear.

"Who saw *that* coming?" Taylor mutters, when we've hoisted ourselves off the fire escape onto our own windowsill and back into our room.

"I literally can't process it," I say in a heartfelt voice. "It's too juicy. . . . I'm too tired. . . ."

"I know," Taylor says, giving such a deep yawn it sounds like she's pulled it up from the soles of her feet. "I'm way overloaded."

"She was always having a go at *you* about being gay!" I say, yawning in return, so hard I almost split my jaw. "Like it was a bad thing!"

I start to pull my clothes off.

"Well, she must feel weird about it if she's keeping it a

secret," Taylor says, her voice already thick with sleep. She kicks off her shoes, her jeans hitting the floor a second afterward.

"I can't believe it," I mumble, undoing my bra and crawling under the covers in my knickers, too tired to put on my pajamas.

"I can," Taylor says, her mattress creaking as she climbs into bed.

"You know what, though? They looked really pretty together," I say drowsily, my eyes closing, exhaustion hitting me like a ton of bricks to the back of the head.

Taylor starts to say "Mmn" in agreement, but halfway through she falls asleep and the "Mmn" morphs into a rumbling snore.

*That's so funny*, I think. *I have to tell her she did that.* . . . And then I hear my own breathing heave into a snore as I pass out as well.

# Fifteen

## "GHOSTS AND GHOULIES"

It's dark down here. Dark, and eerie, and very, very cramped. This is the first time since stopping gymnastics (where it really helps not to be too tall) that I've been happy I'm barely five foot three. The taller girls are having to duck every time we pass under a lintel, and they're tripping in their heels on the cobbles.

"None of these young leddies are claustrophobic, are they?" the tour guide, a burly old man dressed in a frock coat and wig, asked Miss Carter ten minutes ago, when we were all gathered in the bright, shiny guest shop, with no idea of the subterranean tunnels into which we were about to descend.

Plum started to say something, but Miss Carter was too quick for her.

"Oh, they're not so claustrophobic they can't visit dimly lit nightclubs on a regular basis," she said cheerfully, raising a guffaw from the guide. "I'm sure they'll be fine."

Still, these tiny rooms, these narrow passages, are enough to induce claustrophobia in anyone. It's the atmosphere, the chilly, damp air seeping through the uneven brickwork, and the ghost stories at which the guide is hinting that make us shiver. He herds us into a room that's mercifully big enough for us all to stand at one end, huddled together for warmth and companionship, as he paces at the other, pounding the cobbled stone floor with his silver-topped cane for extra emphasis as he explains to us with relish exactly where we're standing. We climbed down a wooden staircase two stories below street level, but it feels as if we're buried alive.

"Up there," he says, reaching up to the ceiling with his cane and tapping it, "up *there* is the center of Edinburgh. The Grassmarket, the Royal Mile. Edinburgh's finest Old Town streets, thoroughfares any capital city would be proud to boast. Perhaps you young lassies have been there already, spending some of your fathers' hard-earned money on the shiny trinkets you love, eh?"

"Sexist," Taylor mutters in my ear.

"But down *here*"—he swings his cane down and pounds the stone floor, so loudly that Lizzie whimpers in shock— "down *here* is where the poor people of Edinburgh lived, three centuries ago. No toilets down here! None of the modern luxuries you're used to! The rich people's servants would shout *'Gardez loo!'* and throw their brimming buckets of waste out the windows! Do you know what I mean by waste, young leddies? Human waste! Buckets of it, running down the streets, the alleys—alleys like this one. Imagine it all, under your feet, day after day. Stinking, nasty filth! Edinburgh was known as Auld Reekie in the nineteenth century, because of all the smoke from the breweries and mills, but it reeked much more with all that excrement, wouldn't you think?"

"He's enjoying this *way* too much," Taylor hisses.

"And not just human waste either!" he continues gleefully. "Right here"—he walks over to the long wall behind him and taps at a series of projecting, ancient metal rings, heavy with rust—"here is where their animals would live! Imagine, living right next to your animals, day in, day out, with them of course adding to the waste that would pour down these stone runnels, down the side of the steep castle rock on which we're standing. . . ."

"There *does* seem to be rather an obsession with *fecal matter* of all kinds," Jane mutters to Miss Carter.

"Who can tell me what kind of animals there would be tethered here?" the guide is asking.

To my surprise, it's Susan who pipes up.

"Cows," she says in her soft, quiet voice. "For milk."

"Exactly! Well done, young lassie! Cows, for milk! And, in due time, for meat as well," he says. "The puir animals would be led in here, never to leave again. They'd be slaughtered where they stood, when they were old, and their blood would run down these gutters—"

"Let me guess," Luce, who's always had a sarcastic sense of humor, suggests dryly. "Mingling with the poo and the wee?"

"No!" he says triumphantly. "Made into black pudding, the fine Scots delicacy whose main ingredient is nice rich blood!"

He rolls the r of *rich* theatrically, and lingers on the word *blood* so long that Lizzie and Sophia giggle nervously and cling together.

"Perhaps we could move on to the *history?*" Ms. Burton-Race says loudly. "Could you explain a little bit about the architecture of this place? I understand where we're standing was originally not closed in like this?"

"Indeed!" the guide says, grinning widely. "Imagine, if you will, that all this above us is open sky, for so it was for centuries. People shopped here, came to visit their lawyers, had their saws sharpened, bought their bread, had their clothes altered. And they lived here too, in these tiny rooms. Where we're standing right now was known as the Fleshmarket. Can anyone tell me why?"

"Prostitutes, I imagine," Plum drawls. "Standing in doorways. Like in Amsterdam. Only without the red lights, because they hadn't been invented yet."

The guide looks completely taken aback. I have to hand it to Plum—at least she's managed to stop him in his tracks. He scratches his head, sending his wig askew.

"*No,*" he says eventually, sounding very disapproving. "Not at *all*. This is Edinburgh, young leddy, not the Continent." He makes the rest of Europe sound like an absolute hotbed of vice. "No, this was where the slaughtermen did their grim business. The butchers. And over there"—he gestures across the room, to another narrow alley—"that was Skinners' Close, where the tanners would make leather from the skins. Och, there'd be a stink in the Fleshmarket and Skinners' Close!"

He's getting back into his rhythm now.

"But of course, then, as I said, there'd be open air above

our heids! To carry some of the reek away! Then, during the seventeen fifties, in came the town council, who built the floors above that you see today, to make their smart Royal Exchange, where people could do their shopping in more comfort. Shutting the people of the closes in"—he lowers his voice to a whisper—"like rats in a maze."

Although we all know everyone would still have been able to get in and out, we still can't help shivering. That's the feeling of being buried alive, bricked up in these passages, with no daylight above us. It's very eerie, and our guide smiles in triumph as he sees our reaction.

"Och, and I haven't even started on the ghost stories!" he says, leading us into a smaller room with a wooden floor that creaks as we file in one by one, since the doorway is so narrow. I'm one of the last, and as I wait in the corridor, a cold breeze glides along the back of my neck, as if a door has been opened somewhere down the passageway.

Only I haven't seen any doors.

I swing around, and out of the corner of my eye, I spot a dark shape slipping across the close, disappearing into a room farther down.

"Who's there?" I say quickly, involuntarily. "Taylor?" I nudge her, my heart racing. "Did you see that?"

"See what?" she asks.

"I thought I saw something—someone—"

"Oh *please*," Nadia says loudly to Plum as I walk into the room. Rough floorboards shift underfoot. "Did you hear that? Scarlett's trying to pretend she saw a *ghost*. How *pathetic* and attention-seeking!"

"There are many stories of ghosts down in the closes,"

the guide says immediately. "A woman in black, called Mary King, comes and goes as she pleases! And I'm about to tell you all the story of the plague that ravaged Edinburgh"—much rolling of the r on *ravaged*—"and the ghosts and ghoulies that haunted the Coltheart family in 1685, in this very room. . . ."

He's indicating that we should all sit on a long bench along the wall. Alison and Luce are already taking places next to each other, and as I meet Alison's eye she nods at me. It's an acknowledgment of the fact that ever since the night out at the Shore, we have what Ms. Burton-Race, in her lectures, would call a détente. That isn't as big a deal as having actually made peace; it's more that you've mutually decided not to be hostile to one another. Luce, seeing Alison nod, looks up as well and actually flashes me a half smile.

*Wow. That's a nice change. I wish I could enjoy it more.* I still think Alison and Luce, with their physical dexterity and their grudge against me, are the most likely candidates for having set the smoke bombs and left me that note, though it would really kill me to think that one of them had pushed me over the stair rail. And Taylor's suggestion that they could have slipped the antihistamines in my water, but that Alison had had a fit of conscience and saved me when it looked as if I might seriously injure myself, or worse, also makes sense.

Well, if it was Luce and Alison behind the attacks, I have the sense I'll be safe from now on. After the Shore, after hanging out with the boys and walking back to school together, they've softened toward me. Neither of them has ever been fake; they say what they mean, and mean what they say. They wouldn't nod or smile at me if they were still furious with me. (Of course, if they knew we'd sneaked out last night to go to a party with Callum and Ewan, they'd probably be livid with jealousy, but mercifully, they have no idea why Taylor and I look so tired today.)

Maybe one day—if I find out the truth, if I can clear them of trying to hurt me—we'll be friends again. I'd like that. But right now, the tables are turned. It's me being wary of them.

I look over to see where Plum is, and notice that she and Susan aren't sitting beside each other. They didn't share a double seat in the coach coming here either; Plum very pointedly plopped herself down next to Nadia, and Susan equally carefully selected a place next to another Wakefield Hall girl. It's the first day on our trip here that the two of them haven't been joined at the hip, and I can guess why. Plum's clearly told Susan that Taylor and I saw the two of them sharing a bed this morning, and they've embarked on a policy of total denial.

Well, I don't care if Plum and Susan keep a distance of a hundred feet from each other at all times or sit in each other's laps. What I *do* care about is that Nadia Farouk is sniggering to Plum about me seeing ghosts and being pathetic, her gold bracelets clinking as she pushes her hair back from her face. And Plum, beside her, is letting her do it.

I know perfectly well that Plum decides who she and Nadia bitch about. Well, it's time to get Plum to shut Nadia's nastiness toward me down for good.

"I might have been seeing things 'cause I'm a bit tired, Plum," I say, sitting down on her other side. "I didn't sleep that well. Is your bed comfortable? Mine really isn't."

I can feel her whole body stiffen.

"And the mattresses are so narrow, aren't they?" I add, not raising my voice, because I don't need to. "Barely room for one!"

"Overkill alert," Taylor mutters.

Everyone's sitting on the bench now, and the guide is shushing us. Plum turns her head to look at me. It's too shadowy in here for me to read her expression, but I hear the one word she whispers at me:

*"Please."*

I've never heard Plum like this. Vulnerable. Pleading. Desperate.

In my time at St. Tabby's—particularly when I was getting my boobs, which caused her to taunt me on a daily basis—I'd have pictured myself jumping six feet in the air with triumph at having finally reduced Princess Plum to begging me for mercy. And it does feel good. I'm surprised, though, that I'm not quite as giddy with euphoria as I would have imagined.

The guide's telling a story in his best creepy voice, clearly intent on scaring the living daylights out of as many of us as possible. But I'm not listening. The fleeting sight of that figure in the corridor has already managed to creep me out so thoroughly that I don't even have room in my brain for a ghost story; I'm scared I'm being stalked by someone who's flesh and blood, not a phantom. Occasional phrases— "disembodied head," "severed arm," "dreadful groan"—float past me, but don't sink in, though I can hear girls around me emitting delighted squeaks of fear.

Plum, beside me, is still as rigid as a statue. I don't think she's taking in a word either. When the guide reaches what's clearly a thrilling climax, and marshals us all up again to continue the tour, Plum's the last to stand, her long legs wobbling in her knee-high boots. I'm almost out of the room when I feel something tug at my sleeve, and I have to repress a squeal of shock.

It's not a phantom or a stalker. It's Plum. But she's white as a sheet, looking as scared as if she'd just seen a ghost.

"*Please*, Scarlett," she whispers plaintively. "*Please* don't tell anyone, or let Taylor tell. I'll do *anything*."

"Don't talk to me," I say, jerking my sleeve free from her grip. "Don't talk to Taylor. Leave us both alone. And make sure everyone else does too."

"I will! I promise! I will!"

She still looks utterly terrified. This, I suppose, is what I've wanted all along from Plum: to have her completely in my power, to be able to neutralize her evil tongue, at least when it's directed at me and Taylor. Plum was an absolute cow to Taylor last term, intimidating Lizzie and Susan into helping her physically bully Taylor, who couldn't stand up to her because Plum knew Taylor's brother's secret.

*Well, Taylor won't need to worry about that anymore*, I reflect as I follow the rest of the group out into the close, leaving Plum behind. Turning my back on her as if she doesn't matter to me. Because from this moment on, she doesn't.

I'll never be afraid of what Plum's saying behind my back again.

And yet the triumph I should be feeling just isn't there.

I hurry to catch up to Taylor, who's waiting for me at the tail end of the crocodile of girls winding their way down the narrow passages. She raises her eyebrows as I reach her, two strong dark lines rising in a silent inquiry.

"Total surrender," I whisper. "Anything we want. She begged me."

"Eew," Taylor says, frowning now, the lines drawing together.

"I know. It's weird. It didn't feel that wonderful."

"I'm not surprised," she says, as we turn a corner. "'Cause—whoo!"

The passage has suddenly widened into a close as wide as a street, dipping away from us sharply; I've lost any sense of which direction we're going in this maze, but I imagine we must be standing on the ridge of the rock on which Edinburgh Castle is built, and this close falls away down one of the steeper hills. Girls farther down the stony slope are giggling and clinging to each other as the guide calls us to a halt.

"Now, I'm sure all you fine young lassies are very used to posing for a photo or two, aren't you?" he asks rhetorically. "Pretty young things like you must have all the boys asking to take your picture!"

"He's kind of like the too-friendly old uncle your mom tells you never to be left alone with," Taylor comments as Jane hisses to Miss Carter:

"I am *not* comfortable with his gender assumptions, Clemency."

The guide raises his cane to the high beam in the ceiling.

"Smile for the camera!" he says. "It'll go off in five seconds—counting down—"

To be fair, he's bang-on about most of the girls here. The St. Tabby's posse is more than used to posing for the cameras, and the speed with which they all hit their marks is impressive: groups form lightning fast up and down the steep slope, hair tossed back from faces, bodies snapped into their most flattering angles, smiles blazing, pouts pursing out. Taylor jams her hands into her pockets and scowls; she hates having her photo taken. And I just stand there, staring up at the beam, as a white light opens up and vibrates for a long, eyeball-searing moment, leaving us temporarily blinded when it finally dissipates.

"That'll be available to purchase in the gift shop when you finish the tour," the guide says, "if you're happy with the way you look—I know the leddies are always complaining about the way they look in photos, aren't they?"

"I'm *definitely* going to lodge a complaint!" Jane fumes as we slip and slide down the slope.

"Did Plum catch us up?" I say suddenly, very aware of the state I left her in: white-faced and shaking. I didn't see her in the photo groups, and it's completely unlike Plum not to have been in the center of one of them.

I swivel round, worried now that she stayed back and might have got lost in the corridors. It's actually a relief when I see her tall figure picking its way toward us, long giraffe legs in tight jeans and high heels, one hand out to the stone wall to help herself balance.

It's what's behind her that makes me freeze. The shadows are thick around the doorway at the top of the slope, but I see it quite clearly now: a dark figure, stocky and square-shouldered, as if the gloom has taken form, coalesced into the shape that is already horribly familiar to me from two nights ago in the night streets of Leith.

I grab Taylor's arm. And this time, I know I'm not going mad: I know Taylor can see it too, because she turned when I did, and she's looking in precisely the same place I am.

"Look!" I say, sounding almost frenzied. "*There!* Look! There *is* someone!" My other arm shoots out and I point at the doorway, my hand shaking with emotion.

Plum spins round, alerted by my frantic voice, and stares into the doorway too as the shape slides back, into the dark, blending imperceptibly into the shadows behind it until it disappears completely.

"Come on, girls!" Aunt Gwen calls impatiently from farther down the slope. "There's been enough dawdling!"

But I'm taking off in the opposite direction, in the direction of the shadow. Taylor grabs my arm, physically stopping me, pulling me back.

"Scarlett! We've got to go—your aunt's calling—"

Impatiently, I jerk at my arm, but Taylor's grip is like a vise.

"Let me go!" I say urgently. "I can catch whoever it is! They've been following me—I can catch them—"

"Scarlett—" Her face is right in front of mine, her brows dragged together in one straight line. "Scarlett, there's nothing there, okay? I didn't see anything! We have to get going!"

"*Girls!*" Aunt Gwen sounds furious. "Come *on*!"

The seconds are ticking away; whoever was standing

there at the top of the slope, watching us, has had a chance now to slip into one of the many little rooms or closes in the maze up above. I'll never catch them now. My shoulders slump in frustration and anger.

"There *was* someone there! The same shape that was following us in Leith!" I insist to Taylor as she pulls me down to join the rest of the group. "You *must* have seen him!"

"I didn't, Scarlett," she says, shaking her head. "I'm really sorry."

I wrench my arm free.

"I don't believe you," I say, tears of rage pricking at my eyes. "I don't believe you didn't see it—it was right *there*!"

"*I* saw something," Plum volunteers, skittering down the incline and nearly falling into it. "There was definitely someone in the doorway. I saw it too."

"Oh please," Taylor snaps. "You're just lying to suck up to Scarlett."

"I'm *not*!" Plum insists as we all reach the bottom of the gradient and turn in to a small room with open wooden struts that look as if they're barely managing to hold up the ceiling. There's hardly room for all of us. I shuffle in, pushing forward through the cluster of girls and teachers to get as far away from Taylor as I can—I'm furious with her for stopping me from chasing that shadow figure.

But as I reach the front of the group, I see a truly creepy sight.

Dolls. A wooden trunk full of dolls, set against the stone wall, more dolls spilling out of it, some arranged on a shelf above, their beady eyes staring sightlessly in front of them, glassy and dead, as if they're gazing at ghosts only they can see. It's like something from a horror film, and for some reason it affects me really strongly. I freeze, transfixed. There must be over a hundred of them, their beige plastic skin gleaming in the harsh glare of the single lightbulb hanging overhead, their cheap acrylic hair bright and fake.

Behind us, the guide is gleefully telling the story of the dolls. I catch snatches of it as I stare, hypnotized, at the trunk and its contents.

"And so, when the psychic came into *this* room—well, she didn't even come in, poor leddy, she stopped there on the threshold and said she felt so cold she couldn't move, like a presence was haunting it . . ."

Some of the dolls are bald, like babies with grossly over-sized swollen heads, shiny in the light.

". . . eventually she did a séance or some such and got in touch with the spirit of a puir wee dead lassie called Flora, who said she wanted her dolly . . ."

Lizzie, next to me, starts to sniff in sympathy with Flora.

". . . and when she made the documentary, we found ourselves swamped with dollies for Flora. They come from all over—Australia, Canada, even China, people have sent dollies from round the globe. The leddy said Flora told her she died of the plague and her mummy left her here. . . ."

Lizzie starts to cry, which sets off Susan. Sighing, Aunt Gwen reaches in her bag for a packet of tissues and extracts a couple, handing them over to the girls. As Susan leans over to take them, sniffing and sobbing, her head grazes against the hanging lightbulb; Susan's as tall as a model. It's just a brush of her scalp against the white plastic protective cage round the bulb. Susan barely notices. But it sends the bulb, hanging from a thick white safety wire, swinging back and forth.

I know I shouldn't look back at the dolls. I know I shouldn't. But I can't help it; the impulse is stronger than common sense.

So I do.

It's a huge mistake. My nerves are already wound tighter than elastic on a spool; I'm groggy and vulnerable from lack of sleep; and I'm totally freaked out, not just from seeing that shadow-shape again, but even more from the fact that Taylor once again denied seeing it when it was plainly in front of her.

*Is it Taylor playing these awful tricks on me? Is she in league somehow with the person who's following me? She must be— why else would she deny she saw something that was right there—something I saw with my own eyes!*

The swinging lightbulb is sending pools of light and patches of shadow back and forth, back and forth across the trunkful of dolls. It makes their eyes glitter and their expressions ghastly. And as it moves, it catches the shape of one of the dolls propped up on top of the pile, magnifying its shadow hugely against the bare stone wall. For an awful moment, with its squat, bulky body and round head, it looks almost exactly like the shape I saw in the doorway just now. Only this one is reaching out toward me with one stubby, clawlike hand.

I'm completely overloaded, still in a flood of panic at seeing that menacing shape in the doorway at the top of the close. I'm deep in a maze of confusing passages, being followed by a dark, mysterious figure, with my best friend turning on me, doing her best to drive me crazy by telling me I can't believe the evidence of my own eyes. Everything's upside down: I can't trust Taylor. Which makes me so insecure it feels as if my head's going to explode.

I realize that I'm barely able to breathe. And the next thing I know, I'm swaying dangerously on my feet, and the room's going black.

# sixteen

## SOMETHING'S VERY WRONG
## WITH ME

I should be mortified, totally and utterly mortified, at making such an awful scene over a trunk of kids' dolls and a swinging lightbulb. And deep down, I *am* thoroughly embarrassed, but it's a dull sensation buried under layers and layers of other emotions that are much sharper and more stabbing. Fear. Confusion. Panic.

Someone's caught me and is holding me by the shoulders, keeping me on my feet. It's Jane.

"Has anyone got a paper bag?" she's asking urgently. "She's having a panic attack—it helps to breathe into a paper bag—"

"It's like that shadow on the wall! Like that shadow we saw up there!" Plum squeals. "I know why she's screaming! She saw something at the top of the slope in the doorway—she said someone was following her—"

"Wee Flora's just a story, lassie," the guide says, sounding very worried. "There's no documentation for it; we've just got the psychic's word for it. She might have made it all up, y'know—"

"Throw some water on her!" Miss Carter recommends.

I really can't breathe now. Dark spots are spinning before my eyes. My head's tightening, as if my skull's shrinking, and my body feels lighter and lighter, my legs as wobbly as jelly.

And then someone grabs my arm in a grip even tighter than Taylor's and starts dragging me out of the room. I feel every single finger digging into me, separate and distinct, the thumb sinking into my tricep muscle, and the pain is sharp and clear and hugely welcome, because it's an instant distraction from my panic. I gasp in shock and drag in a long, merciful breath as I'm pulled out into the corridor and up the incline, then shoved into a stone embrasure, an old window frame onto which I slump. It's an improvised chair; the hand stays on my arm and the other hand comes down on the back of my head, shoving it between my knees.

"Blood to the head stops a faint," Aunt Gwen's voice snaps above me.

"Oh, well done, Gwen," Miss Carter says, trotting up the slope in our wake. "Very well done. What on earth is going on with Scarlett? I know she had period issues on Arthur's Seat, but I'm beginning to think we have a serious nerve disturbance here!"

"Her mother was very unstable," Aunt Gwen says grimly. "A lot of these problems start at puberty, you know."

"Oh *dear* . . ." Miss Carter clicks her tongue.

I try to speak, but my head's still swimming. Aunt Gwen

242

is a foul, evil witch who can't resist an opportunity to bitch about my mother, and yet she's the only person who had the wit to save me from fainting. I suppose I should be grateful to her. Which is incredibly annoying.

"I'll take her back to Fetters and let her rest," Aunt Gwen says. "It's the best we can manage for now."

"Absolutely," Miss Carter agrees. "I really don't think that silly little ghost story was remotely upsetting enough to cause something like this. Plum was saying Scarlett hallucinated some sort of shadow, isn't that right? We'll have to get her checked out by a doctor once we're back at Wakefield."

"One thing at a time," Aunt Gwen says. "Scarlett, lift your head up now and take deep breaths from your diaphragm. You *can* control yourself, and you *will*."

It's amazing that Aunt Gwen's rough treatment is actually working. But it is. She's let go of my arm by now, but it's still throbbing, and the pain's a focus for me to concentrate on. Pain I can deal with. Panic's much harder. By the time I raise my head as Aunt Gwen commands, the black spots in my vision have gone, and my head isn't spinning anymore.

"Miss Carter, what's happening?" Taylor sprints up the slope, sounding as frantic as I just felt. "Is Scarlett okay?"

"Goodness knows, Taylor," Miss Carter sighs. "Her aunt is taking her back to Fetters to lie down. We'll see what the nurse has to say."

"I'll go back too!" Taylor says immediately. "She shouldn't be alone. I can sit with her in our room—"

"I think I'm more than capable of taking care of one hysterical teenager, thank you, Taylor," Aunt Gwen snaps.

243

"No—Miss Carter, Miss Wakefield, *please* let me come!" Taylor sounds hysterical herself. "She's my best friend, *please*!"

"I suppose it couldn't do any harm—" Miss Carter starts, but I interrupt her.

"No!" I say loudly. "I don't want her!"

"*Scarlett!*" Taylor almost wails. "Scarlett, you *have* to—"

"I don't have to do anything!" I yell. "I *know* you saw that ghost—no, *not* a ghost, it was something real—I *know* you saw it, and you're *lying*! Not just now, when we were coming back from the Shore as well! That's twice you've lied about it!"

"It's not—I can explain—" Taylor begins, but Aunt Gwen's voice cuts through us like a knife through butter.

"This situation is completely out of control," she snaps, her voice as tart as a lemon. "I am taking Scarlett back to school *immediately*. Miss Carter, will you please escort Taylor McGovern back to the group *now*, before the girls work each other up to any further heights of childish hysteria?"

"Come on, Taylor," Miss Carter says, turning away. "This isn't helping Scarlett at all."

I look at Taylor; she's white as a sheet. Pushing past Miss Carter, she runs up to me, dropping down next to me so she can be level with my face.

"Scarlett, let me come with you!" she pleads. "*Please!* I can explain everything—just let me come back to school with you—"

"Leave me alone," I say angrily, my voice echoing off the stone walls. "I can't trust you anymore! *Plum* saw that thing—whatever it was—it's *mad* that you're the one who kept lying to me, and *Plum* didn't! Everything's so messed up, I don't know what to think!"

Aunt Gwen pulls me to my feet.

"This is clearly a case of a friendship getting too close," she says over my head to Miss Carter. "We see it much too often, don't we? It's the bane of single-sex schools."

"*What?*" Taylor jumps up, yelling at Aunt Gwen. "That's bull! You're the one who told Scarlett she couldn't see her boyfriend! If you were worried about me and Scarlett getting too close, why didn't you let her see Jase?"

"Jase Barnes is Scarlett's boyfriend?" Miss Carter says in surprise, before she shakes her head. "This is getting *completely* out of control," she says firmly. "Gwen, you're absolutely right. Taylor, you will come with me this instant to rejoin the group."

"But, Miss Carter—"

"*Now!*" Miss Carter barks at her, with all the authority of a gym mistress more than used to making reluctant girls jump on command.

Aunt Gwen is already marching me back through the narrow underground passages as expertly as if she had spent her life down in these closes. In a matter of minutes, we're climbing the wooden staircase again, emerging into the gift shop, startled faces turning to stare at us as we exit through the heavy iron-framed door into the daylight. The Royal Mile is bustling, and I balk at the number of people on the pavements, the sightseeing buses lumbering past; it's too much for me to deal with. Too much reality, too much confusion.

But it certainly isn't too much for Aunt Gwen. Maybe

she really is the best person to be taking care of someone in as highly emotional a state as I am right now; she hails a black taxi and has me inside, slumped on the backseat, almost immediately. The familiar ticking noise of the cab's engine is loud and comforting, and in the fifteen minutes it takes us to drive back to Fetters, we don't exchange a word.

Aunt Gwen doesn't take me to see the nurse, for which I'm also grateful; that woman was nasty enough to me last time I collapsed. I can't imagine how sarcastic she'd be at the sight of me coming in twice in three days with fainting symptoms. Instead, I'm marched through the main hall, up five flights of a back staircase, and through a series of fire doors to a modern wing of the school so tucked away behind its Victorian Gothic facade that I didn't even know it existed. This is clearly for the teachers—Aunt Gwen has her own suite of rooms, which are as spacious and luxurious as the pupils' are cramped and old-fashioned.

*So this is where a lot of the school fees go*, I think, the cynical granddaughter of a headmistress. *Bet they don't let the parents anywhere near this wing.*

Aunt Gwen chivvies me into the sitting room and indicates an armchair while she bustles off into the adjoining kitchenette. I peer around and notice a bedroom off one side of the sitting room, and what I assume is an en suite bathroom beyond it. The living room is very nicely furnished, with a leather sofa and two matching armchairs round a coffee table, floor-to-ceiling bookshelves, a desk, and two huge windows with views over the parking lot to the Fetters football pitches beyond.

"Here, drink this," Aunt Gwen says, coming back with

a mug of tea and setting it down in front of me on the coffee table—on a coaster, naturally. "Plenty of sugar in it. That's always good for a shock." She takes a seat in the other armchair. "Oh, and open that window next to you," she adds, nodding at it. "Cold air will do you good as well."

There's no disobeying Aunt Gwen; I stand up obediently and twist the chrome handle, cracking the heavy, double-glazed window open as little as I can get away with. The breeze is sharp on the back of my neck as I turn away, and I must admit, she's right; it does wake me up, even as I'm shivering.

I sit back down in the armchair and pick up the tea, blowing on the top to cool it down. Aunt Gwen has brewed it as strong as she could.

"Drink it all," she commands, fixing her bulging, green gobstopper eyes on me.

One of Aunt Gwen's most effective powers is her ability to not say a word, which is a lot harder than you'd think. Under her basilisk stare, I dutifully drink down my entire mug of tea. The sugar and caffeine rush, combined with the cold air blowing over my face, dispels the last wisps of dizziness from my meltdown; I set the mug on the table, feeling as good as I can, considering that I just threw a major wobbly and am now seated in front of my horrible aunt, doubtless about to get one of her special, nerve-crunching lectures about exactly what's wrong with me.

I take a deep breath and brace myself for the onslaught. But her first question takes me completely by surprise.

"Are you still in contact with Jase Barnes, Scarlett?" she asks, leaning forward and smoothing her tweed skirt down over her knees. "Taylor McGovern said just now that he was your boyfriend. I told you in no uncertain terms to break it off with him earlier this year. And I certainly assumed that after all that unpleasantness with his father, and Jase's disappearance, the two of you were no longer in touch."

I bite the inside of my lip and prepare to tell a string of lies. There's no point having a confrontation with Aunt Gwen; I live in her house, and she made it very clear to me months ago that if I kept seeing Jase, she would do everything in her power to turn my life into even more of a living hell than she's managed to do so far.

"No, Aunt Gwen," I fib, sliding one hand under my thigh so I can cross my fingers. It may be a silly superstition, but this isn't just any lie; it's to do with Jase, and after what happened last night at the quarry party—blood rises to my face when I think about it—I'm more protective than ever of our relationship.

It isn't enough, though. Aunt Gwen doesn't look remotely convinced.

"He's gone," I say. "I haven't heard from him since he took off. We weren't even seeing each other when all that happened. I just wanted to help him because I was sure he was innocent."

To sell the lies, I call on the memories of how awful I felt when Jase didn't ring me for all those weeks, and how even more awful I felt when I thought we'd broken up. It's like being an actress, when they tell you to think of something really sad, like your dog dying, so that you can cry on cue; I feel my face sag in misery, my mouth turning down at the corners.

From Aunt Gwen's expression, I see immediately that it's worked; she's nodding in satisfaction.

"The Barnes family are nothing but scum," she says, settling back in her armchair and crossing her legs. "Look at the grandmother! And that pathetic creature Kevin married!"

*I don't think I've ever heard Aunt Gwen say a nice word about another woman,* I reflect, *but she's particularly nasty about poor Dawn.* Jase's mum isn't exactly the Brain of Britain, it's true, but she means well, after all, which is more than one can say about Aunt Gwen. It's odd that I think of Jase's mum by her first name, rather than calling her Mrs. Barnes, but when you meet Dawn, you know that treating her like an adult just doesn't feel right. In a maturity contest between her and Lizzie Livermore, I honestly think Lizzie would win.

"You really don't like Dawn—Jase's mum," I observe.

Aunt Gwen's eyes bulge.

"There's nothing to dislike," she snaps. "Dawn Barnes is simply a nothing. She wasn't even that pretty when she was younger, let alone now."

*Harsh,* as Taylor would say. But you just have to look at Aunt Gwen to understand why she might be catty about another woman's looks. Poor Aunt Gwen didn't have much luck in the beauty department; she takes after her father, and my grandfather's craggy, masculine features and big, sturdy build don't translate well to a female. Of course, Aunt Gwen could make more of an effort—do something with her frizzy sandy hair, dye her eyebrows, wear clothes that make her look less like she's in an Agatha Christie village mystery

249

from the 1940s, with her twinsets, pearls, and orthopedic-looking sturdy shoes. But it's true that the raw materials don't give her much to work with, and the thyroid disease that makes her eyes bulge out like an angry frog's is very unlucky.

I don't look anything like Aunt Gwen; I'm a dead ringer for many of the Wakefield women in the family portraits. Small frame, white skin, blue eyes, dark curly hair. My mother was actually a distant cousin of my father's, so I have Wakefield blood on both sides, which explains why the resemblance between me and a lot of the previous Wakefields in crinolines and bonnets and, later, bustle skirts, is so pronounced. I know Aunt Gwen hates me for this, but it's not exactly my fault, is it?

And without meaning to be too much of a bitch, I do think Aunt Gwen should be more careful about commenting on other women's looks. I mean, people in glass houses shouldn't throw stones.

I close my eyes for a moment, feeling a little woozy. I squinch the lids shut tightly, shaking my head, in an attempt to wake myself up.

"So you're not still in contact with Jase Barnes?" Aunt Gwen asks. "You don't have any idea whether he's planning to come back to Wakefield?"

"No," I say, opening my eyes again. *Why is she going over this?* I wonder. *I already said I wasn't.*

I turn toward the window a little, letting the air blow onto my face. I'm feeling a bit dizzy again. Probably because I got so little sleep last night—or rather, this morning.

"I think I should go and lie down," I say to Aunt Gwen, stifling a yawn.

"Not yet," she says with a shake of her head. "We have a lot more to talk about."

*Really?* I think. *All you seem to be asking me is the same question about Jase, over and over again.*

"I just feel a bit woozy," I say apologetically.

"Stay where you are," Aunt Gwen says calmly. "You're fine in the armchair."

It's true, the armchair's very comfortable, squashy and yielding; it's just that it's hard to relax in Aunt Gwen's presence. No, I amend that; it's impossible.

"Did you ever wonder, Scarlett," Aunt Gwen continues conversationally, "why I live in the gatehouse? Not the family wing of Wakefield Hall? There's a whole floor, almost, of the Hall, that was being done up for your father and mother. And now it's closed off, and I'm in that tiny little cottage where the lowest member of staff used to live."

My eyes widen.

"I *did*, actually," I admit. "Wonder about it, I mean."

She nods.

"It was my mother's idea," she says. "After your parents died. She wanted me to move in there with you, bring you up; she wanted me to bond with you. Be a sort of substitute mother, I imagine." She snorts in contempt at this idea. "Crammed together in that horrible little box—what was she thinking?"

She leans forward again.

"But of course, you realize her *real* motive," she adds.

"She was terrified. Terrified that I had something to do with your parents' being killed. She couldn't bear to think about it. So she made me take you in and bring you up, to prove to herself that she didn't believe it. And, I assume, to make sure nothing happened to you. She didn't think I could risk anything happening to you when you were in my care."

My mouth is hanging open; I'm dumbfounded. This is so unexpected, so hard to process, that there's nothing I can think of to say.

Also, my head feels like it's stuffed full of cotton wool, and my lips don't seem to be working very well.

"And she was right, wasn't she?" Aunt Gwen smiles. It's like watching a crocodile bare its teeth. "I couldn't have risked you having an accident when you were small and vulnerable, could I? It would have been much too suspicious."

"But *Mr. Barnes* killed my parents!" I manage to get out. "He knocked them off their scooter—he ran them down with his van!"

Aunt Gwen raises her hands and claps once, mockingly.

"Why don't you try thinking for a moment, Scarlett? You're supposed to be a bright girl. Did it ever occur to you to wonder why Kevin would bother to do something as senseless as run over Sir Patrick and Lady Wakefield? Why would he have taken a risk like that unless he had something huge to gain? What, did you think he was a homicidal maniac? You're as big an idiot as your mother, that brainless little fluffball. Kevin killed your parents so that I could inherit the Hall, my dear. We were in it together."

I simply don't believe this. She's playing a horrible joke on me, torturing me, knowing that no one will believe me

252

when I tell them what she said to me, because it's so impossible and outrageous.

I try to shake my head, but it's as heavy as lead. Something's very wrong with me.

"Don't you like what I'm telling you, Scarlett?" Aunt Gwen says, smiling even more now. "Then why don't you leave? I won't try to stop you."

I push my hands down on the arms of the chair, but I can't lift myself. I'm almost paralyzed; my bones might as well be made of polystyrene, my muscles of cotton wool. I can't brace myself against the chair; my arms collapse instead.

"Antihistamines always had this effect on you," she informs me. "I gave you one when you were small and had hay fever, and you went out like a light." She looks reminiscent. "It was *very* tempting, I can tell you! But, as I said, it was too soon. I made a note of the active ingredients in the pills, and I bought some more last week and put them in your water bottle. I was hoping you'd fall off the edge of that mountain and split your head open." She shrugs. "Well, I didn't have much luck with that, did I?"

"Taylor said . . . antihistamines . . . ," I mumble.

"Taylor's a clever girl," Aunt Gwen agrees. "That's why I was so relieved when you didn't want her to come back with us this afternoon. Goodness knows what's going on between the two of you, but it worked out perfectly for me. Your tea had four pills crushed up in it—you should be very drowsy by now. I just hope you can take in what I'm saying. It would be a disappointment for me if you couldn't, frankly."

253

"You—and Mr. Barnes?" I say, my lips almost numb.

She nods abruptly.

"We were—together, when we were younger," she says, and now she looks wistful, almost vulnerable. "But it was impossible, of course. He was the gardener's son, and I am a Wakefield! Ridiculous! But Kevin was always ambitious. When I made it clear to him that no one could ever know that we were seeing each other, he got furious. Really angry. Kevin had a terrible temper. He tore off and married the first woman he met, that stupid little nothing, Dawn." She's frowning now. "But naturally, that didn't last. How could it? She bored him to death. So we began seeing each other again. And it occurred to both of us that if your father was out of the picture, my mother would be a lot more generous to me."

She looks directly at me, her eyes flashing.

"Patrick was always her favorite," she says bitterly. "The son—her firstborn—serving in the army, marrying a Wakefield cousin, for God's sake! He did everything right in her eyes! And then, when they had you, and it was clear that you were going to be a perfect tiny little Wakefield clone, it was as if I didn't even *exist* for my mother anymore. Everything was Patrick's, *everything*. I thought if he wasn't around anymore—and your mother, too, because my mother just *drooled* over her—that it would all be different." She sighed. "I wanted you gone too, of course. That would have been best. But Kevin wouldn't do that. *Not a little girl*, he said. That was too much. He turned out to have some scruples."

She laughs, without a hint of humor.

"But it was too much for him anyway, wasn't it?" she says resentfully. "He couldn't cope with what he'd done. He was weak, weaker than I ever expected. After running down your mother and father, he dived straight into a bloody whisky bottle. God, it was so infuriating! He'd barely even look at me afterwards—he blamed me for talking him into it, when it was his idea just as much as mine." Her eyes narrow. "Pathetic! Catch me ever falling to pieces like that! At least my mother never made the connection. But I know she suspected I was involved somehow, I *know* it. Otherwise I would never have been sent to the gatehouse. And made to look after you. *God*, those were the worst years of my life. Waiting, waiting, until enough time had passed, and you were old enough so it wouldn't look suspicious. Till I could finally get rid of you and be the only heir to Wakefield Hall, whether my mother liked it or not."

She raises her eyebrows.

"I thought this would be the perfect opportunity—up in Scotland, a different location. It has to look like an accident, of course. The smoke bombs were *such* a good idea, weren't they? I knew no one would ever think a teacher would do something like that. And that note I put in your room!"

Aunt Gwen is almost beaming with perverse pride. "*So* clever! With all those St. Tabitha's girls around, there were bound to be some who you'd had a fight with! I know exactly what teenage girls are like—best friends today, deadly enemies tomorrow. Ugh, such a waste of an excellent plan!" She sighs. "If you'd only been killed falling down that staircase . . . I gave you a hard enough push, God knows! It

255

would have been absolutely perfect. They'd have looked at the smoke bombs, found the note, and thought it was a prank that went horribly wrong."

I'm pushing down on the arms of the chair now frantically, with everything I have, trying to get my feet underneath me to take my weight, but my legs keep collapsing. I'm never getting out of this chair under my own steam. Panic is rising in me. It might seem totally unbelievable that I haven't freaked out before now, but the antihistamines make me feel as if I'm being wrapped in layers and layers of padding; it takes ages for anything to sink in, to seem real. Let alone a story as insane as Aunt Gwen's.

I know it's true, every word of it. She's relishing telling me all this; I can see the malicious gleam in her eyes. Everything fits—especially because it slots in the last puzzle piece to Mr. Barnes's hit-and-run killing of my parents, his motive for doing that. And it explains why both Mr. Barnes and Aunt Gwen were so violently opposed to Jase's and my falling in love with each other.

"It's time," she says, standing up. She tugs down her skirt, smoothing it out, a banal, everyday little gesture that somehow intensifies the horror of what she's about to do.

I shake my head frantically, a scream building inside my skull, wanting to explode from my mouth; but I can barely manage to make any sound at all.

"I have no idea why on *earth* you've been babbling about all this ghost nonsense," she says almost cheerfully. "You've never seemed that sort of silly, childish girl. But it's perfect for my purposes. You've had two collapses in three days. You're acting so hysterically every single teacher is concerned you're on the verge of a nervous breakdown. So, my story will be very simple: I brought you up here to talk to you and see how you were, Scarlett, because I was worried about you. After all, you are my niece. I left to make another cup of tea, but when I came back, the window was open. And you were gone."

She walks toward me, reaching down and pulling me out of the armchair. I can't believe how strong Aunt Gwen is; I try to struggle but I have nothing at all to do it with. *No juice*, Taylor says, when we've worked out so hard our muscles feel soft as toffee and we're too knackered even to lift the remote to change the channel on the TV, lying there watching a blah program rather than mustering the energy to find something we're actually interested in. And right now, I have no juice, not a drop of it. Aunt Gwen hauls me up and out of the chair, gripping my sweater rather than my skin, and I know this is so she won't leave any marks on me that might be suspicious. My feet flail at the ground as she frog-marches me over to the window.

"You opened it yourself, of course," she's saying complacently. "That's why I got you to do it, in case anyone was suspicious—your fingerprints are all over the latch. You wanted to get some air, but you leaned out too far. A tragic accident. I'm not stupid enough to try to fake a suicide— even though it's terribly common among teenage girls, apparently. Though if that's what the police choose to believe . . ." I feel her shrug as she nudges the window open with an elbow and starts to shove me through the frame, out onto the ledge.

Desperately, I do the only thing I can think of. Fighting

her isn't working; the antihistamines have sapped my muscle control. Instead, I slump against her, making myself a dead weight. My feet catch on the windowsill, and she curses, trying to lift me. The rubber of my trainers catches on the paint of the wall below, providing resistance against her attempts to haul me up.

She's swearing now, a stream of filthy words pouring from her—in any other context it would totally shock me that Aunt Gwen has this kind of vocabulary. I'm hanging from her grip like a huge, unwieldy doll, and I feel her knee come into the small of my back, boosting me, shoving my legs so they fold up enough that she can hoist me through the window frame.

I'm trying to push back, fall back on top of her, make myself so heavy that she can't maneuver enough to make the final shove. It's freezing out here, the wind icy on my face, lifting my hair, my fingers feeling numb with cold, and it's sapping me. I'm exhausted, shocked, and dazed from the drugs she's given me; part of me still can't believe that it's my aunt who's doing this, my own flesh and blood. My aunt, who's made several attempts to kill me, and is going to succeed this time . . .

My neck wobbles, tipping my head forward, despite my best efforts. And that's fatal for me. An adult human head weighs about ten pounds—I had that dinned into me for years at gymnastics, to remind me to tuck my head in when I somersaulted. The extra weight helps with the rotation.

And now it's helping Aunt Gwen, tilting my body in the direction she wants it. Forward. Out the window. Off the ledge. Chin resting on my chest, I'm looking straight down at the ground below. It's hard concrete: the empty parking lot. Not even a car that might break my landing.

Aunt Gwen's planned this perfectly. There are no lawns below, no soft grass. No question that this fall will kill me.

I close my eyes, not brave enough to watch myself plummet into space.

And then my head spins dizzily as I'm dragged back so abruptly that I hit my head against the side of the window. Pain shooting through my skull, I tumble awkwardly onto the carpet inside, my knees shooting up into my chest, rolling into a ball to protect my face and chest, because Aunt Gwen and someone else are struggling, trampling each other, feet shuffling right next to me, one tripping over my leg as I scramble as best I can to get out of the way.

My back pushes against the armchair. I curl up against it, eyes snapping open, staring in disbelief at what I see: Aunt Gwen and Taylor, swaying back and forth in the window embrasure. But no, not Taylor; that's what I'm finding so hard to process. It's a male version of Taylor, built on a bigger scale; the same shaggy hair, the same wide shoulders, the same strong features.

My brain's firing so slowly that it takes me a ludicrously long time to work out what's blindingly obvious.

"Seth!" I say finally. "You're *Seth*!"

He swings round at hearing his name, momentarily distracted, his heavy fringe tumbling across his eyes, his hold on Aunt Gwen slackening. Aunt Gwen, gasping for breath, reaches out, hand rising like a claw to scratch at his face. I scream a warning to him. Seth looks back and slaps her hand away just before her nails can make contact with his skin.

And that's what sends her off balance. Her feet slide from underneath her, her legs shoot up. She snatches desperately for the window frame, and misses. It looks as if she's sitting down in thin air. Her skirt bunches up around her knees, her bottom tips back. Her head jerks madly, her eyes bulging more than I've ever seen them before; her mouth opens in a scream.

The last thing I see of Aunt Gwen is the soles of her shoes as she falls off the ledge, back into nothingness, her scream thin and faraway. The scream of someone who knows she's already dead.

## seventeen

# "I LOVE YOU VERY MUCH, SCARLETT"

I'm sitting quietly, turning something over in my hand. A pendant on a silver chain, a bright blue stone that I used to think was an aquamarine, in a simple silver setting. It used to belong to my mother; my father gave it to her on my fourth birthday, because it was the same color as my eyes. Wakefield blue, she called the color, and my father must have gone to a lot of trouble and expense to find it.

When Mr. Barnes deliberately knocked my parents off their scooter that summer day, when he stopped the van he'd been driving to make sure they were dead, he took this pendant from my mother's neck. Like a trophy. And he gave it to his wife, Dawn, Jase's mother, who never wore it, because she was suspicious about where it came from—he told her not to wear it out in public, not to show it off to anyone.

Dawn, who couldn't say boo to a goose, wasn't brave enough to ask any awkward questions. Scared, intimidated by her increasingly drunken and violent husband, she put the pendant in a drawer and pretended it didn't exist. And years later, when Jase and I started seeing each other, Jase remembered the necklace his mother had left behind, and thought I might like it, because it matched my eyes.

I loved it from the moment he gave it to me; I wore it constantly. Until Lizzie Livermore, who, if nothing else, is an expert on expensive jewelry, looked closely at it and told me it wasn't an aquamarine at all. It's a round-cut blue diamond, very rare and very valuable. And when I learned that, I started to trace the story of the pendant, like tugging on a loose thread that ends up unraveling a whole garment.

Of course, now that I know it's a diamond, I wonder how I could ever have thought it was anything else. It sparkles as I hold it to the light, and though it glints brightly, the layers of blue beneath are velvety, with a depth that— according to Lizzie—is too rich for a semiprecious stone, but is characteristic of a diamond.

I never let Aunt Gwen see me wearing it, because Jase had given it to me, and she was so opposed to our relationship that she was quite capable of confiscating any present from him. But of course, that was before I knew the truth about the necklace, what it really was. I realize, thinking over the whole story, that it would have driven Aunt Gwen crazy to know that Mr. Barnes had taken my mother's necklace for Dawn. To me, that says that although he killed my parents in a conspiracy with Aunt Gwen, it was purely for financial benefit. His feelings must always have been with his wife, if he bothered to lean down and snatch this pendant off my mother's neck for her.

I swallow hard at the image this calls up. It's horrible. And it was all for nothing. If anything, Aunt Gwen was worse off after she had her brother and sister-in-law killed; not only did her lover, Mr. Barnes, turn into a drunk, her mother—my grandmother—marooned her in the gatehouse with an orphaned four-year-old.

All for nothing. I can't think about it too long; the pain and the waste are too overwhelming. If I let myself think about what my life would have been like if I'd grown up with my parents alive—parents who loved me, and would probably have had more children, so I'd have had little sisters and brothers to play with—it makes the biggest lump come up in my throat.

And then I think, the first time this idea has ever come to me: *If I had a younger brother, it would be him who'd inherit Wakefield Hall, not me. Because the whole estate is entailed on a male heir, if there is one.*

It wouldn't be fair. I feel a rush of resentment rise up in me at the thought—and not just resentment, but a love for Wakefield Hall I didn't even know I had. The centuries of history, the beautiful old central wing; the maze, the lake, the terraces with their views over Lime Walk. It'll be all mine one day. It's a huge responsibility to take care of it, to keep it as perfectly as my grandmother does. The weight settles on my shoulders. I've always known it was there, and now I've accepted it.

The idea of my parents having a boy after me, a boy who would take that all away from me, is harder to bear. For the first time, I feel something in common with Aunt Gwen. I have an inkling of the anger and resentment she must have felt, growing up knowing that her brother would, one day, have all of Wakefield. Aunt Gwen wouldn't be cast out without a penny, of course. There's plenty of family money to go round. But it must have been really bitter for her to realize that just because her brother was a boy, he was the crown prince, and she was a very distant second.

I can't ever forgive her for what she did to my parents, and what she tried to do to me. But at least I can understand it, a little.

"Scarlett? Scarlett!" Penny, my grandmother's secretary, has to call my name twice, I'm so lost in thought. She leans over her desk, waving her hand to catch my attention. "You can go through now. She's ready for you."

The entire Wakefield Hall contingent came back on the train from Edinburgh first thing this morning. We only got back to school half an hour ago, and Miss Carter brought me straight to my grandmother's suite of rooms. I've got my pull suitcase here, propped up against the wall, and for a moment I debate taking it in with me, before Penny gestures to me to leave it where it is.

I pause with my hand on the doorknob. I can't believe I was seriously considering dragging and bumping my suitcase into my grandmother's elegant, exquisitely decorated study. I must be feeling even more disoriented than I realize. I'm dreading this interview with my grandmother. It's all still sinking in, probably because I was zoned out for most of yesterday, knocked out by the trauma of my struggle with Aunt Gwen, the shock of her death, all heavily overlaid with the antihistamines she'd given me. The strain of keeping my story straight to the police was horrendous, even with Seth backing me up.

We kept our version of events as simple as possible:

Aunt Gwen was taking me up to her room to make me some tea when Seth walked into the school, making a surprise visit to his sister while traveling through Edinburgh. Aunt Gwen naturally offered Seth a cup of tea too, telling him he could wait with us until the rest of the school party got back from their excursion; I felt dizzy, Aunt Gwen kindly opened a window to give me some cool air, leaned out too far, slipped, and fell in a terrible freak accident. Seth coached me over and over before the police came, telling me not to add any extra details that might catch us out, focusing completely on putting across the most basic story possible.

Even so, the police didn't like it at all. I wanted Seth to go before they came, telling him he shouldn't be mixed up with them, but he'd refused, saying that they wouldn't believe a story this implausible unless there were two witnesses. Seth turned out to be right; they questioned us for hours, trying to find holes in the story, convinced that we were in some sort of conspiracy. It helped that everyone, especially Taylor, swore up and down that I'd never met Seth before, which made it incredibly unlikely that we would have got together to plan something as extreme as killing my aunt; in the end, with no evidence to the contrary, and both of us telling the same story, there was nothing they could do but let us go with great reluctance.

Seth was amazing. I was pretty much a total wreck, and he was a tower of strength: calm, detached, clearheaded, focusing not on Aunt Gwen's awful death, or what she'd tried to do to me, but on the single task of selling our story to the police. He seemed so much older than me; I know he's twenty, which is quite a bit older, but honestly, it was like talking to an adult, one I could completely trust. I liked him and was intimidated by his poise in equal measure. And it made me realize why Taylor's so confident in so many areas: with a brother like that to model yourself on, how could you not be?

Afterward, I was so shattered they put me straight to bed. I passed out, sleeping through until Taylor woke me this morning in time to pack and catch the train; and then, in the first-class seat Miss Carter had thoughtfully booked for me, I passed out all over again, watched over by her and Jane. It's extraordinary how the aftermath of extreme stress can knock you out utterly and completely as the adrenaline floods out of your system, leaving you just a drained, exhausted shell.

But as I eventually turn the handle and step into my grandmother's sanctum, the sight of her shocks me to the core. However bad I felt yesterday and today, she looks infinitely worse. Lady Wakefield is always perfectly poised and groomed, her white hair smooth, her twinset and pearls exquisitely appropriate, her blue eyes bright and sharp. This afternoon is no exception; she doesn't have a hair out of place. But her face is a pale, fragile mask, white as paper and massed with lines, like tissue that's been crumpled in someone's hand; her eyes are faded and full of pain.

I'm supposed to call her Lady Wakefield in term time, because I'm a pupil at the school and she's the headmistress. My grandmother imposed that rule on me as soon as I came here as a student, and she's very strict about it.

But, running toward her, full of worry at how frail she looks, I forget it completely.

266

"Grandma!" I exclaim, plopping down on the upholstered footstool next to her chair, taking the hand she's holding out to me.

"Oh, Scarlett . . ." To my utter amazement, she starts to cry. It should be frightening, my grandmother crying, showing her vulnerability, because she's always so strong. But actually, surprisingly, it comes as a huge relief. "Scarlett," she sobs, "you're all I have left. . . ."

She raises her other hand and strokes my hair gently, something no one has done for a long, long time. It's so comforting that tears form in my own eyes. I lean against her knees.

"I'm not going anywhere, Grandma," I assure her, trying to find words that will make her feel better. "I'm right here—I'll always be here. . . ."

"Both my children, gone," my grandmother sobs quietly. "And Sally, lovely Sally—she and Patrick adored each other, they were such a happy couple . . . how could this have happened? How could my family have come to this, just one Wakefield left, apart from me? I thought Patrick and Sally would have a whole family of their own, running around the gardens, playing on the lawns . . . and now it's just you left, Scarlett. Just you."

She's still holding my hand, so tightly that her rings are cutting into me, but all I do is squeeze hers back, too choked up to be able to say a word.

"It's my fault," she says desolately. "I loved Patrick better, and Gwen knew it. Children always know if their mother has a favorite. Poor Gwen, I never felt the same about her, and I couldn't pretend to. She was her father's pet, but he died too young. If he'd lived, maybe everything would have been different . . . maybe Gwen would have been less bitter, less resentful . . . but he died, and I miss him every day. . . ."

I never knew my grandfather; he died a long time ago, well before I was born. I've seen photographs, of course. That's how I know Aunt Gwen took after him. Thinking of Aunt Gwen makes me shiver, and my hand tightens even more on my grandmother's, holding on to the only relative I have left, the only one I've ever been able to trust.

"I should never have let Gwen bring you up," she says. "Never."

Patting my hand, she reaches into her pocket for a handkerchief; nothing as common as tissues for my grandmother. She dabs her eyes as she continues:

"I wanted to have you here, at the Hall. That's what Penny suggested I do. Hire a nice nanny to live in, furnish your parents' room, keep you under my own eye. But Gwen was in her thirties, a much more appropriate age to bring up a child. And Mrs. Bodger had just moved out of the gatehouse into the old-age home at Wakefield—countless generations of children grew up in the gatehouse. I remember all the little Bodgers playing in the garden. It was a very happy little family home. I hoped that you and Gwen would come together, make your own little family. Redeem what had happened, somehow." She gulps. "I meant it for the best, Scarlett. If I was distant with you, it's because I didn't want to undermine Gwen; she was in loco parentis with you, after all. I didn't want to tread on her toes."

*How much has she guessed?* I wonder as she blows her

nose with perfect elegance: Lady Wakefield could give princesses lessons in etiquette. *From the way she's talking, she must have some idea of what happened between me and Aunt Gwen yesterday afternoon. If she really believed it had just been a tragic accident, she'd be asking me questions about it, talking very differently. She'd be mourning Aunt Gwen. Concerned whether I'd been traumatized by seeing the fall, still in shock at Aunt Gwen's horrible death.*

*But I'm not hearing any of that. Instead, my grandmother's telling me that she should never have left me alone with Aunt Gwen. That she has a half suspicion, at least, that Aunt Gwen wasn't trustworthy as far as I'm concerned.*

"I had no idea that anything was wrong. . . ." She gulps. "Well, it would be more honest to say I didn't *want* to have any idea that something might be wrong, Scarlett," she says piteously. "My son was gone, and so was his wife. Gwen was my only daughter. My only living child. How could I bring myself to believe that she . . ." She trails off, squeezing my hand tightly. "I *never* thought any. harm would come to you," she says more strongly. "*Never.*"

I remember Aunt Gwen telling me yesterday that she thought her mother suspected what she had done. I hadn't truly believed her. Because if my grandmother left me in the care of the woman she thought might have killed my parents—a woman who would have a motive to kill me, too—that would have been incredibly irresponsible of her.

And if there's one word that doesn't describe Lady Wakefield in any way, it's irresponsible.

I look up at her, into her blue eyes. I sense she did have

a tiny inkling that Aunt Gwen might be capable of murder, but I sense too that she's spent every day of her life since my parents' death suppressing that instinct with every ounce of willpower that she possesses. There's absolutely no way that my grandmother would have decreed that I was going to live with Aunt Gwen if she had truly believed that inkling. She would never have risked my life.

No, she's spent all these years telling herself firmly that being with Aunt Gwen was best for me, that we were bonding. Which is really tragic, because my grandmother actually wanted me with her, in the Hall, and I would have loved that too. Aunt Gwen's suggestion that I was forced on her as some sort of perverse punishment for her crime was just typical Aunt Gwen nastiness, designed to make me feel as bad as humanly possible.

My grandmother loves me, and wanted what was best for me. She wanted me to grow close to my aunt, so that I'd have a relative left who loved me when she eventually died. And I can't blame her for refusing to believe the truth about Aunt Gwen: what parent could believe their daughter killed their son without solid, cast-iron proof?

"I made a mistake, Scarlett," my grandmother is saying now as she clasps my hand. "But I meant it for the best. You believe that, don't you?"

I can't manage to speak, but I nod vigorously as I sit back on the footstool, wiping my eyes with my sleeve. It's a measure of how upset my grandmother is that she doesn't immediately snap at me for not having a handkerchief of my own. Instead, she takes a deep breath and sits back herself, her spine once more poker-straight, folding her handkerchief and slipping it into the pocket of her cardigan.

"Well, I've made more than one mistake," my grandmother says more firmly. "And there's nothing I can do to redeem those. My daughter is dead." She swallows, but she has herself under control now, and some color is coming back to her cheeks. "Gwen was never happy," she adds. "She shouldn't have stayed at Wakefield. She could have taught at any school she wanted to. Goodness knows, there were always offers; she was considered one of the best geography teachers in the country. Eton . . . Winchester . . . Cheltenham . . . a mixed school, where she could have had a wider circle of acquaintances . . ."

*Men, Grandma means. Male teachers, who might have been interested in Aunt Gwen.*

"I should have put my foot down. Insisted that she take one of those opportunities," my grandmother continues. "It might have been the saving of her. Instead, she became unhealthily obsessed with Wakefield, I'm afraid. I thought she understood that, as your father's daughter, you would naturally be my heir."

"That doesn't seem completely fair," I venture, thinking of Callum's family, the McAndrews: how Dan had been due to inherit everything just because he was born a few minutes before Callum, his twin brother. Like winning the jackpot, completely by chance.

"It's how it works in Britain, Scarlett," my grandmother says, looking at me seriously. "In the old families, everything is held for the most senior member of the next generation.

The title, the estate. It means that the ancestral homes are passed on with enough land and inheritance to maintain them. That's why we still have so many beautiful stately homes—look at Chatsworth, or Castle Howard. They are intact because they passed down from the oldest son to the oldest son, without being split up between the rest of the family." She touches the pearl necklace she always wears. "Even this is a family heirloom," she adds. "Held in trust, to be passed down to the next generation. I couldn't sell it even if I wanted to."

"So if I had a younger brother, he'd inherit Wakefield Hall," I say. "And he'd have the title, while I don't."

"The baronetcy can only be inherited by a male," my grandmother, who's Lady Wakefield because she married Sir Alexander Wakefield, confirms.

"That isn't fair either," I say. "I just mean, if Aunt Gwen was upset about it, I do sort of understand."

My grandmother reaches out to squeeze my hand again.

"I'm used to the way things were always done," she says quietly. "It's hard for an old dog to learn new tricks, Scarlett. But a truly good parent, or grandparent, hopes that their descendants will improve on how they lived their lives. If you don't think it's fair—and poor Gwen may well have felt the same—the remedy is in your hands. You will be able to do what you want with the Hall when you inherit it. If you feel that your youngest daughter, not your oldest son, is the right person to take it over—or if you want your children to share it in a trust—you'll decide that for yourself."

My expression must be appalled, because she actually

manages a smile as she looks down at me, the first one that I've seen on her face today.

"You should see yourself when I talk about children you may have," she says, her eyes brighter now. "Utterly horrified! Don't worry, Scarlett. I'm much more interested in your educational than your reproductive prospects." She sighs. "And, of course, your immediate residential ones."

I'm still working through this as she adds:

"You can't stay on in the gatehouse by yourself, of course. Not that I imagine you'd want to."

I hadn't even thought about where I would live now, with Aunt Gwen gone. The idea of being on my own in her house, fending for myself, is overwhelming; for a moment I picture myself staying there by myself, with Jase visiting me, and although maybe that should be exciting, the image is actually more scary. Too much, too soon.

"I don't think I could manage," I say honestly. "There's so much responsibility in running a house. I mean, I can wash my own clothes, but . . ."

I think about doing the shopping, running out of things I always forget, like dishwashing tablets, cream scrub for the bath, that mildew spray Aunt Gwen was always nagging me to use in the shower. . . . It isn't glamorous, it's frightening. After the unbelievably dramatic year I've had, I just want to be a nearly-seventeen-year-old for a while. By which I mean, as entirely irresponsible as possible.

"Especially with exams to do," I say nervously. I feel as if I'm being a coward, but when I look at my grandmother, she's nodding sympathetically.

"I'm very keen on young people taking responsibility," she says, "but it would be absurd for you to be suddenly catapulted into adult life. I think the best solution is for you to live in the dormitory wing during term time, with the other students. If you move in there now, that will give us enough time to plan a set of rooms for you here in the Hall with me. They'll be yours in the holidays, for as long as you want them. You know I'm hoping that you'll eventually make your home here, Scarlett. This will be the first real step to making that happen."

"Thank you," I manage to say.

"We'll put you on the same floor as Taylor McGovern in the dormitory wing," my grandmother adds. "I know you two are close."

I nod, overwhelmed.

"You've been through much too much in this last year," my grandmother says. "More than any sixteen-year-old should have to cope with. But I think you have an old head on young shoulders, Scarlett."

She utters these words very firmly; she sounds like the Lady Wakefield I've known, and been intimidated by, forever. But when I glance at her, I read doubt in her gaze for the first time, as if she's trying to convince herself.

"I'll be okay, Grandma," I assure her. "I really will."

She heaves a deep sigh, one that seems pulled up from the very soles of her feet.

"I hope and pray you will, my dear," she says very gently. "Now why don't you go and find Taylor, and start to move your things over to your new room in school? And have a think about what you want to keep from the gatehouse.

274

Any piece of furniture you want, make a list and give it to Penny. But you might want to have a whole fresh start—leave it all behind. It's entirely as you wish." She smiles. "I have plans for that house."

And then she reaches out to me, takes my face in both hands, and kisses me on each cheek.

"I love you very much, Scarlett," she says softly. "I never want you to have a moment's doubt of that."

I leave her study with my head reeling. Lady Wakefield, my grandmother, actually showed emotion in my presence. She cried in front of me. She talked about her feelings. She talked about what I wanted, as if I were a real human being. She acted like a grandmother.

I've lost an aunt who hated me, and found a grandmother who loves me instead.

I can live with that.

# eighteen

# "LIKE THERE'S NO *THERE* THERE"

Taylor's waiting for me in Penny's anteroom; she jumps up on seeing me, looking excited.

"Matron just told me," she blurts out, "you're coming into the dorm! They're moving me so you can have the room next to me! It'll be really cool!" She grabs the handle of my suitcase. "I'll take this over, and then we can go get the rest of your stuff. Matron said we can use the porter's trolley."

Penny smiles at me. "Lady Wakefield's having the estate builder come in tomorrow to look at the rooms in the old wing of the Hall," she informs me. "To see how much work they need to make you a place of your own. We thought you'd like your own little kitchenette. And bathroom, of course."

It's ridiculous how small things can make a real difference sometimes. The thought of actually having my own bathroom that I don't have to share with anyone, where I can soak in the tub as long as I want without Aunt Gwen banging on the door, or try those semipermanent dyes I've been longing to experiment with, safe in the knowledge that if I get a drop or two on the bath mat Aunt Gwen won't rip my head off and shove it down my throat, is really amazing. I'm beaming as I leave Penny's office.

"I'm so psyched!" Taylor says happily. "It'll be so cool to be next door to each other!"

"I'm going to get my own bathroom," I say dreamily. "I wonder if they'll let me pick the colors? And I'd really love one of those baths that go in the middle of the room. . . ."

"Ooh, those are amazing," Taylor says, momentarily distracted. "*Super*-romantic!"

I sigh in bliss.

"Look, Scarlett—" Taylor's been bumping my case down the back stairs, but she stops at the bottom, looking at me. "I didn't get a chance to be alone with you before—you were totally zonked out yesterday, and Miss Carter's been around all day today—I need to talk to you about Seth." She hoists the case up as I hold the back door open for her. "So you understand why I was acting so weird."

"Oh, I think I understand," I say as she follows me out into the fresh air. "I had a lot of time to work it out."

We're at the side of the Hall, walking down a little stone path that leads around the building and comes out onto the top of the many stepped terraces that fall away, one after another, to the expanses of lawns beyond. I walk over to the stone balcony at the far end of the terrace, and prop myself up on its wide balustrade, swinging my legs, looking down at the ornamental Italian garden on the terrace directly below.

Taylor sets down the case and follows me over.

"You got Seth to come over from wherever he was," I start, "because you were worried about me."

"Cornell," she says. "He was at college. He got emergency leave."

"Wow." I look at her. "You must have been really worried."

"I was *freaking out*, Scarlett," Taylor says, starting to pace back and forth; she can never stay still when she's nervy. "'Cause after that note in our room, and your getting pushed down the stairs, I did think it was Alison and Luce, okay? It all pointed to them. Blast from the past, you know?"

I nod.

"I thought it was them too," I admit.

"But the next day, it didn't *feel* like it was them," Taylor continues, still pacing. "They didn't seem triumphant, or smug. They were just the same as the day before; snotty, standoffish, pretending we didn't exist. That's not how girls act when they've pulled off some huge prank that gets everyone in school out of bed, and fire engines showing up. Plus one of them shoved a girl who used to be their best friend down a flight of stairs. I mean, that's huge." She pauses, leaning on the balustrade with both hands as if she's doing press-ups. "So I took a good look at all the girls in the group. And I couldn't see *anyone* who seemed different from the day before. That didn't feel right."

She leans farther onto the balustrade, bending her arms, keeping her body straight, like she's going into plank position.

"And then I thought: if it wasn't a girl, it had to be a teacher. Which seemed, like, nuts. Until I went through the list of all the teachers who were there with us. And I ended up with your aunt."

Taylor's not looking at me now, but straight ahead, across the lawn. It's still half-term, and most of the other girls on the school trip have gone back to their homes until spring term starts next week; there's no one on the lawn, just a couple of herons flying overhead, dipping down behind the ivy-covered fence that encloses the lake.

"Which seemed nuts too," she says quietly. "But my parents always say to think the unthinkable. And it seemed that pushing you over a stair rail was really harsh. I mean, you dropped your friends to go to a party. That sucks. They had a complete right to be angry and not be friends with you anymore. But you could have been killed when you went over that banister, which is totally out of proportion to what you did. So I was, like, what's the motive here? Who would benefit if Scarlett got killed?"

She turns her head to look me straight in the eye.

"And the answer to that was really easy," she says simply. "It was standing out a mile."

"You're going to be a really good secret agent," I say dryly.

"I wasn't sure, not for ages," she says. "When your water got tampered with—it had to be your water, it was the only thing you ate or drank after breakfast, and we all had the same food then—your aunt had the spare keys to the coach. She could really easily have sneaked out and put something in your water. And Alison actually caught you when you fell. Sure, that could have been Alison feeling guilty about going too far with the prank from the night before, but it made much more sense to just think she was innocent in the first place."

I nod. Taylor's line of thought is unarguably clear.

"So your aunt had motive, opportunity." Taylor pushes herself to standing again, ticking the points off on her fingers. "Two attempts in two days—and both of them happened when I was around, so obviously I couldn't protect you on my own." Her mouth draws into a tight line of remembered stress. "I IM'd Seth and told him what was going on. *Major* panic. He was amazing. Really amazing. He got straight on a plane. But Scarlett"—she's grimacing now—"I couldn't tell you what I suspected! I mean, she was your *aunt*! Your mom and dad are dead, you're not exactly close to your grandmother—you wouldn't have anyone left if I was right. And if I was wrong, I'd have made you feel even crappier about your aunt—"

"It's okay!" I hold up a hand to stop her apologies. "I get it, I really do! I'd probably have done exactly the same thing."

Her shoulders sag in relief.

"Of course," she says, shoving her hair back from her face, "the irony was that Seth turned out to be completely sucky at shadowing you without being spotted." She rolls her eyes. "He was too worried about me. He thought I might be in danger too. So he got way too close, just in case anyone tried to do something to us, so he'd be there to defend us. But that meant you saw him. Which," she adds with the kind of withering sarcasm you'd only use about a close relative, "is because he did the worst job of surveillance *ever* in the history of the *world*. I could hear him a mile off! He might as well have been walking along next to us! When we were coming back from the Shore, and I told you it was just dry leaves on the ground making that noise, I was just *dying* inside with embarrassment that my brother was being so totally *lame!*"

Taylor's expression is so contemptuous that I can't help giggling.

"I mean, *please*," she finishes, shoving her hands into her pockets. "*Humiliating*. And down there on the ghost tour! You spotted him twice—I mean, he was just standing there in plain sight! I could have killed him! What did he think was going to happen to us with a whole lot of girls and teachers around? What an idiot!"

"He did save my life," I point out in his defense. "And he was fantastic afterwards, too. I'm worried I didn't thank him enough. He really came through when I needed him."

"Yeah, well. There is that," she acknowledges, rocking back on her heels. "God, Scarlett, I've never been in such a state in my life when your aunt took you out of that ghost tour. Finally, she was going to be alone with you. And you were so wound up I knew she could have gotten away with murder—all the teachers and girls would have told the police that you were totally hysterical. If your aunt had managed to push you out that window, no way would they have done an autopsy and found out you had antihistamines in your system. They'd have said you were having a meltdown, maybe that you were trying to get attention, and that you slipped and fell out the window."

I nod, slowly. "I couldn't let you come with us, though," I say. "It wasn't that I didn't trust you—"

"No, it *was*," Taylor interrupts. "And you were right, okay? You *shouldn't* have trusted me. I told you that you didn't see something you saw with your own eyes. I lied to you. You must have thought you were going crazy."

"Honestly, I didn't know what to think," I admit. "I was so confused."

"I texted Seth right away," she says, "and told him you were leaving with her, and to follow you and make sure you weren't alone with her. He got a cab, and the only sensible thing he did at all was to get into the school and find where you both were." She shivers. "It sounds like he got there just in time."

I nod. "I was so dozy with the antihistamines, Seth said he was worried the police would think I was on drugs."

"Well, it turned out okay," Taylor says. "He flew out of Edinburgh this morning, back to the States. The police said he could leave. I mean, they're agreeing it was an accident."

"It *was* an accident," I say simply. "He was just fending her off. She tripped and fell all on her own."

We fall silent for a while, thinking over the crazy events of the last few days. Here, on the terrace of Wakefield Hall, where everything is so still and quiet, it's almost hard to believe what we went through in Edinburgh.

"I just want to go to sleep for a week," I say fervently, slipping down from the balustrade. "Let's go and get my stuff into my new room. And then we could bike to Wakefield village and get some decent food. The kitchen's even worse in holidays than in term time."

"Um, Scarlett?" Taylor comes up behind me as I take the handle of my suitcase. "There's something else I wanted to talk to you about. . . ."

I dart a glance at her and my eyebrows shoot up in

surprise; she looks—I have to think hard to find the word, because it's one I would never associate with Taylor—*insecure*. She's staring down at her feet as we walk along the terrace, refusing to meet my gaze; her hands are shoved into her pockets as if she's trying to root them down to Australia.

"Okay," I say, suddenly madly curious.

"You and Jase," she starts, "you're, um, all good, right?"

I feel a blush spread across my face as I think about that night under the stars at the quarry party.

"Definitely," I say, happily embarrassed. "More than ever. We sort of, um, did stuff. Not, you know, *it*," I add quickly, in case she worries about me. "But, um, *stuff*. And it was wonderful."

"Well, that's cool," she says, kicking a stray pebble against the wall. "I'm happy for you."

"Taylor?" I stop at the top of the stone staircase that leads down to ground level, leaning on the suitcase handle. "You're sounding totally weird."

"That's 'cause I did stuff at the party, too," she says, and to my utter surprise, I notice that her cheeks are red too. Really red. Like ripe tomatoes.

"Cool! Why are you looking so guilty? You didn't do anything with Jase," I say confidently. I have no idea what's going on here, but that at least I'm sure of; I can't think of another reason why she's looking so embarrassed, though.

"No!" She looks horrified. "*God*, no!" And, if possible, she goes even redder. "With, um—"

"With Ewan!" I say cheerfully. "Oh, Taylor, that's brilliant! I could tell he really liked you!"

"*No,*" Taylor says, doggedly pressing on, her entire face the color of a postbox by now. "With *Callum.*"

"You *what?*"

In my amazement, I knock the handle of my suitcase, which tips toward Taylor. She jumps out of the way to avoid it, but much more awkwardly than she normally would; she bumps into a big stone vase planted with peonies, and falls back into it, bottom first, as my suitcase tips head over foot and crashes down the staircase before I can catch it.

The expression on Taylor's face is priceless. She hates to be out of control; she hates to do anything clumsy. Her eyes are wide in shock, her mouth hanging open, as she stares at me above her knees, which are almost as high as her head because her bum's landed deep on the soil in the vase. I'm giggling hysterically at the sight of her.

"Pull me out!" she yells furiously, wriggling in the vase; the more she moves, the more flowers she squashes. "Pull me *out!*"

Through my laughter, I manage to walk over and take her hands. It's really hard to get her out of the vase without tipping it over, as she's fairly low down; I have to haul her up bodily while propping the vase with my foot at the same time. By the time she's standing back next to me, the carefully planted peonies are completely flattened; I look down at them and start to laugh all over again.

"I've got flowers all over my butt!" Taylor exclaims crossly, twisting round to slap at the bum of her jeans, which sets me off even more. "It's not *funny!*"

I bite my lip, take a pull at myself, and shake my head.

"It's all your fault," she snaps. "You threw your suitcase at me."

"Sorry," I say meekly.

"I was telling you something really big, and you threw your suitcase at me!" She finishes dusting soil off her bottom.

"You have some petals down there. . . ." I reach out to pick them off where they're caught on her back pocket, but she slaps my hand away.

"So"—I start down the staircase, hoping she'll follow— "you snogged Callum?"

"It was an accident," she says in a small voice from behind my shoulder.

I retrieve the suitcase, which doesn't seem to have broken, and start to pull it round the walkway to the dormitory wing.

"That sounds interesting," I say, keeping my voice deliberately neutral.

And then it all bursts out from her in a flood as she dashes to walk beside me.

"I always liked him," she confesses. "Even when we were up at Castle Airlie. But obviously, it was all so messed up then—and you kissed him at the airport, so I didn't think about him anymore. Well, not *much*," she adds honestly. Taylor's always brutally honest. "But I thought we'd never see him again, and you'd kissed him, so that sort of made it clear that I wasn't going to have a chance with him. Then we bumped into him at the gig, and I thought he was *gorgeous*. But you and Jase were sort of broken up, and you'd kissed Callum before, so I just sat back to see what would happen with you two."

"Ewan was really into you," I comment.

"I know. He was putting his arm around me and kissing my neck at the party when we went off to explore, so I had to tell him I didn't like him that way and not to do that anymore."

"Wow. Is that what you really said?"

"Sure!" Taylor sounds baffled. "I'm always really straightforward with boys."

"Good for you," I say, bouncing my case round the corner of the building. "I think I'd make up a lot of pathetic excuses. Your way's much better."

"So then it was a bit awkward," she goes on. "We hung out with some other people and played bongos for a while—"

"You're really good at those," I comment.

"I know," she says smugly. "I'm better than Seth. He hates that. Anyway, we decided to come back and see what you were doing, and Callum said you'd gone for a pee, so we hung out, and I started playing bongos and Callum was playing his violin and Ewan saw some people he knew and went off to play with them, and I sort of lost track of time." She clears her throat. "I mean, I knew your aunt wasn't going to sneak up and attack you at a quarry party, so I wasn't worried about you."

"Was Seth there?"

Taylor snorts. "*Right*. I was really going to tell my older brother to follow us when we snuck out to go to an all-night party with boys," she says contemptuously. "Sometimes I can totally tell you don't have brothers."

I bow my head, duly reproved. We've reached the fire doors for the dormitory; Taylor holds them open. I bump my case through and pick it up as we climb the stairs.

"So we stopped playing, and Callum said we sounded amazing together, which we did," she goes on. "And then we just looked at each other for a bit, and suddenly, um, it was obvious that we had a connection. It was like the music made it happen. And he looked really surprised. Like he hadn't been expecting it at all. But then he sort of leaned toward me, and I asked if, you know, anything had happened with you. Because he was into you before, I could tell. And he said yeah, you'd kissed, and it was weird cause there was nothing there, and he thought that was partly why you'd gone off. And I believed him."

"It was true," I confirm, looking at her as we reach the top of the stairs. I pause, seeing her relax in relief. "And it *was* weird. Like plugging something in and turning it on, but then it just doesn't work."

"I've had that with boys," Taylor says. "It's like there's no *there* there."

I giggle.

"Exactly."

"And the next thing, we were kissing," she says, blushing now, her cheeks on fire. "I think it might have been me who kissed him first."

"And there was a *there* there," I say cheerfully.

"Um, *yeah*. So we totally lost track of time. And then I

freaked out and rang you, and you were with Jase, and I said to Callum you'd got back with your ex, and he said it was weird you'd never mentioned him, and I said it was a messed-up situation, and then he said . . ."

She trails off.

"Go on," I prompt.

"He said, 'Why are we talking about them when we could be doing this?' and he kissed me again. A lot," she finishes, grinning from ear to ear.

"Oh, Taylor." I reach out and put an arm around her shoulder, hugging her awkwardly. "I'm really happy for you."

"We're going to try to go on seeing each other," she says, shrugging, trying to sound cool, when it's blindingly obvious that she's anything but. "Sort of see what happens. But it was—" She gives up trying to be cool, and looks directly at me, fire-engine red, her eyes shining. "It was—" She gulps. "I mean, neither of us ever felt anything like that before. We both said it."

"Poor Ewan," I say wryly.

"Yeah, Callum felt a bit bad," Taylor admits. "Apparently Ewan'd been going on about me a lot."

"It's chemistry, though," I say, thinking of me and Callum, and me and Jase. "I thought I had it with Callum, but maybe it was just the drama of the situation. Or maybe it was there before, but now all I can think about is Jase, so I don't have it with anyone else. Anyway, that's chemistry—you can't fake it and you can't change it."

"So true," Taylor says dreamily.

"You know what? I'm *starving*," I say, realizing all of a sudden that I haven't eaten for ages. Which is very unlike me. All the pent-up tension from the last few days is drain-ing away; Jase and I are stronger than ever, I've started a real relationship with my grandmother, and Taylor and I have confided everything in each other and come out the other side.

Taylor looks as if she's unloaded the weight of the world off her shoulders.

"Me too! Hey, we don't have to bike to the village right now. I forgot I've got cookies in my room," she offers. "Chocolate chip."

"I could eat a whole tin," I say, setting off down the cor-ridor.

We're almost at her room when a bedroom door opens and Plum's head pops out.

*Damn*, I think. *I totally forgot.* Plum had to come back to school with us when the field trip finished early, because her parents are skiing in Verbier and not due back for two days; all the other Wakefield Hall girls had parents who could come and pick them up from King's Cross station. I assumed we would try to stay out of her way as much as possible, but there's been so much else going on that her presence in school was pushed to the back of my mind.

She looks as if she's been crying. Her eyes are swollen and puffy, and I think it may be the first time I've seen Plum without any makeup at all.

"I was waiting for you," she says, emerging into the cor-ridor. She's wearing a big T-shirt that comes down to midthigh, the kind you sleep in, and baggy pajama bottoms; her hair's greasy and pulled off her face in a messy ponytail. I've never seen Plum looking the same age as us before, rather than years older and layered in effortless sophistication.

"I wanted to talk to you about"—she gulps—"you know. What you saw the other night. Or what you think you saw."

"*Please,*" Taylor says witheringly. "We know what we saw."

"Susan had a nightmare," Plum says weakly. "I was just comforting her. . . ."

"You're not really going to try that, are you?" Taylor interrupts. I glance over at her; she gives me an "I'm taking this one" look.

I nod. After all, Taylor's the one Plum taunted for ages about being gay, as if it were some sort of crime. Plum kept mocking Taylor for being butch. Taylor deserves to get satisfaction for that. Taylor plants her hands on her hips and stares Plum down.

"There's nothing wrong with being gay!" she says to Plum. "Just admit that you are!"

Plum takes a deep breath.

"Maybe I'm bisexual," she mutters, shamefaced.

"No one actually *cares* what you are," I chime in.

"It's just sad when you have to lie about it," Taylor says coldly. "And call other people gay, like it's an insult or something. It's tragic."

Plum's hanging her head.

"Please don't tell anyone," she whispers.

"Oh yeah, Scarlett and I are really going to rush right out and gossip about your private life," Taylor says. "You're the most fascinating subject ever! We never talk about anything else when we're by ourselves! We're *almost* as interested in you and Susan as you are in me and Scarlett!"

Plum's clearly on the verge of tears.

"Look, rub it in as much as you want," she mutters. "I deserve it. I completely deserve it. I've been a total bitch to both of you. You can torture me as much as you want, just *please* don't tell anyone. . . ."

"Why does it even *matter?*" I can't help asking. "The only person who seems to think it's a big deal is you. Even when you were going on and on about Taylor and me being a couple, none of the other girls really cared."

"Self-hating," Taylor says. "Like I said, totally tragic."

Plum raises her head, her eyes big with fear.

"My dad would have a *fit*," she breathes unhappily. "He's expecting me to make a really good marriage. *No one's* gay in our world." She catches herself. "Or at least they're not out. If my father knew, he'd cut me off without a penny—"

"Nice," Taylor interrupts. "So money's more important to you than being yourself."

"It isn't—but . . ." Plum's voice trails off. She looks hopelessly at me.

"I never thought I'd say this," I comment as Taylor turns away, "but I feel sad for you."

Plum swallows hard.

"I'll agree with every single thing both of you say from now on," she promises as Taylor walks off down the corridor. "Honestly I will."

"Eew!" I recoil, revolted. "Yuck! I don't want you to do that!"

The thought of Plum sucking up, as desperate as she was on the ghost tour, running after me like a Lizzie-like puppy, makes me want to throw up.

"Don't be a bitch," I say simply. "Just stop being a horrible bitch. Not just to us. To everyone."

From Plum's appalled expression, I can see that she's going to find that much harder than sucking up.

I start to walk off, pulling my suitcase. Then a last thought stops me, and I stop, swinging around.

"And, Plum, for what it's worth," I add, "I thought you and Susan looked really beautiful together."

That does it. Behind me, I hear Plum burst into tears; she slumps against the doorframe, crying her heart out. I wonder if I should go back, try to comfort her, but there's nothing I could say to make her feel any better. At least, there's nothing I can think of. Perhaps it's a failure in me. Perhaps I'm not compassionate enough. Or maybe it's that Plum's atrocious behavior to me over the years has burnt me out.

I'm not comfortable hearing anyone sobbing like that, not even my worst enemy. But my feet are carrying me away down the corridor in Taylor's wake. And I have no impulse to turn around and go back.

I park my case outside Taylor's room for the meantime, since there's no one here to trip over it.

"Matron said they'd move us after you pick out what stuff you want from your old bedroom," Taylor says, already plopped down on her bed, peeling open a pack of chocolate chip cookies. "I miss Oreos," she adds wistfully. "These just aren't as good. I'd've gotten Seth to bring some over from the States, but he flew out in kind of a hurry." She stuffs a cookie in her mouth. "The FunStix are *unbelievable*," she says, spewing crumbs over her T-shirt. "They're like straws. You can drink through them. Isn't that amazing? Cookies you can *drink milk through*."

"I don't know why you Americans are so obsessed with milk," I say, scooping a whole handful of cookies out of the packet.

"Makes us big and strong," Taylor says, spilling more crumbs as she talks.

"Honestly," I comment, "even if I were gay for you before, watching you stuff down those cookies would turn me straight. Never let Callum see you eat."

Taylor goes bright red at the mention of Callum's name.

*Hah*, I think happily. *I'm going to have a lot of fun with this.*

And then I think: *Oh God. Was I like that when Jase and I got together?*

"What?" Taylor says, looking up at me, her boob area now a crumb shelf.

"Nothing," I say as my phone pings in my pocket, signaling an incoming text. I pull it out eagerly. And I'm not disappointed.

"Ooh!" I say happily. "Got to go!"

"I don't need to ask you why," Taylor says, reaching for more cookies. "You've gone as red as a London bus."

Trust her to get the last word.

*nineteen*

## BORING AND NORMAL

I stuff down the handful of cookies I've grabbed as I go, wanting (a) to avoid Jase being put off by seeing me gorge, and (b) to give my face enough time for the blush to fade. But though I achieve (a), (b) was a waste of time; as soon as I see him leaning against the huge wrought-iron gates to the Hall, next to his parked bike, I know I've gone red with excitement all over again.

It's so unfair that Jase is darker than me, dark enough for a blush to be much less obvious on his caramel skin. But as soon as he spots me, his golden eyes light up, and he opens his arms wide for me to run into; I hurtle into him so fast I knock the breath out of him, and he's laughing as he hugs me back so tight he squeezes the breath out of me in return. I squeal with everything I have left as he picks me up and swings me around in a big circle, my legs flying out almost parallel to the ground. I cling to him for dear life, my hair whipping round my face, and I have a flash of memory: my father doing this to me when I was really small, my little hands gripping the collar of his shirt, my mouth wide, screaming into his face with delighted terror.

It doesn't last. I try to picture his face, but the memory fades as quickly as it came. *No one's done this since I was tiny,* I think. There wasn't another adult who would have picked me up and swung me through the air after my parents died. I've been craving touch ever since, longing for someone to hug and hold. No wonder I loved gymnastics so much; you're endlessly being pushed and pulled and squashed flat and thrown through the air by big strong hands.

*I must ring up Alison and Luce,* I resolve as Jase sets me down. *We could go and get a coffee, talk about what's been going on with them since I left St. Tabby's. Maybe go to some gigs in London together. Wow.* I grin. *I sound really grown-up.*

"Nice to see you smiling," Jase says, finally setting me down on my feet again.

I'm dizzy, but that's not why I throw my arms around his neck; I pull his head down and kiss him and kiss him till we're both reeling, backing him against the gatepost, wrapping myself around him, kissing him with total and utter abandon.

"Wow," he says, when we finally pull apart, gasping once more for breath, our mouths soft and moist, our eyes shining. "I didn't get back a moment too soon. . . ."

"Do you realize, this is the first time we've ever been able to kiss properly in daylight!" I say happily. "Isn't that amazing?"

"Yeah," he says, his arms still wrapped around me, his expression suddenly serious. "I can't actually get my head

295

round it yet. I keep expecting my dad or your aunt to come shooting out of a rosemary bush and start screaming at us to get away from each other."

We stand there, looking at each other, the fact that both Mr. Barnes and Aunt Gwen are dead truly sinking in.

"I want to say I can't believe it," I say in a smaller voice. "But I can. I keep seeing her falling, over and over again."

"Oh, baby—" Jase pulls me tighter, so that my head snuggles into the hollow of his collarbones. "Are you having nightmares?"

"No," I say simply. "I'm happy that she's gone. I don't even feel awful about it. She always hated me, and then she tried to kill me. I can't feel anything but incredibly relieved."

Jase heaves a long sigh against me. "Fair enough," he says. "I'm the one who's having nightmares, to be honest. I keep seeing that ambulance pull up outside the school. And them carrying a body out on a stretcher, all covered over."

"Oh, Jase—" I pull back, looking up at his face.

His full lips are drawn together, the skin across his cheekbones tight. Because I was so zonked by the antihistamines Aunt Gwen gave me, I pretty much passed out after the strain of keeping it together for long enough to talk to the police. And I'd lost any sense of time. My phone was turned off—they made us do that for the ghost walk—and it hadn't occurred to me, in all the commotion, to turn it on again. Jase, who'd been hanging around outside the school, hoping I'd be able to sneak out and see him for a bit, saw me come back in a cab with Aunt Gwen and then an ambulance rushing up the drive forty minutes later. No wonder he was freaked out.

"I thought it was you," he says quietly. "I really did think it was you."

"I'm so sorry I didn't ring!" I say, my face creasing into a grimace of apology. "I was really zonked—"

He presses both my hands.

"I asked them," he says. "The paramedics. They wouldn't tell me much, but they did say"—he pulls a sort of ironic grin as he makes a stab at the Edinburgh accent—"one of them did say, 'Dinnae worry, pal, this cannae be your gurrrl-friend.' And the other one went, 'Not unless his name's Oedipus, eh?' And then they both laughed a lot."

"Wow," I say, my eyebrows rising. "Black humor."

"Oedipus married his mum, right?" Jase says. "I remember that from school."

I nod. "They were talking about Aunt Gwen being a lot older than you."

"Hey!" He grins wider. "I may not have gone to private school, but at least I learned something at the comp, right?"

"Did you know it was Aunt Gwen's body?" I ask, boosting myself up to sit on the stone wall.

"Nope." He shakes his head. "They wouldn't let me see her. Said she was pretty bashed up. But obviously, I was doing my nut by then. I didn't know what to do. After everything that happened with my dad, I was worried about being there when the police showed up. So I went back to the bike and started ringing you. I rang for *hours*."

"I'm sorry!" I wail. When I turned my phone back on this morning, I could have died, listening to his frantic messages—and I didn't even know it could log that many missed calls. "Thank God for Taylor," I add. She'd come back to school, seen Jase across the road on his bike, and rung him as soon as she had some idea of what was going on.

"No, *I'm* sorry," Jase says intensely. He moves toward me where I'm sitting on the wall. "I wasn't there to look after you. I hate that I wasn't there. I hate that Taylor's brother had to save you instead. I should have guessed somehow— I should have been there for you—"

I reach out my arms to him, and open my legs, wrapping them around his waist, hugging him in reassurance. He's stiff against me, frowning in anger at himself.

"Jase, how could you have known?" I ask, trying to be as reassuring as I can. "All you saw was me coming back to school with my aunt. How could you possibly have known what she was going to do?"

He hangs his head. I reach out and rub his curls, feeling them crunch in my palm; they're squashed from being under the motorbike helmet. Jase set off this morning from Edinburgh, but it takes a lot longer on the bike than it does on the train. He's only just got back to Wakefield.

Or so I thought.

"I've been to see your gran," he says, looking up at me. "Just now."

"Really?" My eyes widen.

"She rang me when I was on the road," he says. "Asked me where I was, said to come and see her if I was anywhere near Wakefield. I said I was on my way back, to see you." His eyes gleam gold, a little defiantly. "I thought I might as well say it straightaway. That we're still together."

I gulp, still stroking his hair.

"She was never the one who made a fuss about it," he goes on. "Your gran was always nice to me."

"She thinks you're a good boy and a hard worker," I say, doing my best to imitate my grandmother's impeccable upper-class accent.

"Well, I bloody am!" he says, and unexpectedly, his face cracks into a huge smile. "She's bloody right!"

"What did she want to see you about?" I ask.

"You ready for this?" he says more seriously. "She wanted to see if I'd like to live there." He nods back at the gatehouse, where, until so recently, I lived with Aunt Gwen.

"Wow," I say. "It didn't take her much time to work everything out, did it?"

He grins. "That's your gran for you. She said you wouldn't be living there anymore. But I can't go back to my dad's old cottage, and she'd like me to stay on the estate. There's a job for life for me here, I know that. Running the grounds."

I nod. Jase loves gardening; it's the one thing he's inherited from his dad.

"And what did you say?" I ask, my heart rising in nervous anticipation of his answer.

I don't know if Jase will want to stay at Wakefield, not even for the moment, let alone long-term. Just a few months ago he told me that he didn't know if he'd ever come back, that the guilt of what his father had done to my parents meant that he wasn't sure if we could ever be together. Now it seems that the two of us are okay; but my future is tied to Wakefield, my inheritance, and if Jase can't face being here, it doesn't bode well for us as a couple.

He heaves a long, slow breath, and I feel the blood drain from my fingers and my toes as I wait for his answer. I've gone very cold. So much rides on how Jase feels about this, and there's nothing I can do to change his mind.

"It's all changed now, hasn't it?" he says soberly, looking over my shoulder at the bulk of the Hall.

"What do you mean?" My voice is almost infinitesimal.

"Well"—he looks back at me—"your aunt was as bad as my dad, wasn't she? They were in it together."

I nod. We managed a short conversation this morning, before he set off down the M1 for London; enough for me to fill him on Aunt Gwen's revelations to me yesterday.

"So don't you see?" His eyes are intent, shining bright as stars as he looks down at me. "Your family—my family—they're as rubbish as each other. At least, the bad seeds are. My mum, your mum and dad—nothing wrong with them. But my dad and your aunt were both bastards. They did their best to ruin our lives."

I swallow hard as Jase mentions my parents. But I nod in agreement with every word he's saying.

"So I don't have to feel bad anymore," he explains urgently. "See? My dad, your aunt—they were shits. My dad killed your mum and dad. Your aunt tried to kill you. So we've both got shitty horrible relatives. We're even."

Blood floods back into my face as I realize what he's saying.

"I don't have to feel guilty," Jase concludes triumphantly. "Or that I don't belong here anymore, 'cos my dad did something so awful that I don't deserve to be here. I don't have to stay away from Wakefield." He beams at me. "I love it here, Scarlett. I mean, I was born here, I grew up here. It's the only home I've ever known. And I had all these ideas for it too. My dad'd never listen to me—he just wanted to keep things as they'd always been. But I was thinking the Hall should grow its own fruit and veg, you know? Make the estate more self-sufficient. There's so much space, we could use it for all sorts. Bring back the old kitchen garden and the orchard, keep hens, maybe some pigs and sheep— get all the girls here working to grow their own food, learn about farming—"

He breaks off, stepping back, running his hand over his hair, laughing at himself.

"Wow, I'm getting carried away!" he says. "But I've been sort of flying ever since I heard about your aunt. I feel like I've been freed." He spreads his arms wide, his motorcycle jacket hanging open over his T-shirt, a huge smile on his face. "Like, it's not just me! It's not just my family that's all messed up! It's yours too! We're just the same!"

I'm giggling now in sheer happiness.

"We can have a party to celebrate!" I suggest. "Only people with horrible relatives invited!"

"They'd have to be really bad, though," Jase says. "Hard-core stuff."

"Okay, it'd be small and highly exclusive," I agree. "Oh ick, I sound like Plum."

And then it occurs to me that, by the sound of things, Plum is the only person I know who'd qualify for an invitation. Taylor's parents are obviously fantastic; you just have to look at her enviably high self-confidence level to see that. Alison and Luce's are equally lovely. Even Lizzie

Livermore is coddled and adored by her largely absent tycoon father.

While Plum's expression of absolute fear when she talked about her father spoke volumes. And though she has Susan, Viscount Saybourne would clearly come down on Plum like the wrath of God if he ever found out about his daughter and her girlfriend. Whereas Jase and I are free, finally, to kiss in public.

I'm much better off than Plum. What a strange feeling that is.

Jase snaps his fingers in front of my face.

"And when I do that, you will come out of your trance!" he says, like a stage magician.

"Sorry," I say, back to reality. "All right, no party. Just the two of us in the Appalling Relatives Club."

"Works for me," he says, smiling down at me.

I look at the gatehouse behind him. If I manage to blot out all memories of Aunt Gwen, of how much I dreaded coming back here and having to call it home when it was no such thing, I can see that it's a charming little cottage, like something out of a fairy tale. Red shutters at its windows, wisteria trained around the door. You wouldn't exactly think it was the obvious house for a nearly eighteen-year-old boy, but it's very generous of my grandmother to offer it to Jase.

"Are you going to live there, then?" I ask, nodding toward it.

He glances back too, then turns back to me.

"Not yet," he says seriously, and my heart sinks. "I'm just not ready for all that."

"All what?" I ask, my voice tiny again.

"Running my own place. Having to be all grown-up. Because it's your gran's house, and she's doing me a big favor. I'd have to be really careful, y'know? What if I wanted to have some friends round, have a party or something?" He pulls a face. "It wouldn't be respectful. I'd be looking over my shoulder the whole time."

"So what are you going to do?" I say, and I'm amazed he can hear me at all, because I'm sure by now my voice has gone so high and squeaky that only dogs can pick up the frequency.

He cups my face with both his hands, his eyes glowing affectionately.

"Don't worry, Scarlett," he says gently. "I'm not going far. I'm still going to start my estate management degree at college in the autumn, down Havisham way. I've met a couple of lads who've been doing the part-time course there this year, that I've been on, and they've all signed up for the degree course too. Nice lads—we have a good laugh together. We thought we'd find a place we could share in Wakefield village. It'll probably be pretty slobby—three boys sharing—but I'll have my own room, and you can come and visit all the time. We can practically live in each other's pockets if we want to."

Panic drains from me in a lovely clean rush, like water pouring from a fountain. I realize I've been holding my breath. And then, as I inhale with great relief, I realize something else: I'm not just relieved because Jase isn't planning to move miles and miles away. I'm also grateful that he's chosen not to move into the gatehouse.

*Huh*, I think. *Why is that? You'd think I'd be desperate for him to be living here, so close to me!*

"It's all been so weird and crazy, ever since we got together," Jase is saying. "Like you said, we haven't even been able to kiss or hold hands or anything, without worrying that my dad or your aunt are going to pop up like jack-in-the-boxes and start yelling at us. We haven't had a chance just to hang out, do what we want. Be ourselves."

I nod fervently in agreement.

"And if I move in to your aunt's old house," he continues, nodding back toward it again, "that'll feel weird too. I mean, it's your old house! It'd almost be like you were there as well!"

"Like we were going from sneaking around to almost living together," I agree, finally understanding what he means.

"*Exactly*," he says thankfully. "I mean, we're really young. We should be doing stuff that—you know, normal teenagers do."

I grimace.

"I don't even know what that *is*," I admit sadly, slipping down from the stone wall.

"Oh, baby . . ." He enfolds me in a hug. "We'll find out together, all right? From now on, it's all going to be as normal and boring as we can possibly get."

I hug him back just as tight. It doesn't sound at all romantic; no one but me, probably, would have a rush of love and gratitude at hearing the words normal and boring applied to their relationship by their boyfriend.

But I feel as if Jase and I have been strapped to a roller-coaster ride for longer than we even realized. We got so used to being thrown around, bounced up and down, dropped precipitously from great heights, that now it's as if we're finally unbuckling our straps and staggering out, wobbly-legged, heads dazed, onto solid ground again. Not quite trusting it yet. Clinging to each other for security, just as we're doing now.

I'm smiling against his chest, feeling it rise and fall with each breath, my mouth pressed against the lovely firm pectoral muscle over his heart. This is so new and wonderful, being able to stand here with Jase, in daylight. No panic, no fear of being yelled at. Just to stand here with him, listening to him breathe, wrapped in his arms, my head against his heart.

If this is boring and normal, that's how I want my entire life to be from now on.

"Come on!" He pulls away from me, beaming, every line of his face creasing into a huge smile of pure happiness. His eyes are crinkled up, his full lips wide and merry. "Let's get on the bike and go for a ride!"

"Cool!" I say excitedly, zipping up my jacket.

Jase flips open the seat and throws me the spare helmet.

"Where are we going?" I ask as I put it on.

"Nowhere," he says blissfully. "Anywhere. Wherever we want, as long as we want. You don't have to be back in a hurry, do you?"

I shake my head. No curfews, no Aunt Gwen with her beady eyes waiting for me; I'm free as a bird.

"We could grab some dinner out," Jase suggests happily. "Fish and chips or something."

I'm about to agree when a thought strikes me.

"We should bring food back for Taylor," I say conscientiously. "I can't go out on our first night back and leave her by herself—"

Jase is already holding up his hand.

"Of course," he says. "We'll get a takeaway and bring it back. Sorry, I should've thought of it myself. We can't leave her alone."

A wave of love sweeps over me; I must have the nicest, most thoughtful boyfriend in the world.

"I'm so lucky to have you," I say, gulping back tears. "I love you so much, Jase. I think you must be the nicest, sweetest—"

"Stop it!" He grabs me, swings me up as if I weigh nothing at all (which is very far from being the case) and plops me down on the seat of his motorbike. "Enough soppy stuff! We're going for a ride!"

I'm laughing as he swings his leg over and settles in front of me, putting the key in the ignition.

"Will you give me a proper lesson?" I ask, leaning forward. "On how to ride this?"

"*Maybe,*" he says, drawing the word out long. "If you promise to stop the soppy stuff, okay?"

"I will," I say.

"And never call me sweet again."

"Promise," I say, but I'm crossing my fingers.

"I love you, Scarlett," he says as he kicks down and fires up the bike, and the gravel beneath us spits up as the wheels spin and we shoot off down the drive.

"I love you, Jase!" I yell into his helmet, and even though the noise of the bike is deafening, I know he's heard me, because he speeds up, knowing my arms are tightly wrapped around his waist, and tips up the front of the bike. For a few delirious seconds, we're leaning back, still flying along but only on the back wheel now. I tilt my head and look up at the sky through the visor, dizzy with ecstasy as Jase pulls a high and dramatic wheelie.

The front wheel bumps down again, and Jase hits the accelerator, going even faster. I close my eyes and drop my head to nestle against his back, overwhelmed with happiness. Wakefield Hall is behind us for now; we're spinning away from it, wherever we want to go.

Nowhere. Anywhere. Escaping: putting everything behind us.

And we won't go back until we're more than ready.

# ABOUT THE AUTHOR

Lauren Henderson is the author of several acclaimed "tart noir" mystery novels for adults, as well as the witty romance handbook *Jane Austen's Guide to Dating*, which has been optioned for film development by the producer of *Legally Blonde* and *10 Things I Hate About You*. Lauren was born and raised in London, where she lives with her husband. Her first three novels about Scarlett Wakefield, *Kiss Me Kill Me*, *Kisses and Lies*, and *Kiss in the Dark*, are available from Delacorte Press. Visit the author online at laurenhenderson.net or myspace.com/mslaurenhenderson.